RENDERED

RENDERED

Harriette Gill

iUniverse, Inc.
New York Lincoln Shanghai

Rendered

iUniverse books may be ordered through booksellers or by contacting:

iUniverse
1663 Liberty Drive
Bloomington, IN 47403
www.iuniverse.com
1-800-Authors (1-800-288-4677)

ISBN: 978-0-595-48278-8 (pbk)
ISBN: 978-0-595-60365-7 (ebk)

Printed in the United States of America

iUniverse Rev. 10/17/08

Dedication

I dedicate this book to my family.

- My grandmother, Lynchie McGuire Francisco, whom I never knew but whose writing ability I inherited.
- My mother, Madonna Francisco Trimble, who was first and always a teacher and always wanted me to write.
- My dad, Harry Trimble, who loved me unconditionally and thought I could do anything.
- My sister, Brenda Ravenhawk Culpepper, who has been my best friend and confidant all my life.
- And my husband, Mike Gill, who gives me the wings to achieve my dreams.

"*The greatness of a nation and its moral progress can be judged by the way its animals are treated.*"

—Mohandas Mahatmi Gandhi

Foreword

The story and characters in this book are entirely fiction. However, horse slaughter is real and is going on even today. At this writing the last operating horse slaughter plant in the United States has closed due to an Illinois law banning slaughter being passed.

There are now no horse slaughter plants operating in the United States; however, our horses are being transported to Canada and Mexico where they meet a more brutal death than they did here.

Until federal legislation banning the transport of horses for human consumption is passed, our horses will continue to be brutally killed and sent overseas for human consumption.

Horses are an American icon. They have carried our men in battles, domestic and abroad, carried settlers all over America by wagon train, horseback and stagecoach. They once carried the mail across this land. They have rounded up cattle and sheep and plowed our fields. The American West is symbolized by cowboys and horses. Our horses deserve better than to end up on a foreign dinner plate.

I would like to recognize the 1986 Kentucky Derby Winner, Ferdinand, for making me aware of the atrocity of horse slaughter for human consumption. In 1989 Ferdinand was put to stud. In 1994 he was sold to Japan. "Much to the outrage of many horse racing enthusiasts, reports indicate that in 2002 Ferdinand was sent to slaughter in Japan with no fanfare or notice to previous owners. Ferdinand's death was the catalyst for the Ferdinand Fee, an optional donation program to fund keeping old racehorses alive."[1]

Outraged at how anyone could think of a horse as a delicacy to be eaten, I started writing, poems about my own horses and dogs at first, and now my first book. At age 55, I have fulfilled my mother's dream for me.

---

1. Wikipedia, "Ferdinand," http://en.wikipedia.org/wiki/Ferdinand_%28horse%29.

CHAPTER 1

▼

Jett stood at her kitchen window watching her daughter, Savannah, playing outside. Savannah was talking and gesturing and carrying on quite an animated conversation. Jett couldn't hear what Savannah was saying, but she could hear the laughter every now and then as her little girl continued to hold the rope in her hands and raise her tiny hand to stoke the head of Star.

Star is a horse; he is Savannah's best friend, maybe even her only friend outside of Jett. Savannah spends almost all her time playing, talking to and taking care of Star. Why is this unusual? Well, you see, Star is an imaginary horse.

Jett poured herself another cup of coffee, walked back to the table and sat down. She glanced over to the corner where a bucket of water, a plastic feed container and some hay were spread. She shook her head but couldn't help but smile. Savannah had insisted Star have access to food and water in the house. After all, he slept in her room!

Maybe Jett should have put a stop to the Savannah's imagination; she knew many of her friends thought she and Savannah were both slightly crazy. But Jett remembered her own childhood imaginary playmate. Her parents had been concerned when she wanted an extra plate set at the table and constantly carried on conversations with her friend. It worried her parents enough that they took Jett to the family doctor. He assured them it was not unusual for a child to have an imaginary friend. In fact, he had told them, it showed a good imagination and intelligence.

The fact that Savannah's friend was a horse didn't make Jett think there was reason for concern. She figured sooner or later Savannah would outgrow this phase of childhood. Right now, the child was dealing with the loss of her father and if she needed Star to help her, then Jett wasn't about to make things harder for her daughter.

It wasn't all that surprising that Savannah's imaginary friend was an animal. Jett and Blake both loved animals and both had been raised with a string of loyal dogs. Blake had had a horse at his grandfather's ranch when he was growing up and had told Savannah horse stories since she was in the cradle. Jett had never had a horse, but had asked for one every birthday and Christmas when she was a child. Her dream had been to own a horse, and she was sure one day she would.

Jett sat her coffee down and thought back on all that had happened to her in the last few years. When Blake died she was sure she would not survive, but she knew she had to for the sake of Savannah. Savannah had been the apple of her daddy's eye, and Blake had been the love of Jett's life.

Jett remembered the first time she had seen Blake. It was the first day of her sophomore year of high school. She and her two best girlfriends, Maggie and Julie, were checking out all the boys in the hall when Blake walked by. At first they had giggled at his looks. The usual dress in Brannon for boys was khaki pants and oxford cloth button down shirts. Blake stood out in his checked cowboy pearl buttoned shirt, jeans and a belt buckle that looked big enough to be a saucer! He was also wearing cowboy boots, another unusual sight in their school. Blake did not seem to be aware that everyone was staring and giggling at him.

Jett remembered how even then that had impressed her. He was who he was and was comfortable with it. He wasn't trying to change himself for others. He had been born and raised in Texas, cowboy country. When his dad got a job transfer, the family had to move to central Kentucky, and Blake was not happy. Changing schools wasn't fun anytime, but even less when you were a senior and had left all your friends behind in Texas.

Jett had a schoolgirl crush on Blake that never developed into anything. She doubted he even knew her name much less would be interested in her. She thought he was so handsome with his black hair and unusual brown eyes. Jett always noticed a person's eyes first. Her usual choice of color was blue eyes. She never really liked brown eyes, but Blake's weren't just your average dark brown eyes. They were the color of fine bourbon backlit by a candle, rich translucent amber. They were clear, hard to describe, like a marble you could see through the layers of color. She thought maybe his eyes would change shades with emotion, but it was a few years before she got to see her guess was correct.

The word had quickly gotten around school that Blake was more than just a cowboy. He was also a computer whiz. He could do anything on a computer. Rumors had it he had hacked his way in to even high security websites without ever being detected. It wasn't long before Blake was a well-respected man on campus. He helped build a website for the school and also built several computers. Jett couldn't comprehend how computers even worked, much less how to order pieces and parts and put one together. All she knew was how to turn one on, check her email and use her word processing program for writing letters or school papers.

After Blake's graduation from high school he joined the Air Force. The men in his family had all done their service for their country, and Blake was no different. He figured he would put in his four years and then go to college on the GI Bill when he left the service.

Life sometimes doesn't work out the way you plan and that was true for Blake, too. When Blake took his Air Force admission tests he scored so highly on the electronics part they thought the test score was wrong. Blake had noted on his areas of interest that he would like to work with computers, but they had no idea the kid was a computer genius. Why was a kid like this joining the service when he could be in college or making big money in a corporate setting? The Air Force didn't care why; they were elated to have this kind of talent and planned to put Blake to good use. Blake did his normal basic training at Lackland Air Force Base in San Antonio, Texas. While most of the young recruits were suffering from the hot Texas weather, Blake loved every minute of it. He was home, back in Texas and better yet San Antonio had been his home. He'd spent many hot summers working the fence lines of his grandfather's ranch and enduring the near desert-like heat. Basic training was a piece of cake. His long limbs were muscular and defined and his skin soon turned copper, bronzed in the Texas sun. Blake's mother was of Cherokee ancestry, and Blake had inherited the black hair, high cheekbones and dark skin of his mother's people.

Jett did not see Blake again until a couple years after she graduated from high school. After high school, she enrolled part time at the local business college. She got a job as a teller at the bank, and they let her work her hours around her school schedule. She liked her banking job and thought she just might make it a career choice. She started taking classes that would help her learn more about the banking industry. The bank was delighted Jett was taking such an interest. They told her they would help with her tuition if she stayed at the bank.

It was while working at the bank one afternoon that she saw Blake. She knew of the terrible car crash that had taken the life of both his parents. Blake was an only child, and she knew he would take the death of his parents very hard. He had come in on emergency leave from the Air Force to handle his parents' funeral arrangements and handle any necessary estate issues.

Jett had sent flowers to the funeral home with a sympathy card for Blake, even though she doubted he even remembered who she was. When he walked in the bank that day, the sight of him make her heart beat faster. The years since she had seen him had changed him. He had lost any traces of being a teenager. He had grown and filled out some, too, she noticed. His t-shirt was straining against his chest and biceps, his stomach was flat and those long legs were once again making her heart stir.

He was walking straight to her window. She could feel herself blush, the heat rising to her face. Oh, please she thought, don't let me stammer like an idiot. I'm a professional, I can handle this…She smiled her best banking smile and said,"Hello Blake how can I help you?" He wanted to cash a check. No problem; even though he didn't have an account, this had been where his parents banked.

"Jett," he said, "I want to thank you for the flowers and card you sent for my parents. It's been a very rough week and that was very kind of you."

She could hear the slight tremor in his voice as he struggled for composure. Jett told him how sorry she was and how she had come to know his parents from their bank visits. "They were both so proud of you," she told him. "Your mom and dad both always told me where you were stationed and how proud they were of you for serving your country. They told me you were probably the most important enlisted man they had, that you had given them computer ideas and set up networks and even written some programs for the Air Force." Now, he was blushing from her praise.

"Well," he said, "I'm sure I'm not as important as mom and dad thought I was, but it is nice to know they were proud of me." "Hey," he said, "Would you like to have dinner with me? … I mean, I'm sorry I don't even know if you're dating anyone. I know you're not married because your name hasn't changed…" He was now the stammering one.

"I'd love to have dinner," she said, "What time?"

He told her he would pick her up at 7:00 and confirmed she was still living at home with her parents. They had a great dinner and afterwards took a long drive out in the country. He told her that he had re-enlisted for another 4 years after his first four were up. He was thinking after the end of that he might rejoin civilian life. He found himself really pouring his heart out to Jett. He certainly had not intended to do so, but he found she was so easy to talk to. Unlike most people, she really listened. Not only that, he could tell she genuinely was interested in listening. He told her he was, of course, the only child and the only heir in his parents' wills. He had been surprised to find out his mother and dad had mortgage payoff insurance on their farm so he was going to own it free and clear. Also, his mother had taken out a bunch of accidental insurance policies, and since they died in an accident all of them were paying. That combined with inheriting the balance of his father's retirement funds meant Blake had quite an inheritance coming to him. They both had life insurance also, and the loss of life insurance from the car was going to be more money. Blake was a little overwhelmed about all this unexpected wealth and grieved about the loss of his family.

Jett asked if he had decided whether to keep the farm or sell it. Because he was born and raised in Texas, she thought he might want to return to civilian life there. He answered that for right now he was keeping the farm. He was going to try to find someone to look after the grounds and he would come home as often as he could to make sure everything was okay. This was great news for Jett; she hoped she would be seeing a lot more of Blake.

What happened in the following months was the stuff of fairy tales. She and Blake kept in constant communication through phone calls and email. She knew she was in love with him long before the words were actually spoken. She found herself thinking of him every moment of the day, wondering what he was doing, wondering if he was thinking of her, too.

Because of all the estate issues Blake had to deal with, he requested the Air Force transfer him to Wright–Patterson AFB in Dayton, Ohio. They approved his request. It really didn't matter much where his home base was, he traveled a lot to different bases anyway. The way his schedule worked he had most weekends off duty. This made it easy for Blake to come home on the weekends to Brannon, to see to the farm and also to see Jett. On the weekends he didn't have time to drive down, Jett drove up to Dayton to spend time with him. They had both fallen hopelessly in love with one another. Within six months, Blake asked Jett to marry him.

They decided to keep the farm and move into it as their home. They went through his parents' house deciding what they would keep and what they would sell or give away. With that done, Blake gave Jett the okay to change anything she wanted in the house and to decorate it the way she wanted.

She had always loved Blake's house. When his parents moved here they had had it built for them. It was a sprawling stone ranch house built with southwest design. The rooms were large and airy and the kitchen was a cook's dream. The master bedroom suite was almost a house in itself! It had double walk in closets a sitting area and a large bathroom complete with Jacuzzi. The floors were hardwood plank style in light oak in the great room and bedrooms. The kitchen and bathrooms were done in all tiles. There were three other bedrooms besides the master bedroom, and each had its own bath. The great room had a huge stone fireplace and a cathedral ceiling with exposed wooden beams in the ceiling. All the windows had plantation shutters.

They decided to update the house with paint colors of Jett's choice and new leather living room furniture. They sold the master bedroom furniture and replaced it with a vintage- look iron, king size bed. They found a chest of drawers and dresser with mirror that looked just right with the bed. Jett found she loved decorating the house and had quite an eye for color and décor. With just a few changes it no longer looked like Blake's parents house, it looked like Blake and Jett. They turned one of the bedrooms into a computer room-office for Blake. Blake's old room they left as he had left it, full of his childhood things and, for now, Jett loved it just the way it was.

It had taken six months to do the changes they wanted to make to the house. It was almost a year from the day Blake walked in the bank until the day they were married. The wedding was small and just a few school friends, Jett's parents and some of Blake's parents' friends attended. It was an intimate candlelight ceremony in the small, quaint country church Jett had attended her whole life. She chose a floor length, ivory silk dress that was form fitted to her slender body. The neckline was intricately beaded and was cut low enough to accent the bust line. Instead of a full veil, she wore a garland of white roses and babies breath with ivory lace attached, running down the back. Her bouquet was white and blush pink roses. She wore a single strand of pearls around her neck and earrings to match. She had left her hair in its natural style. She had seen too many wedding photos that didn't look natural because of "prom" hair dos, and she didn't want to look back at their wedding pictures 20 years from now and wonder what the heck she had been thinking when she had worn her hair that way. Jett's hair was thick with a natural wave that fell to her shoulders. Her hair was the color of honey and had a natural shine and gloss. Her eyes were blue or green depending on whom you asked and what she was wearing. She was a beautiful bride and as she joined hands with Blake before the minister, he thought she was surely the most beautiful woman in the world and he the luckiest man. When they exchanged rings, she gave him a platinum band engraved inside with "I love you forever". He had a band made to go with her engagement ring. Her engagement ring was a two carat princess cut diamond set in platinum; the band was an eternity style with princess cut diamonds also set in platinum all around. Blake only wished his parents had lived to see this day.

When Jett and Blake discussed a honeymoon destination, Jett's first thought was a beach, maybe even Hawaii. Blake wanted to take her to Texas, to his own hometown of San Antonio. He promised she wouldn't be disappointed and she wasn't. They spent their first night as man and wife in their newly redone home.

The next morning they flew to San Antonio for a week-long honeymoon. They reserved a suite at the Marriott on the River Walk in downtown San Antonio. Jett fell in love with the city at first glance. She loved the River Walk. The San Antonio River wound its way thru the heart of downtown. At river level shops and restaurants lined the walking paths. The landscaping was lush and no matter how hot the day you could walk in the shade along the river. Restaurants had outside tables so you could enjoy a dinner or lunch or just a cold margarita while watching the brightly colored river taxis going up and down the river.

They walked to the Alamo and Jett was astonished to see it was in the heart of downtown. In all the old movies, the Alamo had been in the middle of nowhere; now the Old Fort was the main tourist attraction. As they walked inside the walls and through the fort, looking at the artifacts Jett could imagine all that had happened here. After they toured the Alamo they sat in the park across the street and enjoyed an ice snow cone, just the thing to beat the Texas heat.

They spent hours that week walking along the river, exploring old stores, and shopping the Mexican marketplace. Jett found some wonderful Talavera tile mirrors she thought would look great in the house along with a great old wooden sugar mold with candles to be used in candelabra. They dined at the restaurant at the top of the Tower of the Americas, took in the view from the top where they could see for miles in every direction. Jett could see why Blake loved Texas. They rented a car and Blake took her on a tour of the old missions and out to see the ranch his grandfather had owned, where he had played cowboy and ridden his first horse as a child. They also made a stop at the nursing home where Blake's aging grandfather lived. Blake hardly recognized this shriveled old man as his once robust pa-paw. Harrison Edwards was in his nineties and suffered from Alzheimer's. It was so sad to see him this way. Blake thought once he might have seen some recognition in the old man's eyes. He was very depressed when they left the nursing home. He told Jett as soon as they got home he wanted to look into donating money for Alzheimer's research; he might not be able to cure his grandfather, but he certainly wanted to try to help so someone else might not suffer the same fate one day.

They spent a week walking the old town, listening to Mariachi Bands while strolling along the river eating great food and exploring all the charm of San Antonio. At night they made love and explored the secrets of one another's bodies. It was an intense week of fun and love, one that neither wanted to end. Too soon, it was time for them to return to Kentucky and for Blake to report back to Wright–Patterson for duty.

Jett kept her part time job at the bank and when not traveling on duty, Blake came home most weekends. By the time they'd been married 6 months, Jett was pregnant. They had been a little surprised it hadn't taken any longer to get pregnant. Jett had always had very irregular menstrual cycles, and the doctors told her it might take them a while to conceive. Instead of worrying about it, Jett and Blake had laughed and said they planned to do a lot of practicing to get pregnant. They were both delighted when Jett missed a couple of periods and began to get queasy in the morning. Missing the periods didn't really say too much given her irregularity, but getting morning sickness was what they had been waiting for.

A doctor's appointment confirmed she was indeed pregnant and everything seemed to be just fine. Jett now spent her spare time deciding how to turn the spare bedroom into a nursery. Ultrasounds told them the baby was most likely a girl so Jett had the room painted a pale pink with white baby furniture. She found a great rocking chair, too, and sat it right beside the bed. The room was large enough that she also added a daybed preparing for nights up when the baby needed feeding so she could grab a nap, too. Savannah Grace Edwards was born right on time with her proud father in the delivery room. Seeing the love and tears in his eyes as he held his baby girl, made Jett's heart soar with love for him. He was going to be a great daddy.

The next four years went by quickly, Blake stayed in the Air Force. Jett had resigned herself that Blake would never be a civilian until he retired, although every time he said just four more years…

When the war in Iraq started, Blake came home and told Jett he was going to have to go over for about a month and help set up all the computer networks. He assured her he would be completely safe, and it would be nothing to worry about. Jett didn't like the idea of Blake going but she knew he couldn't argue with orders.

The end to their storybook marriage came with that trip to Iraq. Jett got an email from Blake that day saying he going to catch a ride with an

Army supply truck to another location to help with a computer problem and would email her back as soon as he could. That was his last email. The truck was hit by sniper gunfire and everyone was killed. Jett remembered having nightmares that night, dreaming of Blake saying goodbye and that he loved her and would always be with her. She awoke with a sweat soaked nightshirt and a thumping heart. She heard Savannah crying and ran to check on her. Savannah was four and she loved her daddy more than anything. When Jett tried to calm her and ask what was wrong, did she have a bad dream, Savannah sobbed that she saw Daddy and he told her he loved her and for her to be a good girl and he would send someone to take care of her and mommy.

Jett held the sobbing child and hushed her cries while all the time her own heart was bursting. It was no coincidence to her that both she and Savannah had had such a dream. She knew deep in her heart that Blake was not coming home. The next day she tried to make nothing of the dream and didn't mention it to Savannah. Savannah seemed out of sorts all day, whiny and not herself; she kept crying for her daddy. Every time the phone rang, Jett's trembling hands could hardly hold the phone. She checked her email dozens of times, hoping for word from Blake. Finally the call came; Blake was confirmed dead. The timing was right when both Savannah and Jett had the dream.

Jett thought she would surely not be able to live through those next days. The hardest thing was to tell Savannah her daddy wasn't coming home alive. How do you explain death to a four year old? Savannah just nodded her head sadly. She said she knew her dream was true. She had looked up at Jett with Blake's own eyes and asked, "Who's going to take care of us mommy? Daddy said he'd send someone." Jett only held her tighter, and told her they would be just fine and they would take care of each other.

It was the next day that Star came into the household. With all the plans of bringing Blake home and the funeral arrangements, at first Jett didn't realize Savannah had an imaginary playmate. She was so relieved to see Savannah didn't seem to be grieving and was out side playing. It took a few days of listening to Savannah's four year old language skills and excited words to understand they had a horse in the house. Daddy had always told her he'd get her a horse and now he had sent her one.

CHAPTER 2

▼

Lester and Bernice Puckett lived in the hills and hollows of Eastern Kentucky. They lived in a shack of a house as far up Puckett Branch as you could go. As a matter of fact, there wasn't even a road to the house. Ending about four miles from the little shack, a paved road gave way to a gravel road and then to a rutted-out dirt road before coming to a dead end. The Pucketts walked the rest of the way in to their house. Lester could have cleared out a road in to his house, but the fact was he liked it isolated. Lester Puckett owned 20 acres of woods and hillside up Puckett Hollow; his brother owned the rest.

Lester didn't take to people much. He was a hard man living a hard life and not enjoying any of it. Bernice was a battered wife, barely resembling the girl of her youth. Bernice had the defeated look of a trapped animal. Her cotton shift hung with no shape on her slim body. Her hair was dull and her eyes were smudges of blue in a pale, pinched face. She could have been anywhere between 30 and sixty. It was hard to tell by looking at her. Life with Lester had not been kind.

About the only work in Eastern Kentucky was coal mining, and Lester worked in the mines and hated every minute of it. He came home every night covered in the black of the mines, his back bent from working in cramped spaces all day.

Lester and Bernice's house had electricity although it was stolen. Lester had rigged the lines and run a bypass on the main power line to his house. There was no meter. Heat was provided by an open fireplace in the living room. The kitchen had a stove, an old Sears refrigerator, and a sink. There were no cabinets, just some shelves that held a few dishes and pots and pans.

Another set of shelves held rows of canned fruits and vegetables Bernice had grown and canned for the family.

Water was provided by a well, and Lester had put a pump in to get the water to the house. Every night when Lester got home, Bernice had a washtub of water heated and ready for his bath. The water quickly turned black from the coal dust as Lester washed away the day's work.

Lester believed in living off the land. He hunted year round and was an excellent shot. The woods were full of small game and the family rarely didn't have some kind of meat that Lester had killed and skinned himself. He was as good with a knife as he was with a gun.

Bernice had a garden and was expected to raise enough to feed the family throughout the summer and can enough for the winter months. She raised corn, potatoes, tomatoes and beans. There were wild strawberries and blackberries in the woods that she picked to make jam. Lester would bring in apples from town, and Bernice would make apple butter and dried apples for the winter.

They usually had a couple pigs in a pen out back that they would raise and fatten up to kill in the fall. The meat from the pig was good for bacon and sausage along with rib meat, and chops and roasts. All in all, the Pucketts were self-sufficient. They didn't need much outside of what they grew or killed. They bought the staple items, flour, sugar and milk from the little country store at the mouth of the hollow.

Bernice and Lester had twin sons, Elvis Puckett and Aaron Puckett. Bernice had named them after Elvis Presley and his twin brother that died Aaron. Bernice loved to hear Elvis sing. When the boys were born that cold January 8th, she knew she was going to name them after Elvis. She thought them being born on his birthday was a sign. It was a hard birth. Lester didn't put much faith in doctors so the only help Bernice had when her time came was her mother. It was a miracle the boys lived at all, born under such conditions. Bernice, severely weakened, managed to survive the birth, too, although she was never able to have any more children.

At first glance Elvis and Aaron were identical twins. I say at first glance because until they opened their eyes or until you examined them really closely they looked alike. Two things set them apart. Elvis was born with two thumbs on his left hand. The second thumb was more the size of a little toe, but it was there, growing at the joint of his thumb.

Had the boys been born in a hospital the extra digit would have been removed with little problem, but being born at home, it was left alone. Aaron's distinguishing feature was his eyes, one blue the other green. Many people thought the boys were cursed being born the way they were. Rural mountain people had a lot of strange beliefs. The boys were always considered oddities and grew up with people and other kids staring at them and calling them names.

Lester was determined to raise the boys to be a tough as he was. He was bitter the boys were not normal and blamed Bernice that it was so. Lester drank, and when he drank he was mean drunk. The boys grew up under the heavy hand of their father's beating, watching their mother getting beaten as well. They hated their mother and father. They hated their father for being the mean son a bitch he was, and they hated their mother for being weak and not protecting them and for bringing them into this world to begin with.

The boys were smart but because of the sneers from the other kids, they hated school and skipped whenever they could. When they missed too many days, the truant officer would show up at the house and threaten Lester about keeping the boys in school. This always meant another beating. The boys swore to each other they would kill their father one day and be free from Puckett Hollow and the hell they lived in.

Lester saw his chance to quit working in the mines. Everybody was claiming black lung back then and getting on disability. It meant going to some doctors, but Lester figured if he could draw some money and not have to work it would be worth the hassle. The disability didn't take much proving. In those days if you could prove you had ever worked underground in the mines you could "get on the draw". Of course he had worked in the mines, plus he had smoked all his life so his lungs were bad. He qualified for benefits with no problem. That gave him even more time to hunt, get drunk, and beat Bernice and the boys.

The only good thing the boys could say about Lester is he did teach them how to hunt, shoot, fish, skin a deer or any kind of game they killed. The boys were natural hunters; they could sit for hours, motionless, waiting for a good shot. Yes, Dad taught them well. He taught them how to survive.

The boys were inseparable. They were so close they could literally read each others' thoughts. If one was sick, the other could feel the symptoms. They needed few words to communicate with each other. All through school they kept in the same room and took the same classes; they didn't like being separated. Teachers who tried to put them in separate classes soon gave up.

Always, they were the subjects of ridicule for being different. They called Elvis "Thumbs" and Aaron "Two-Tone" because if his different eye coloration. Most people found it hard to look at Aaron very long. His blue eye was as cold as ice, and his green eye held no light. The eye almost looked reptilian. Neither boy had any emotion in his face. They lived behind a mask. They were bullied and picked on but neither ever backed away from a fight and the boys, though not big were strong and tough and could whip boys twice their size.

At their full growth they were each about 5'8 and weighed about 150 lbs. They were lean and wiry but strong from hard work and the way they lived. They loved to watch war movies on the little black and white TV they had and thought when they got old enough they would run away from home and join the Marines. They couldn't wait to leave home.

One night Lester was drunk and looking for a fight. The boys had warned him a year ago they wouldn't be taking any more beatings, and they wouldn't be allowing him to beat their mother. Bernice had pneumonia and was in bed barely breathing, her thin body racked by deep coughs. They could hear her gasping for breath. They had tried to get her to go to a doctor, but she refused. Now she was dying, and the boys knew it. Actually, they discovered they didn't care. Long ago they had stopped caring for anybody or anything except each other.

Lester went into the bedroom and demanded Bernie get up and fix him something to eat, but she was too weak to even raise her head. The boys heard Lester swear at her and saw him grab her arm and try to drag her out of bed. They told Lester to leave her alone Lester came at them with murder in his eyes. He would teach those sons of a bitch to tell him what to do. He threw a punch at Elvis, and Aaron picked up a cast iron skillet and hit him as hard as could on the side of the head. Lester crumpled to the ground. The boys took one look at each other and decided what to do. It was time. Lester was knocked out cold, and their mother was good as dead. They were leaving. The boys took a few belongings, some money they found in their dad's wallet, and walked out, leaving Puckett Hollow for good.

Then, they had argued for the first time. Elvis wanted to kill their father and burn down the house. Aaron wanted to also but talked Elvis into refraining. It wouldn't be the smart thing to do because they would end up in jail for arson and murder.

Aaron and Elvis walked and hitchhiked to the nearest town, Williamson, West Virginia. They slept in the hospital's waiting room. Back in the country it was nothing to see people all hours at the hospital asleep in chairs or on the floor. You didn't leave your kin when they were sick. The boys knew they wouldn't be questioned if they came in quietly and didn't make a fuss.

They used the restroom the next morning to freshen up a little then walked into town to the Marine recruiting office. They walked in and told the recruiter they wanted to join up. The recruiter took one look at the odd pair in front of him and started to say something smart, but something in the dead look of their eyes told him not to. He did tell them he didn't think they were old enough and asked if they could produce birth certificates to prove their age. Elvis put his hand, the one with the double thumb on the desk and said, "Look, we were born at home and we don't have no birth certificate. We're old enough. We just turned 18 on January 8th. I'm Elvis, this is my brother Aaron, and we want to join the Marines but we have conditions."

Once again the recruiter stifled a snicker, "Who did these kids think they were—one with 3 thumbs and one with two colored eyes—telling the U.S. Marines what they were going to do?" They had balls— he'd give them that much. Because of Aaron's eyes and Elvis's extra digits, many people made the mistake of thinking the boys were dumb or mildly retarded. People tended to speak louder than necessary to them. The boys realized this at an early age. It really pissed them off. Why did everyone think because they were different you had to talk louder or slower like they were stupid? They could feel the rage gathering inside.

Elvis once again spoke, "We want join up but only under the condition that we stay together. We stay together through basic and then stay together wherever we're sent after that. And you don't have to talk loud. We hear you just fine. Just because we're different don't mean we can't hear."

"Look, you boys have to pass a test. We don't take just anybody walks in off the street to be a Marine. We're looking for a specific kind of man, and I'm not sure you boys could make the cut."

Aaron spoke this time, his odd eyes staring intently at the recruiter. "We'll take your test. If we make over 90% will you take us, specify we stay together, and give us a chance?"

The recruiter nodded, "Okay boys, I'll call your bluff. You both score over 90% on the test and then pass the physical, you're in." He put the boys in separate rooms and gave them the test. He didn't think those two had a snowball's chance in hell getting 90%. When he graded the tests, he could hardly believe it. Both boys had scored exactly the same, 95%. They had missed the same question—unbelievable! Maybe it was true that twins were really in tune with each other. These two certainly were. Well, he would hold true to his word. He signed the boys up, fudging the date of birth, and told them they would need to go to Huntington, West Virginia, for their physicals. If they passed there, they were on their way to being United States Marines. He even gave them bus fare to Huntington. He was beginning to like these boys. Little did he know, he had just signed the way for Aaron and Elvis to get the training they needed to be the killers they were born to be.

Aaron and Elvis reported to Huntington for their physicals and passed with flying colors. The boys were in excellent health, physically fit with acute hearing and perfect vision. They were on their way to boot camp!

The U.S. Marines are known for their ability to weed out the inferior, the weak, and the less than dedicated. Boot camp in the Marine Corps is rough. Any weakness is sought after and zoomed in on to try to break a recruit. The Marines want only the best, only men who can face tough choices and do what has to be done. Marines have to be able to carry out any order without question. If the Puckett boys had a weakness, it was this last quality. They hated authority. They had been beaten their whole lives for trying to think their own way. If they were to become Marines, this was going to be the obstacle they needed to overcome.

Going though the lines at boot camp every recruit looks pretty much the same. All hair is cut short, all clothing is alike, and all boys look the same. With Elvis and Aaron, the sergeant saw right away he had a couple different ones, identical twins. "Well, well. This is going to be fun," he thought. When he noticed the extra thumb and two color eyes, he knew he was going to weed out these inferior specimens.

The sergeant was right in their faces screaming obscenities at the two, making fun of their eyes and hands. The boys' faces reddened, but neither blinked. They set their jaws and stared straight ahead, stony masks for faces. They were determined to be Marines; they could put up with anything for 6 weeks. After all, they had been putting up with ridicule their whole lives.

The sergeant soon saw these boys were tough. They were in excellent physical condition. They did their daily runs with ease and never faltered under any conditions. When the company went to the rifle range the first time, the sergeant again was in their faces. "Can you shoot, Thumbs?" Sgt. Brown asked.

"Sir, yes sir!" Elvis replied.

"What about your two-toned brother, can he shoot straight?"

"Sir, yes sir, my brother and I will out shoot any man in the company, sir."

"Is that a fact?"

"Sir, yes sir, that's a fact."

Brown thought he had them this time, how dare they be so arrogant, the first sign the boys couldn't take the heat. "Tell you what," he said, "if you boys don't shoot better than the rest of these boys, all of you are going to do 10 miles with heavy packs. I know you boys aren't popular to begin with, so let's see how you do after you screw up and I punish the whole platoon."

Again, the boys' faces held no emotion. They looked straight ahead. Brown let everyone else shoot first, put some pressure on these boys, let them sweat it out a bit.

When it came their turns, the boys burned up the targets. They'd been shooting and hunting their whole life. This was a piece of cake. Brown could hardly believe his eyes when he saw the tight grouping of their shots, all in the bull's eye. "Well, well," he thought, "I've got myself a couple of genuine shooters…"

The boys also breezed though survival training. They had to admit, their dad had been a mean man, but he had certainly taught them everything they need to be a good Marine. They could out shoot, out hunt, out smart anyone in the woods. They had lived in survival camp their whole lives. When they heard the other recruits complaining at nights, they laughed to themselves. Hell, compared to the Lester Puckett household, the Marine Corp was like 4-H camp.

After boot camp, the boys did let their father know where they were. Lester was actually kind of proud that the boys had joined the Marines. They found out their mother had died a week or so after they left home. The pneumonia had finally killed her, just as they knew it would.

After their 4-year stint was up in the Corps, the Marines tried to get the boys to be career Marines, promising to send them to sniper scout school for training. They were the best natural shooters the Marines had seen in a long time. Elvis and Aaron were tempted, but they declined. No real wars going on, no one to kill, why stay in and have someone tell you what to do for the rest of your life? No, thank you, they'd had enough. They had a couple cousins who they liked pretty well. One lived in Illinois; the other lived in Brannon, KY, not far from Lexington. It was while visiting Bobby Dean in Illinois, they saw a help wanted sign at a slaughterhouse. This wasn't an ordinary cattle slaughterhouse. No, this was a horse slaughterhouse. Killing was killing. It didn't matter much what, so Elvis and Aaron thought they would apply for a job and stay with their cousin for a while.

Although most people hated the work they did there at the slaughterhouse, the boys loved it. They loved the copper smell of blood. They loved to see the fear and fright in the eyes of the horses. They loved to kill. Being in the Marines had only enhanced that thrill of killing. They loved the sense of power they felt when they killed.

Most of the workers in the plant were illegals or people who couldn't find work anywhere else. Aaron and Elvis quickly gained rank in the plant and were put in management positions. Still they liked it best right on the kill floor. They would sometimes go out to the pens and hand-select a few of the horses to kill.

When the workers saw Aaron and Elvis do their handiwork, they soon learned these were not men to fool with. They were feared by the workers. Aaron and Elvis would sometimes shoot the horses, or sometimes they slit their throats. What made other men shudder made Aaron and Elvis smile.

When a particularly pretty horse came through, a palomino, or nice spotted or paint horse, the boys really took their time. They took great pains to skin the dead horses, keeping as much of the hide intact as they could. They knew how to skin a buck and how to tan the hides; horses would be no different. They soon had their house filled with horse skins on the walls and on the floors as rugs. They were so good they managed to skin the horses with manes attached. Some of the hides were beautiful. Soon they saw with a discreet word put out they had a way to make some extra money with these hides.

Normally all the scrap meat, bones and waste were sent to the rendering plant. No one took a count of the actual parts that came and went, so a few hides missing weren't missed at all. They also saw another sideline business with horses' tails. They had seen in magazines where show horse owners sometimes use tail extensions to fill out and give more volume to the horses' tails. Any good looking coloration of tail hair was cut off and sold. The workers in the plant saw what was going on, but no one dared cross the brothers. One illegal worker, Pedro, mentioned it to the brothers one day, hinting that he was going to tell the boss unless they paid him a little cash on the side to keep quiet. The next day Pedro did not show up, nor the next. In fact, no one ever saw him again.

That was the first kill.

CHAPTER 3

▼

Margaret (Maggie) May was one of Jett's girlfriends all through school. For as long as anyone could remember Maggie wanted to be a police officer, like her dad, Wyatt. Back in high school when other girls had been worrying about a date for the prom, the perfect hairdo or a new dress, Maggie had her head buried in a true crime book or a mystery novel.

Brannon is in the heart of Bluegrass Country. Horse farms scatter over several surrounding counties. The gently rolling fields and green grass are perfect for raising horses. This area of Kentucky has a lot of limestone. It is thought the limestone is one of the things that make the grass so good for the young horses. It gives them essential elements that grow strong, straight bones.

Brannon got a boost in local economy when the Japanese automaker Ho Supawa decided to build a plant there to manufacturer their most popular car, the Shinzui. Ho Supawa in English roughly translates to horsepower and Shinzui means spirit. The cars sold literally as quickly as they came off the assembly line. Brannon grew almost overnight to accommodate new residents that moved to the area to work.

The little town of Brannon and the community surrounding it did not have much in the way of real crime. The auto plant bought more residents and more commuting traffic to the town, but it was still a nice place to live and work without much fear. As police chief, Wyatt's job was more administrative than the days when he was a patrol officer. Back in those days, Maggie used to love to ride with her dad in the cruiser and out on calls. She had always been adamant about wanting to follow in her dad's footsteps and have a career in law enforcement. As Maggie got older and more insistent he took her with him more and more. He thought if she were intent on being in police work he would teach her what he knew and also expose her to some hazards of the job just to see if she was tough enough. He taught her how to shoot both handguns and rifles. He taught her about gun safety, how to assemble and disassemble a gun, how to clean and care for it. Maggie proved to be an eager and good student. She asked intelligent questions and never grumbled about anything he asked her to do or re-do.

The first time he took her with him to an automobile accident he thought she might give up the idea of police work. Some people can't take the sight of blood and death. The first couple of wrecks were just fender benders with no real injuries sustained to any of the parties involved. But one Friday night a call came in and the code the dispatcher used was one for a traffic fatality. Wyatt warned Maggie when she said wanted to go with him that this was going to be a bad accident. She still said she wanted to go. When they arrived at the scene, it was even worse than Wyatt had anticipated. It was a three-car crash. One car still had an occupant trapped inside, and emergency personnel were calling in the Jaws of Life equipment to free the trapped motorist. Another of the cars had suffered so much damage it was hard to tell what had happened or what kind of car it had been. The driver was dead, and the passenger had been thrown from the car. The driver of the third car was bleeding badly but was conscious and responding to basic questions.

Because Brannon was a relatively small community, Wyatt was pretty sure both he and Maggie would know some of the people in the accident. The driver in the trapped car Wyatt recognized as a friend of Maggie's from school. The passenger who was thrown from the car was a girl who looked to be of high school age, too, maybe another friend of Maggie's. The girl was badly injured and was in hysterics from the crash. She was hurt, scared, and pleading to know if Robbie was hurt. Robbie was the dead driver. A logical conclusion was this young couple was out on a Friday night date. This was one of those times when being a police officer was tough. It always seemed worse when there were young people killed. Kids riding along, laughing one minute without a care in the world, and in the next instant their lives are changed forever.

Wyatt cautioned Maggie before he let her out of the cruiser. "There is one dead, and I think you know him and probably the passenger thrown from the vehicle. It's not pretty over there, Maggie. There's a lot of blood and a lot maybe you wouldn't want to see."

Maggie took a deep breath, set a determined look on her face and told Wyatt she was ready to see. This was going to test Maggie, could she really handle the bad part of police work, could she keep her head in the face of personal feelings for victims where there was great injury and death? She was about to find out if her dream to be in police work could become a reality.

Wyatt had been surprised and proud of the way Maggie handled herself that night. She was calm, professional and level headed. She spoke in slow, soothing words to the hysterical girl and managed to calm her down before the ambulance took her to the hospital. Wyatt could tell she was struggling with emotions as she saw Robbie, the dead boy, in the car. His head had shattered the windshield and there were gashes in his face, his eyes were open wide, and his mouth was agape with a silent scream of death. Still, she held herself together and joined her dad trying to reconstruct the wreck. Wyatt knew after that night there was no use in trying to discourage Maggie from police work. She had the job in her blood, and he would help her go as far as she could. He wished he had been successful in changing his wife's mind when Maggie was born. She was determined to name the baby Margaret, after her grandmother, whom she adored. Wyatt understood, but still he knew the baby girl he held in his arms would be subject to jokes all her life if she were named Margaret. Maggie would be what she would be called, and Maggie May would be the brunt of many jokes and teasing. Rod Stewart's Maggie May was a classic rock'n roll song. It was inevitable. Wyatt knew all about jokes. Even though he liked his name, after he joined law enforcement, he had had his share of Wyatt Earp jokes.

Maggie had heard her share of Maggie May songs in high school and that followed her throughout college. She wearied of it, but took it in good humor. She decided if she reacted, it would only make people worse, but if she just laughed with them, then pretty soon it wouldn't be an issue. She had been correct. Maybe some day when she married and lost the "May" last name she would be free of Maggie May, but that wasn't a day she was actively pursuing. The only thing that really mattered to Maggie was being a police officer. She had gone to Eastern Kentucky University and majored in law enforcement with a minor in psychology. She was really interested in the criminal mind and what made someone turn to a life of crime. She knew sometimes people turned to crime because of circumstance; however, she also felt there were a great number who were just born with a streak of evil and didn't care about right and wrong.

After college Maggie had gotten a job with the Lexington, Kentucky police department. The Lexington, Kentucky police served all the city and Fayette County. She was at the very top of her class of new recruits and her dad beamed with pride as she was sworn in as an officer. Maggie started like all new recruits as a patrol officer, handling traffic and general duties. She longed to be a homicide detective, but knew she would have to put in her time and go through the ranks. In the meantime she started taking graduate classes in psychology at the University of Kentucky.

She stayed two years in Lexington working patrol and the vice squads before she decided to try her luck applying with the FBI. She was called for an interview, flew to Quantico, and was accepted! Her dream was finally coming true. She was going to be Special Agent Margaret May.

She had to endure the rigorous training of the Academy and the ruthless teasing about her name. She loved every minute of it. She had always kept herself in great physical condition and it paid off in training. She had run and lifted weights since high school and also had taken Tae Kwan Do in addition to already having been a local police officer with some case experience. She could already envision herself head of some major crime or serial killer task force. Maggie May, super agent, to the rescue.

Maggie had wanted training to be a profiler, but the Academy decided she needed some field experience instead. They sent her to the field office in Chicago, Illinois for her first assignment. In Chicago she was issued her weapon, a Sig Sauer P226 9mm, her FBI credentials, and her body armor.

There was no lack of crime in Chicago, and Maggie loved every minute of it. She saw some horrible things, learned a lot about the Mob and gang wars and handled some pretty gruesome crime scenes. Still, she was hoping for the one big case that would take her career to the places she wanted to go. She spent her spare time searching the FBI data bases looking for unsolved crimes, putting in searches for missing persons, and playing with different key words trying to find anything that had slipped through the system. She got a lot of hits for unsolved missing persons. This in itself wasn't unusual she supposed because there were a lot of runaways and transient people who didn't want to be found. That didn't necessarily mean they were dead. But she had a gut feeling about this, and any cop knows you follow your gut, so she was going to keep at this. Something wasn't right. There were far too many unsolved missing persons cases going back for several years in several states of the Midwest. She started going back through newspaper archives to read stories. It was always the same. The missing person had simply disappeared from the face of the earth. Most of the missing was young girls or prostitutes, but some were people who just never came home. In all these cases there was nothing amiss in their personal lives, no problems either personal or financial that would make people run. They just simply disappeared without a trace. None of their bank accounts was ever accessed, and none of their credit cards was ever used. These especially were the cases that made Maggie's hair on the back of her neck stand up. She felt something very bad was out there that no one had put together yet.

CHAPTER 4

▼

The slaughterhouse was not in town. It was out away from everything. In addition to the slaughterhouse, BFI also had its own meat processing and packing area and its own rendering plant. The smell from the slaughter waiting pens and the rendering plant was so bad that no one wanted to live downwind from it. It remained a pretty isolated area.

Aaron and Elvis had quickly learned the entire process from kill to finish and worked in either area wherever they were needed. They learned how to butcher and cut the select cuts from meat so that it was ready for packing to be sent overseas. Horse meat wasn't eaten in the United States, but there was a market for it overseas in Europe and Japan. Back home in Puckett Hollow Aaron and Elvis had hunted and killed just about every kind of game in the area. They didn't see a thing wrong with eating horses, no different than cows to them. They took some horsemeat home with them one night just to try it and found they liked it. Who was the government to tell them what they could and couldn't eat?

With the money they made from their extra sales from hides and horsehair the Pucketts bought guns. They loved guns and spent their spare time going to local gun shows and even to Chicago to buy guns. In a few years they had quite an extensive collection. They bought some from shows, some from pawn shops, some from locals that needed extra cash, some right off the streets of Chicago. They knew some of the guns were probably hot, but they didn't particularly care. They had AK 47's SK's, Uzis, and every caliber handgun. They had revolvers and automatics, rifles and shotguns, assault weapons and target pistols. They kept their collection in gun safes locked up, and they told no one what they had.

They had bought an old house on five acres of mostly wooded land not long after they began their job at the slaughterhouse. Their cousin Bobby Dean had decided to move back to Kentucky so they couldn't stay with him any longer. They had fixed the house up and had fenced the property in. They kept the gate locked at all times. They had been trained since childhood to be self-sufficient and they carried much of this with them. They had a garden every summer, growing as much of their own food as they could. They found an old widow who canned and froze what they grew, and gave her half of it for doing it for them. It was a good deal for both parties.

They bought an old white van and took it on hunting trips. In the back they had an old freezer. This allowed them to ice down their deer when they went on longer hunting trips. They had a late model pickup truck they used to go back and forth to work. They had come into some unexpected money after their father died. A strip mining company had approached them about buying their land in Puckett Hollow. Their uncle had already sold out so they boys figured they may as well, too. They didn't ever want to live back there again anyway.

Aaron and Elvis splurged a little on a hunting trip to Canada with some of their inheritance money. They wanted to get some big game. They had a guide, and only three other men were on the hunt. One of the guys named Vinnie, a small wiry guy with slicked back black hair, a heavy Italian accent and an attitude was from Chicago. He bragged about being the best shooter and made fun of the eyes of Aaron and Elvis' third thumb. The older man who was with Vinnie shut him up with just a nod of his head. "We'll let the shooting do the talking," the man said. There was something in the twin's eyes that told the man these men were not just the misfits that people took them for on sight. The other man on the hunt was a retired banker out for a wall trophy. Aaron and Elvis thought unless an animal died of old age in front of the man, he wouldn't be bagging a hit.

By the end of the hunt Aaron and Elvis were the only ones who were taking home a kill. Elvis had taken a grizzly down at such long range no one but Aaron could believe he'd made the shot. Aaron just smiled and said, "Nice shot, brother," like it was an everyday thing. Aaron got a huge elk, like Elvis's, a one-shot kill. The group was even more stunned when Elvis field dressed and skinned the bear with precision. Both brothers were going to have the heads mounted by a taxidermist, but Elvis wanted the bear hide to add to his collection at home. A nice bear skin would look great next to his bed. Vinnie wasn't bragging anymore, and the older man was looking very thoughtful at the two brothers. He asked the brothers to join Vinnie and him for dinner that night.

At dinner he asked Elvis and Aaron where they lived, what they did for a living, where they'd learned to shoot like they did. All week the man had only been referred to as Mr.G. It was obvious Vinnie worked for Mr.G, maybe even a bodyguard for him. By the accent and attitude, Aaron and Elvis had pretty much figured out that Mr. G was some kind of Chicago mobster and Vinnie was his hit man. Vinnie was very subdued during dinner. Aaron and Elvis could feel the hate rolling off him. Jealous of the attention Mr. G was giving them, he was seething.

Elvis and Aaron didn't talk much, but they did tell Mr. G they were from Eastern Kentucky and their dad and the Marine Corps had taught them how to shoot and hunt. They told him they worked at the slaughterhouse.

Mr. G. looked thoughtfully at the men and then asked, "Who do you think Vinnie and I are?"

Aaron stared his odd eyes directly at the old man and said, "Well, don't rightly know, but me and Elvis figure you and Vinnie are some kind of mobsters that like to hunt. We figure you're the boss, and Vinnie is either your bodyguard or hit man or both." Elvis nodded in agreement.

"You men have a great talent for shooting, and on occasion I could use a couple of good shooters. Your pay would be high and in cash. You are wasting your time where you are now. I could make you very rich men." Mr. G gave them a card with a phone number on it. "You ever want to work for me, call this number." With that he summoned the waiter for the bill, and he and Vinnie left for their rooms.

CHAPTER 5

▼

The day Pedro threatened Aaron and Elvis they knew they would have to take care of him. When the work day was over, they were driving home when they saw Pedro walking down the road. No one was around, no other traffic in either direction. They had driven the van to work that day because the truck had had a flat that morning, and they didn't have time to fool with it. This worked out much better.

"Hey Pedro, need a lift?" When Pedro climbed in the back of the van, they asked him where he was headed. "I am staying at the church in town right now; I am saving all my money to send to Mexico to bring my wife and daughter here. The Padre at the church lets me sleep in the basement and do odd jobs for my rent."

This was perfect. They offered Pedro a home cooked meal at their house and told him they would take him back to the church afterwards. They told him they had fresh garden vegetables and were grilling steaks. They could see the man's mouth watering. When they got home, Aaron went around opening the back door of the van. When he opened it, he met Pedro with a knife and killed him with a stab to his heart. They rolled him in an old blanket they had in the van and after they had their dinner, drove back to the slaughterhouse. They were on a high. Aaron kept talking about what it was like to see the light go out of Pedro's eyes, what a rush he got from the kill. Animals were fun to hunt, but he'd never gotten the thrill like doing Pedro.

Over dinner they discussed how to get rid of the body. As an idea formulated in his mind, an evil smile curled Elvis's lip, revealing tobacco stained teeth, "Hey, Aaron, let's render him."

The glint in Aaron's two-toned eyes reflected his pleasure, and the high fives sealed the plan. That night, they drove back to the slaughterhouse and processed Pedro. By the time they finished cutting and grinding, there wasn't enough left to identify a human part. They threw him in the rendering boiler with all the carcasses and bones of that day. Next morning when the plant started up, Pedro would be no more than bone meal and dog food; not a single trace of him would be left. It was the perfect murder. More importantly, it set their course for the future. That first kill started one of the longest runs of serial killings in the United States.

Evil had been born in them and the abuse they had suffered at the hands of their father only made it worse. They had joined the Marines in hopes of killing someone. Unfortunately for them, they had gone in after Vietnam and before any of the Gulf conflict, so there was no killing for them to do. Hunting was a way to pacify the growing desire to kill, but once they had killed Pedro they knew there was no turning back. Killing was all they thought about.

CHAPTER 6

▼

Some people seem to live a charmed life. This was the case with Julianna and Daniel Parker. The two had known each other literally all their lives. They grew up in the same town, went to the same schools and chose the same profession for their careers. Both were children of veterinarians who worked in the same practice. Both sets of parents were delighted when Julianna and Daniel started dating in high school and when they both announced desires to follow in their fathers' footsteps.

They chose Ohio State to go to college because of the Veterinary School located there. They both took as many classes as they could together so they could study together during their undergraduate work. Neither had any problem being accepted for the Veterinary School; both were top students with high grade point averages. One of the reasons they did so well in school was they had been around animals all their lives and had spent every summer since they were old enough helping out at the clinic during summers.

The two got married the summer between college graduation and the start of Veterinary School. The parents thought this was a great idea. Both sets of parents were paying all the schooling costs. That meant when Julianna and Daniel graduated from Veterinary School, they would be debt free, a rare thing for any student, much less for a doctor in any medical field.

Julianna and Daniel returned to Central Kentucky and joined the practice of their fathers. It wouldn't be too long before the fathers would retire and hand the practice over to them. Life had been very good for the young couple. They had a beautiful future ahead of them.

They bought a house that had a five-acre tract of land and an old barn. The house was old but had been recently renovated so they didn't expect any immediate expenditure. The barn needed some fixing up, but they were not in any real hurry. Julianna wanted a horse but she knew for at least the first year of work they would be so busy she wouldn't have time to ride or give a horse the attention it needed.

Julianna had ridden for as long as she remembered. There were pictures of her on horses when she was little more than a toddler. Her mother was an excellent rider and had put Julianna on her horse when she was still in diapers. Buck had been a great horse to learn how to ride and she had ridden him until he got too old. He had died while she was away at college and it had broken her heart. Laminitis had taken Buck's life at age twenty-five. Julianna wanted to get a horse and train it from scratch. Daniel had promised her as soon as they got on their feet and settled in they would fix up the barn and get her a horse.

The clinic where they worked served both large and small animals. Julianna was going to stay with small animals, but Daniel was going to treat some of his dad's horse and cattle owners' patients. Daniel spent a lot of time with his dad, going on calls and learning about all the animals that one day would be in his care.

Life went along as good as it could get. The clinic was thriving, Julianna and Daniel were happy, and Julianna was ready for that horse she'd been promised. They got the barn fixed up, and now all they needed to do was find the perfect horse.

The clinic kept one vet on call 24/7 for their patients, both large and small. They had a number of thoroughbred clients in Central Kentucky that needed a doctor available any time day or night. One Saturday after the clinic closed office hours, Daniel's pager went off. It was a call for him to go to one of the larger horse farms to take a look at a young thoroughbred the owner thought might have colic. Julianna decided to ride along because it was a beautiful sunny fall day and she loved riding through horse country, seeing all the miles of white fences with fields of yearling horses running and playing.

When they arrived at the farm, Julianna couldn't take her eyes away from a lone horse in one of the smaller fields. He looked agitated, running back and forth along the fence line and she could see he was in a full sweat. As they passed the field, she got a closer look at the horse. He was beautiful, solid black with a white star on his forehead. His mane was tangled and his eyes had a wild look to them.

"Daniel, look at that horse, wonder what is wrong with him? He looks very unhappy and totally uncared for. Look how tangled his mane is, and he looks like he hasn't seen a brush."

Daniel looked out his side window as they passed the horse, "You're right that is not a happy horse."

After seeing the horse the owner was concerned about and assuring him that the colt seemed to be fine, Daniel asked about the black horse in the field. "Oh, him," Mr. Martin said, "He's crazy, no one can get near him. He belongs to an Arab Prince who bred him and sent him over here to be trained. The Prince travels over here a lot and wants his own horse to ride when he visits. The horse has excellent bloodlines, but no one has been able to handle him. The Prince, who is an excellent breeder and horseman in his own right, failed him as have several other Arab trainers. He sent him here in hopes that someone could handle him. So far, we've had no luck. The Prince has had all the well-known natural horsemen flown in to try their hand with the horse, but so far no progress has been made. I'm afraid he's going to be forced to put him down. Damn shame, he's a fine specimen, but he's damn near killed everyone who gets around him. We can't groom him, last time we had to look at his feet we had to tranquilize him with a dart gun."

Julianna was captivated by the young colt pacing around the field. She knew it was crazy, but she felt a kinship for this wild horse. She walked closer to the fence to see what he would do. He reared on his hind legs and whinnied loudly. As soon as his front legs hit the ground he bucked his back legs and ran off. He was a beauty.

" Julianna, get away from there, that horse could come right through the fence if he wanted to," Daniel yelled. Instead of backing away, Julianna stood very still and locked eyes with the horse that had stopped running and was staring at her snorting from the center of the field.

She started taking to the horse." You're a big boy aren't you? Yes you are, you're a handsome boy, too. I don't think I've ever seen a prettier boy. Why are you so angry? You know I won't hurt you. Can I take a step closer? I promise just one step, and we'll see what you think."

She took a step closer to the fence as once again Daniel yelled a warning. Julianna put a finger to her mouth in a sign to tell Daniel to shut up. Daniel and Mr. Martin both shook their heads like she was not making a good decision. When she took a step toward the fence, the big horse once again whinnied and snorted his disapproval. He came running toward the fence. Julianna tried to stay clam and kept talking to the horse, "I'm not afraid of you and I think you and I are going to be friends. What do you think about that?" The horse did a scooting rodeo back legs halt just a few feet short from the fence. "That's what I thought. You're trying to get the bluff on me aren't you? Well, guess what, I'm on to you. I'm going to stand right here and talk to you a while longer."

The horse stood and looked at her for a moment before he ran the length of the fence and back. She stood on the same spot until he came back in the middle of the field, stopped running and started picking at some grass. "Ah," she said, "That's a good boy. There's no need to be upset all the time. Look at you. Your mane is all tangled, your coat is dull from the need of a good bath and brushing, and you're covered with sweat." The horse raised his head and shook it back and forth, then raised his front hoof and pawed the ground a couple times. She just laughed at him and he presently put his big head back down and started eating the grass again. In just those short few minutes, she felt like she'd made a start with the horse, and her mind was made up. She walked back over to where Mr. Martin and Daniel were still standing and announced, "I want to buy that horse. Is there some way we can get in touch with the Prince to see if he will sell him to me?"

"Julianna," Daniel protested, "We can't buy this horse! For one reason he can't even be touched. He will kill you, and besides that even if the Prince would sell him, we don't have the money to acquire a horse with a pedigree as long as his."

Once again they heard the horse making a racket and turned to see what had provoked him. The Prince or who Julianna assumed was the Prince was walking toward them. He was dressed in traditional Arab robe and head wrap. He looked to be about 6 feet tall, slim, very dark skinned, very white teeth, and with a heavy 5:00 shadow of a beard. Mr. Martin made the introductions.

Prince Shaheen said to Julianna, "Sahara seemed to quiet down a little for you, what did you do?"

"I just talked to him. He is a beautiful horse. Mr. Martin says you have given up on him I would like to buy him if you will sell him." Again Daniel started to speak, but Julianna have him a look that silenced him immediately.

"Sahara is not for sale," the Prince said. "His bloodline has been in my family for years. If he cannot be ridden, he will be destroyed."

Destroyed? Julianna couldn't bear to think this horse would be killed. She knew Arab men did not like to be told what to do by a woman, but she couldn't help herself. "Please, Prince" she said, "Let me try with him. I may not be able to break him, but please let me try."

"What do you know of breaking a horse like this?" he said, mocking her.

"I have ridden all my life. I think Sahara and I can reach an understanding if you will let me try."

The Prince was rather amused at the young woman who stood so defiantly in front of him. She was a little thing, no more than a hundred ten pounds he guessed, maybe 5'1". He had had horseman from all over try to ride this horse, and this young doctor thought she was better than all of them.

"What makes you think you can succeed when all the rest have failed?" the Prince asked.

"I can't explain it," she told him, "I just feel a connection to him. I think for a second I had his attention out there, and he was listening to me. I ask again, let me try, at my own risk. I won't hold you or this farm or anyone else responsible for any injuries I might have. I want to have control over his total care. I will come morning and night to feed him. I want to try to build some trust in him. What do you say? Will you give us both a chance? You have nothing to lose."

"Okay. You have a deal. I will let you try. I will instruct Mr. Martin to leave Sahara to your care. I am leaving in the morning and won't be back in the States for three months. I will come back then and we will make a decision on the fate of Sahara."

Julianna was elated though she tried to stay composed as she thanked the Prince. In reality she wanted to throw her arms around his neck and give him a hug. She was so happy!

The Prince turned and walked back toward the house. Mr. Martin shook his head and cautioned Julianna about the horse. "You be very careful, ma'am. That horse has put three men in the hospital and has bitten, kicked, and charged everyone who has tried to go near him. I hope you know what you're doing."

Daniel gave Mr. Martin a handshake and told him if he had any more concerns on the young colt he'd seen not to hesitate to call. He waited until he and Julianna were back in the truck before he started talking to her. He was trying to keep his voice down, but he had never been angrier with her in the whole lifetime they had known one another.

"What the hell do you think you are doing? You don't know how to break a horse like that. He's a killer. I can't believe you'd even think of undertaking such a task without even consulting me. What makes you think you can do what some of the best horsemen in the world can't do? You've never ridden a horse of the kind this Arabian is. They are high-spirited on a good day. You add crazy and a stallion on top of that, you have to be out of your mind. I want you to call the Prince back and tell him you have reconsidered."

Julianna looked at Daniel, her mouth set in a fine line and her face red with emotion. "You listen to me Daniel, you are my husband but you don't own me, and you do not tell me what to do. I am going to ignore these rantings of yours because I think you are just afraid for my welfare. But let's get one thing clear. I am not calling the Prince and backing out of this. I can't explain this Daniel, but from the moment I saw Sahara something clicked inside me. I have to try. I am the only chance he's got of living. I know I'm not a horse trainer, but there's something about Sahara. I think someone has mistreated him along the way and I don't think he trusts anyone, and that goes doubly for men. For just a split second I thought I saw a glimmer of hope for him. If I haven't been able to get him under saddle in three months, then I will admit failure. At least I will know I did everything I could. Please don't be angry with me, Daniel."

Daniel left out a long breath. "Annie," he said, softening his voice, he usually only called her Annie during the most intimate moments, "You know I can't stay mad at you. I admit you have a way with animals, you always have, but you are my wife, and you will be the mother of my children. I couldn't bear it if this horse hurt you. When will you find time to devote to this project? We are both working long hours at the clinic now."

"It will work out. I will get up early and go over before work to take care of him. In the evenings, I'll go back and do what I can. I will do most of the actual working with him on the weekends. It's not forever, Daniel, just three months. As soon as I think I can get him loaded in a trailer we'll bring him home. The barn is ready and the fields are fenced. What do you say?"

"What can I say? Your mind is made up. I love you. I'll do whatever I can to keep you in one piece."

CHAPTER 7

▼

Victoria Bentley felt a tickle on her nose as she woke up that Saturday morning. She knew without opening her eyes that Precious was awake and had her face inches from Victoria's own, waiting for her to open her eyes. She was so close her whiskers were tickling her nose. As soon as she opened her eyes Precious jumped off the bed and turned around to look at Victoria as if to say, "Come on, get up, I need to go out."

"Okay, Precious, I'm coming." Victoria stretched her body and let out a big yawn as her feet hit the cool marble of her bedroom floor. She found her slippers and shuffled down the hallway to the door, barely remembering to turn off the alarm system before opening the door for Precious to go outside. What time was it any way, she wondered? Good grief, it was already nine o' clock. She had really overslept, and she had a lot to do today before she left to go to her sister's birthday dinner in Bloomington that night. She ticked off a mental list as she filled the coffee pot with water and coffee. She needed her coffee. Her mind was still fuzzy with sleep. She raked her fingers through her hair, combing it with her fingers.

It was a luxury to sleep this late. Haywood was always up at the crack of dawn, and she usually got up when he did so they could have breakfast together before he left for the office. This weekend he was gone on a little golfing trip with a couple of his partners at the law firm where he was the senior partner. Hayward Asher Bentley was a very successful lawyer and a very wealthy man. He was a shrewd businessman as well, having made good investments, owning a lot of real estate. He and Victoria had been married almost ten years. He was 65, and she was 35.

They had met at a Bentley, Goldberg and Williams annual Christmas Party. Victoria had been invited by Hayward the 4th. Victoria was an aerobics teacher and fitness trainer at Gold's Gym when she met Ward. Everyone knew Victoria at Gold's, and she never lacked for dates. Victoria had the perfect body and she worked hard to keep it that way. She had been a cheerleader in high school and was very into the fitness craze of the 80s. She got her aerobics and fitness trainer certification and thought she had the best job in the world. She loved her job, stayed fit, and every man in the club wanted to be personally trained by her. When she went to the Christmas party with Ward that night, she had no idea the turn her world was about to take. At the party she was immediately drawn to a distinguished looking older man with just a hint of gray at his temples. Something about him looked vaguely familiar, but she couldn't quite put her finger on what it was. She asked Ward who the man was. "That's my father," he said, "I was going to introduce you anyway. Let's go on over now."

Ward's date had not gone unnoticed by his father. "My God," he thought, "She's gorgeous. Where in the world did Ward find her?" He had been watching her all night, the catlike way she moved, the way the muscles in the calves of her legs tightened as she walked, the 100-watt smile she gave everyone. She was wearing a royal blue silk cocktail dress that clung to her body's curves and accentuated the blue of her eyes. Every man at the party was salivating over her, and every woman there was jealous. When Ward made the official introduction she had given him a firm handshake, not a limp, clammy cold hand like most woman had. Hayward asked Ward to go get them a glass of wine, any excuse so he could talk to Victoria himself for a minute. He was smitten with this woman, and he was feeling like a fool. He had to be 30 years older than she. She was with his son for goodness sake.

Ward saw the way his father reacted to Victoria. He couldn't believe it. The old man was trying to steal his date! Not only that, Victoria had asked him first who the man was, unbelievable.

It caused a little ripple in the family when Hayward and Victoria started dating. Hayward's first wife, Ward's mother, had died in an automobile wreck, killed by a drunken driver, when Ward was ten years old. Hayward had never remarried; instead, he had thrown himself in to work and building his reputation as a criminal attorney. The Hayward Bentleys had been attorneys for 4 generations and were men to be reckoned with in the courtroom.

Ward really didn't have a reason to be upset with his dad over Victoria. They had never dated before and he had only known her in the gym prior to asking her to the Christmas party.

Hayward courted Victoria with intent and extravagance. Of course, the gossip was she was only after his money and didn't care about him, and he was just being a fool to think otherwise. But the gossip was wrong. Victoria had always been attracted to older men and Hayward was not only older, he had taken very good care of himself and was a very handsome man. He made her feel like a fairy tale princess. She soon realized that she was in love with him. They married less than a year after meeting. He gave her a 5 carat Asscher cut diamond set in platinum for a wedding ring. It was the most stunning piece of jewelry Victoria had ever seen. He told her he gave her that particular cut because of the Asher in his name, to remind her she belonged to him.

Victoria had taken to the good life. She loved living in this beautiful mansion with a maid to do the cleaning and cooking on the nights her and "Ash" decided to eat in. She loved the pool in the perfectly landscaped back yard and the high brick wall around it so she could have complete privacy. Ash had a complete gym put in for her with an area where she could do aerobics if she wished. In addition to free weights and circuit training equipment, she had her own treadmill, stationery bike, and elliptical trainer. She loved not having to go to the gym anymore. Ash lavished her with gifts and every birthday, anniversary, and Christmas bought her an expensive piece of jewelry. For their five-year anniversary he gave her a ten carat princess cut platinum tennis bracelet. During their first Christmas together he gave her a sapphire and diamond right hand ring. She also had two carat each, princess cut diamond stud earrings set in platinum. This past Christmas he gave her an18-inch platinum necklace with 20 carats of princess cut diamonds to match her bracelet. She wore the bracelet and necklace and stud earrings everyday. She found she could wear them with jeans and t-shirt just as easily as she could with evening wear.

Victoria finished her coffee and started thinking again about her agenda for the day. She had to take Precious to be groomed at noon, and then she had an appointment to get a pedicure and manicure. By the time she did that, picked Precious up and stopped by the Dry Cleaners to pick up Ash's laundry it would be late afternoon. She had to be in Bloomington at her sister's at 7:30. From there, they had dinner reservations at 8:00. She was staying overnight with her sister and coming back tomorrow. She wanted to be home by the time Ash got home from his golfing trip. She missed him. No one would believe how much they genuinely loved one another.

"Come on Precious", she said after she fed her, "time to do a quick half hour on the elliptical machine and then hit the shower before I take you to the groomer." Precious, a white Maltese, had been another gift from Ash. He had gotten her as a surprise for Victoria and upon seeing her, she'd squealed with delight, "She's Precious!" So the name had stayed. Both of them doted on the little dog. She was always groomed to perfection, her white fur perfectly brushed, and her little bangs held in a barrette that matched whatever Victoria was wearing.

Victoria got a late start from home that evening and knew she was going to have to make good time to make it to her sister's on time. She was annoyed when Precious started barking in the car. It was her "I need to go to the bathroom bark." About that time, Victoria saw the sign for a rest area in one mile. "Okay Precious," she said, "Hold on."

The Porsche Boxster rumbled off the interstate into the rest area. Elvis and Aaron didn't see the driver, and by the time they heard the big engine the convertible top was closing. "Now, that is a machine," Elvis remarked.

"Damn straight," said Aaron. The name on the vanity license plate read PRECIOUS. The door to the driver's side opened, and the longest pair of tanned, toned legs the men had ever seen rolled out of the car. Attached to those long legs were a black miniskirt and black skin tight tank top on the most perfect body on a woman they had ever seen. The woman had blonde hair that actually looked natural, and even from this distance they could tell her eyes were blue as a summer sky. This was one hot woman. Both the car and the woman oozed sex appeal. The brothers could read each other's minds. They didn't know what turned them on more, the car or the woman. They were both a little dry in the mouth just thinking about it.

They had already chosen this rest stop to take their next victim and had a preliminary plan of how they would do it. They hadn't been there more than enough time to park when the Boxster rolled past. Even better, the Boxster had driven to the more secluded part of the rest area, where people with dogs were supposed to park. It was perfect. She was a gift to them.

As they watched the woman walk toward the rest room, they could see a small white dog, looking through the window watching her every move. The woman could walk. She took long strides and moved like a giant cat, sleek and ready to pounce. This was going to be their most fun yet.

Aaron put the ring on his finger and got out of the car where Elvis had parked it a couple spaces down from the Porsche. The ring had a spike on the palm side, perfect for puncturing a tire. By the time Ms. Precious came out, the tire would be nearly flat, and they would come to the fair lady's rescue. The little dog started yapping as soon as Aaron approached the back of the car. He leaned down quickly and punctured the right rear and passenger tire, then hurried back over to the van. Elvis stayed out of sight in the back of the van.

Victoria walked to the car, opened the door and snapped the leash on Precious. "Hurry up, girl," she said, "We don't have all day." She walked her over to the grass. As she walked back, Aaron got out of the van and walked to where he knew they would pass and threw away a cup in the trash can. He smiled at Victoria, but she just looked away and jerked Precious' leash to get her in the car.

Aaron said, "Nice car. Are you Precious?" Victoria smiled in spite of herself and said, "No, Precious is the dog." Aaron casually looked at the car and said, "Ma'am looks like your tire is low." Victoria looked to the right rear where he was pointing. Damn, just what she didn't need. The tire was almost flat. Now what would she do? She could call Triple A, but by the time they came, towed the car in, and got it fixed, it would be too late to go to her sister's.

Her thoughts were interrupted by the man's voice. "Do you have a spare? I'll change it for you, and get you on your way. I'm in no hurry."

She looked at him and nodded her head. "It's one of those donut spare things, not a real tire. I have another 100 miles to go. No way I can go with the donut on."

"Tell you what," the man said, "There's a Wal-Mart at the next exit, and they have an auto center that could probably plug your tire and get you back on the road in half an hour. I'll take the tire off and you and the little doggie can go with me to Wal-Mart. I'll come back, put the wheel back on, and you'll be on your way."

She surveyed the man in front of her. She knew she shouldn't trust strangers, but this man looked okay. He was clean, wearing jeans and a t-shirt. He had sunglasses on so she couldn't see his eyes, but he had not given off any warning signs to her. He had a country accent and seemed like a good ole boy. She made a decision. She would do it. "Okay let's do it. I don't want to miss my sister's birthday."

" I've got a jack back in my van. Let me go get my tools, and we'll get your tire off." He went back to the van, opened the back, winked at Elvis, put on gloves, and got his tools and jack. He had the tire off in a couple minutes. He put the tire and tools back in his van. He'd ended up not using his jack, instead using the one that came with the Porsche. He was real careful to keep his gloves on and not to leave any prints on the car. He left the car jacked up, told Victoria to lock the car and get her purse and they'd be on their way. Elvis stayed out of sight in the back of the van, Victoria got in the passenger side, holding Precious, and off they went.

As they were pulling out of the rest area, Victoria said, "My name is Victoria Bentley, and I really appreciate you helping me. You're a lifesaver. What's your name?"

"Aaron," he said, "Aaron Puckett and the guy behind you is my brother, Elvis. We're going to have a real good time with you and Precious."

She started to open the door to try to jump out, but the automatic door locks were tightly locked. She started to scream, but a hand came around from behind her and clamped over her mouth. There was something hideous looking on the hand. It looked like a toe growing off the thumb. She shuddered.

"Hey brother," Aaron said, "I don't think she likes your thumb" They both laughed. When she heard them laugh, she knew she was in big trouble; it was the sound of insanity.

Elvis unclamped his hand from her mouth and had the tip of a knife blade at the side of her neck. "Make a move or try to scream and you're dead where you sit," he whispered in her ear.

"Listen," she said, "My husband is rich. He'll pay you anything you want if you'll let me go. I swear, I won't press any charges. Don't hurt me and you can have anything you want."

Aaron said, Anything we want?"

"Yes"

"Well, brother, what do you think??" Aaron waited a minute and then continued, "Yeah, me, too. Elvis said he'd rather hurt you."

"Victoria, Anybody ever call you Vickie?"

" No, my name is not Vickie. It's Victoria."

" Well, la de da," said Elvis from the back. "Vickie's a snob, Aaron, don't you think?" "Now Vickie," Aaron said, "don't get uppity on us cause we hate uppity people. We're gonna have us a little party. You know that chewing gum commercial, double your pleasure, and double your fun? Well that's what it's going to be. You can't see Elvis yet, but when you do, you're going to see except for two things, we're identical twins. This is going to fun. The double mint twins and Vickie are having a party! Hey Vickie, do you have a cell phone? Elvis, grab her purse and see if she has a cell phone. Use your gloves. Yeah, she's got one. Turn it off and throw it out the window. She won't be needing to make no calls tonight."

Again, the laugh that made her cringe. Precious was trembling in Victoria's lap. Even she knew something was terribly wrong. Animals sense things, and she could sense that Victoria was scared to death.

It was dark by the time they got home. "There ain't no houses around here, so there's no use you screaming. Just walk right on in the house nice like. Elvis, stay behind her and don't let her try anything." Victoria had been thinking all the way here. She was fit and she was strong. She may look like a princess, but she was in the prime if her life. She was sure she could out run these guys and if she could catch them off guard, she could get away. This was her chance. She thought back to the self-defense class she had taken. "Use your elbows and step back hard and stomp their foot," she remembered. She dropped Precious to the ground, stepped back and stomped Elvis's foot as hard as she could while at the same time connecting her elbow in his solar plexus with all her strength.

"FUCK!" he yelled, gasping for breath. Victoria took off running, but before she got a few steps from him a sharp pain in the back of her leg sent her to the ground. Elvis had thrown his knife and the blade was sticking deep in her leg. She passed out.

When she came to she was lying spread-eagled, tied to the bed, a gag in her mouth. Elvis and Aaron were looking down at her. They were identical she realized, except for that hideous second thumb and something about Aaron's eyes. They were different colors! It freaked her out. It was creepy looking. His eyes were stone cold, no emotion whatsoever in them. She was terrified, and realized that she was about to pee. She did not want to humiliate herself by peeing on herself. She tried to make a sound through the gag.

Aaron said, "Hold on Vickie, were going to let you talk. We can't understand a damn thing you're saying with that rag in your mouth."

"I need to go to the bathroom," she pleaded.

"Okay, you be nice and you can go. You try to run off again, we're gonna kill your little dog."

"Oh, God," she'd forgotten about Precious. She now saw her laying on the floor chewing on something. "What is she chewing on? She has a delicate stomach and she'll be sick."

"Oh she loves this," Elvis said, "It's a horse hoof. Dogs love 'em."

"A horse hoof," she gasped, "Where did you get a horse hoof?"

"Oh," Elvis said, "That's easy . . . we kill horses for a living, down at the slaughterhouse. Aaron, take her in the living room and show her all the hides we have."

Kill horses for a living? Had she heard correctly? She tried to control her revulsion. She decided to go along as much as possible, keep them talking, maybe buy her some time. Who knows maybe someone would stop by to see them? Please God let someone come by. It might be the only chance she had.

Aaron led her into the living room and her eyes took in all the animals staring back at her from the walls and the hides covering both the walls and furniture. These men were serious hunters she thought. She couldn't help the tears coming to her eyes as she saw all the beautiful horse hides with manes and tails still attached. How could anyone do that to a horse? She tried to focus away from them and say something positive. "Wow, a bear. Where did you find a bear?"

" Oh him, we got him up in Canada, same time we got that elk there. We went to Canada on one of them guided fancy huntin' trips after daddy died and we sold the land back home to the strip mine company. Hey, you might even know two of the guys that were on that trip seeing as how you're from Chicago, and your husband is a big hot shot criminal attorney. One of 'em's name was Vinnie, and the other one went by Mr. G. Mr. G was Geno something, some I-talian name. Vinnie was his bodyguard or something. Geno even offered us a job after he saw the way we took out that bear and elk, said he could always use a couple good shooters."

"Jesus," Victoria thought, "These guys are talking about Geno Giocamo and Vinnie his primary hit man." She and Ash had actually met the two a few months ago in a restaurant. Everyone knew Mama Rosa's was the best authentic home Italian restaurant in Chicago. It was also a well-known mob eatery. They had chanced going down there one Saturday night for dinner. While they were there, the waiter brought a bottle of Dom Perignon to the table. He told them their meal had been taken care of and the champagne as well. When they had asked the waiter who had done this, he replied, "One of our regulars at the back table." Victoria had told the waiter she wanted to personally thank the man and to go ask for an audience.

The waiter had come back and nodded to follow him. As they approached the table, the man known as Vinnie rose and seemed to be scanning the restaurant for any sign of undue activity. There sat Geno himself, Victoria recognized him at once, as did Ash because the man was regularly pictured in the Tribune.

Vickie had extended her hand and said, "I want to thank you for the dinner and the champagne."

" It was my pleasure," Geno had replied. "I had heard that Mr. Bentley was blessed to have a most beautiful wife, but I had never seen you. Everything I heard is true. Mr. Bentley, you are indeed lucky to have a woman like this at your side."

Even Geno could see the love that passed between the two when Ash spoke. "I am the luckiest man in the world. Victoria is my life." She had reached over and taken his arm in hers. Geno had continued, "Come down here anytime at Mama Rosa's. She is a special friend of mine. There will always be a table for you, and you will always be safe here."

Victoria told Elvis and Aaron that she had met Vinnie and Geno a few months ago. She then told them something they didn't know. Vinnie had been shot and killed in a mob hit about a month later. The other Italian mob families had sworn they were not guilty of hiring the hit on Vinnie. Word on the street was it was a Chinese tong that was trying to move in and take some of Geno's action in the city. This was very interesting to the brothers. Maybe they would give their friend Geno a call. They could use some extra money. They hadn't cared that much for Vinnie, but Mr. G had been nice to them. They hated any slant eyes. If they could help Mr. G settle a score and make some money for one hit, it was something worth looking into. They had kept the card with the phone number he had given them all those years ago.

Elvis and Aaron knew their days were numbered at the horse slaughter business. One by one all over the country the horse slaughterhouses had closed. Now there was only one still operating, and there was talk that within a few months, laws would pass that would make it illegal in the US to slaughter horses or to transport horses for human consumption. The company they had worked for all these years knew it was inevitable and had made plans to open an operation in Canada. The manager had even asked the twins to relocate there. They didn't much want to move to Canada, but they didn't have enough money to retire either. The resulting pressure and worry had only made them step up their killing; they were mad at the world. They had been killing people and rendering them, leaving not a trace for twenty years. Pedro had been the first. After him, it became an obsession, a thirst that had to be quenched. They had always been very careful, had taken their victims mostly from hitchhikers, hookers, runaways, people that know one would really miss anyway. They had never seen more than a one or two line blip on the news about a disappearance with no leads, and that would be the end of it. Bolder lately, they had taken victims more frequently and as in Victoria's case, in public areas when it was still daylight. They never kept souvenirs of their kills, and only kept marks to indicate their numbers. With the plant closing and the high profile that Victoria's disappearance was likely to make, this might be their last safe kill for a long time. That's the reason they decided to take their time and enjoy every inch of "Vickie" before they killed her.

After they let Victoria go to the bathroom and see all their hunting trophies, they asked her if she would like something to eat or if she would like to take a shower. Victoria could scarcely believe what she was hearing. These two maniacs were treating her like a guest…maybe they were planning on changing their minds from their original plan and now planned to ransom her. She hoped that was it. She knew Ash would give everything he had to get her back safely. She told them yes, again, if nothing else, buying more time. She said she'd love to have something to eat and a shower. She had only had the coffee this morning. The rest of the day was so busy she had never eaten, and she knew she needed to keep her strength up if there was any chance she was going to get out of here.

She let the hot water beat down on her back, trying to loosen up the knots she had in her shoulders and neck from the tension she was feeling. They had bandaged her punctured thigh from the knife wound, and she hoped it would not become infected. Victoria searched the bathroom for something she could use as a weapon but the men had removed everything before they had let her in there. They had given her privacy, and she took that as another good sign. After her shower, she put back on the same clothes she had been wearing. She had to admit the shower had made her feel better, and she was actually hungry. The men had fixed her a bowl of chicken noodle soup and a grilled cheese sandwich. As she sipped the soup from the spoon and nibbled on her sandwich, she felt much better. Yes, she was going to be fine. The men would contact Ash and after they got their money they would let her go.

CHAPTER 8

▼

By the end of the first week Julianna had made a little progress with Sahara. She had asked Mr. Martin if there was any barn on the farm that was not in use that had a smaller paddock area attached to it. He said yes, there was an old barn with a smaller field adjoining it. Moving Sahara was another problem. They ended up having to lasso him, attaching his rope to a jeep to slowly take him to his new digs. Julianna spent a long time at the fence talking to Sahara, assuring him that everything was okay and they just needed to move him to a new place so she could work with him. He reared and charged and pranced and snorted, but they finally got him moved and managed to get the lasso off his neck. Sahara bolted off to run the perimeter of his new surroundings, squealing his anger, making his disapproval known. Julianna prepared a stall for him with fresh straw, filled a water bucket and put his sweet feed in his corner feeder. When she finished, she went back outside and again talked to the big horse from the fence. He was as wild as anything she had ever seen. She did like where this new area was located. It was away from the normal activity of the farm, and she and Sahara would get to know one another without traffic and onlookers. After he had worn himself out running around the field, he finally settled down and started picking at the grass. Julianna talked to him continuously. She told him she was going to open the barn door so he could go in to eat, She had left his stall door open. She could reach the sliding barn door from the corner of the fence and only had to lean in a little bit to pull it open. Sahara watched her closely, but did not charge as she pulled the door open. When he ran inside she quickly slid the door shut, jumped over the fence and latched the door. She was going to leave him inside for the night.

The next morning before she went to the clinic she went to see Sahara. She talked to him through the barn wall and told him she was there and she was going to open the door so he could go out for the day. She had already made sure his outside water tank was full.

He was whinnying inside the barn and she could hear him pawing the ground. She unlatched the barn door, went back over the fence to the outside, and pulled the sliding door open. Sahara ran out of the barn and around the fence a few times. Again, she continued to talk to him. He calmed rather quickly and got down to the business of picking grass. She slid the door closed and then entered the barn from the front. She quickly mucked out his stall so it would be clean for him in the afternoon. As an afterthought, she decided she would re-open the door so he could go back in the barn during the day if he wanted to. Even though it was fall, the days were still pretty hot and there was no shade in this new field. She pulled the door back open made sure the entrance door to the barn was securely locked, and left for work.

This was the way the whole first week went. She went over every morning, opening the door for him to go out, and then closing it while she cleaned up his stall, then re-opening it for him for the day. In the evenings, she would close the door, put some sweet feed out for him and fill his water bucket, then let him back in for the night. He seemed to be settling in to the routine. He would make a big entrance in to the field every morning, but it was more for show than anything else she thought. She had still not tried to go in the field with him.

The first Saturday she was off she spent the entire day with Sahara, following her normal morning schedule. Then, she just stood at the fence talking to him and watching him for a long time. She had brought a book to read, a lawn chair to sit in, and lunch in a cooler. Except for going to the main area of the farm for bathroom breaks, she intended to spend the day right there. Sahara watched her cautiously but never did anything else. Julianna just sat and watched him, and he would occasionally look up from his eating to see her there. She talked to him almost the entire morning. Up to this time, she had not actually leaned on the fence or made any attempt to go in his territory. After she had lunch, she was going to see what he would do if she tried to lean on the fence.

She waited until his back was turned to her and then she leaned against the fence, interested to see his reaction to even this slight attempt to invade his space. When he eventually turned around and saw her there, he did nothing, just swished his tail and went on picking grass. Julianna wanted to try something else. She had begun to think the horse could actually hear her thoughts even when she wasn't speaking aloud. She hadn't shared this tidbit with even Daniel because she knew he would think she had lost her mind. She decided to try her theory. Leaning against the fence, she concentrated very hard on Sahara, and in her mind, not aloud, called his name. His head instantly shot up, and he looked at her. She knew it! She continued this telepathic conversation, telling him she was going to climb on the fence and sit for a while and that she would never hurt him and she only wanted to be his friend. She told him he could trust her.

She took a deep breath and made her move, all the time silently communicating that she meant no harm to Sahara. When she moved to get on the fence, Sahara squealed his disapproval and reared on his hind legs. He took off on a dead run to the fence. Julianna kept talking to him, telling him this is the way it had to be, she was trying to save his life, she wanted to be his friend, and she was not going away.

Sahara stopped a few feet from the fence where Julianna was sitting. He was blowing air hard through his nostrils, his ears pinned back, and tail swishing angrily. He stared at her and she returned his gaze and tried to make her eyes full of compassion and love, all the time reassuring Sahara she was not the enemy. They both stood their ground, and in what seemed like a very long time, but was, in reality, just a few minutes, Sahara took off in a run around the field to the opposite side and returned to grazing. Julianna was ecstatic. She felt this was a major victory. She wouldn't try anything else today. Tomorrow, she would push her luck a little farther. Before she left for the evening, she once again closed the field side of the barn door while she filled his water bucket and got his food ready. When she scooped his food into his feeder she could hear him breathing under the door, waiting to come in. She again, silently talked to him, explaining she was getting his food and bed ready and she would be opening the door in a minute. She also told him she would be back in the morning and would be spending the day with him and how good he'd been today and how much she loved him.

Julianna talked a mile a minute when she got home that evening, telling Daniel all about her day and about the progress she had made. "And Daniel, he understands me. He hears me somehow even when I'm talking to him only in my head." Daniel looked at her skeptically. "He does," she said. "I tried it several times today. I would call his name in my head, and every time his head jerked up and he looked at me."

Daniel didn't argue with her, he knew it would do no good, but he worried that she was already too emotionally involved with Sahara. He loved her so much, and he didn't want to see her get hurt, either physically or emotionally, but he was afraid this horse was going to do both.

Sunday morning was another beautiful fall day. The leaves were starting to turn colors and the trees were palettes of oranges, reds and gold. Julianna had always loved the fall of the year. One of her favorite memories as a child was helping her dad rake leaves in their front yard. Of course raking leaves wasn't nearly as much fun as falling in a big pile of them once they were raked. She loved the woodsy smell of the leaves in her hair and on her clothes. Instead of scolding her, her dad had played with her and then they'd rake them all back up again. She could see Daniel being that kind of dad, too. They had been talking about having a baby, maybe start trying to get pregnant at the end of their first year in practice. She had on her favorite worn out jeans and a long sleeve Ohio State t-shirt. It was cool enough this morning that she added a sweatshirt but knew once the sun warmed up she would be taking it off. She once again had brought a book to read as she sat watching Sahara, but she doubted she would be reading. Yesterday she hadn't. She just loved watching him. She laughed thinking about the way he looked when he had laid down and rolled over all fours in the air like a big dog. He would wiggle around while on his back. She guessed he was giving himself a good back scratching. Then he would roll the rest of the way over. When he got up, he once again reminded her of a big dog, shaking all over. She had decided today she was going to try to get in the field with him.

If he would just let her in the field without charging her, it would be a major step. This was the end of her first week, and she only had 11 weeks left. When she made the deal with the Prince, three months had sounded like a long time, now it seemed to be going too quickly. One week gone and so far she had only managed to sit on the fence. She and Sahara still had a long way to go. Daniel was off today, too, and said he might stop by after lunch to see how things were going. No one but herself had been around Sahara since they moved him to this field. It would be interesting to see if Daniel's presence would upset the horse. She would tell him this morning that Daniel was coming, so he wouldn't be surprised. Julianna had a theory that somewhere along the way a man had mistreated Sahara, and he didn't trust any man because of it. All the trainers that had worked with him thus far had been men, and none of them had gained the horse's trust.

Julianna started her morning as usual, letting Sahara out in the field, closing the door behind him, then going in the barn and mucking out his stall. With that accomplished, she went back outside and immediately went to and leaned against the fence. She was still carrying on this telepathic conversation with him, telling him everything she was going to do before she did it. He looked up from his eating to see her leaning on the fence, but didn't seem to be concerned. Julianna walked all around the perimeter of the field seeing if Sahara would react. All the time she spoke to him, telling him what a good boy he was, how handsome he was, and how no one would ever mistreat him again. Occasionally, he would look up at her and she could swear he was shaking his head in agreement. She wanted so badly to wrap her arms around his big neck and hug him tight. He needed a good brushing. She wanted his coat to glisten in the sun. It would take a long time to untangle the mess he had in his mane. She told him all this as she was walking back around the field to where she had started.

"So far so good," she thought. "Okay Sahara I'm, going to sit on the fence for a while." She hopped on the fence and although he looked up and ran a tight circle swishing his tail, he did not run at the fence. Much better than yesterday, she thought. "Good Boy," she said, "You're such a good boy." She sat there on the fence until her butt was getting numb. "Sahara," He looked up, "I'm going to jump down in the field." She did.

As soon as he saw her inside the field he squealed loudly and came at a dead run straight at her. She kept talking to him, kept telling him she was his friend, that she was only trying to help him. "Please stop, don't try to hurt me." She stood her ground. She was just about to try to hit the ground and roll under the fence when he stopped, a few precious feet short of her. His eyes held a look of fear, and she could tell he was very close to trying to stomp her to the ground. She kept talking, aloud this time, her voice calm and reassuring even though her knees were weak and her heart was thumping so loud she knew he could hear it. "You're afraid and so am I," she told him," but we've got to learn to trust each other. I will not give up on you Sahara. I'm the only chance you have left."

After she stood there for a minute, she slowly backed her way back to the fence and heaved herself up in her sitting position. Sahara was upset, still pacing back and forth, not relaxed at all. Again, she just kept talking to him in a calm, loving voice.

When Daniel stopped by after lunch, it immediately changed Sahara's disposition. Even though she had told him Daniel was coming and had reassured him that he would not try to approach him in any way, the horse was clearly agitated. He squealed, reared and charged at the fence, running back and forth, blowing hard until he was in a sweat. Julianna finally told

Daniel he had to leave. "You're upsetting him," she said. "I'm making progress. I was actually with him inside the fence for a minute this morning. I don't want to lose the progress I've made today. I'll be home about 5:00." Daniel looked worried and again told her to be careful and not to turn her back on the horse for any reason.

After he left, Julianna once again kept telling Sahara that Daniel was a good man who would never hurt him and that he needed to accept him, too. She spent the better part of the afternoon sitting on the fence watching him. He was a little anxious and kept an eye on her but soon went back to grazing. Before she left for the day, she was going to try again to get in the field with him.

She slipped off the fence as she had done the first time, and he immediately pinned his ears back and pawed the ground. He did not run at her, just stood in the field watching her every move. She took a step forward, just one, and just a baby step, all the while talking to him. He started moving then, running, ears pinned, straight for her. Her throat was dry, but she tried not to show any fear. She kept talking to him, saying "Whoa, boy, it's okay, whoa." He turned just as she was sure he would trample her. She could feel his hot breath as he made the turn. "Whew, that was close!" her knees were like jelly. She knew she couldn't hop back on the fence. She was going to have to stand here and get her legs back. Sahara turned and faced her again, pawing the ground, but did not make another run at her. "Thank God" she thought to herself. Finally, she backed her way to the fence and got back to the other side. That was enough for today. She slid the barn door shut and went inside to get his grain ready and fresh water for his bucket. Once again she could see he was standing right at the door, smelling underneath.

When she got home she told Daniel she had gotten back on the inside with Sahara again. She didn't tell him the details. Some things are just better left unsaid.

She didn't have much time to spend with Sahara the next week. She was still going morning and night, but by the time she left the clinic and drove out to the farm there wasn't a lot of daylight left. She was going to have to do something about that. Soon it would be dark at 5:30. It would be dark when she left work. She had to continue working with Sahara because time was ticking away. She needed more than just Saturdays and Sundays to put in worthwhile time. Every evening she was building the amount of time she spent inside the fence. Sahara seemed to be adjusting okay and she had taken a few steps, albeit small ones, along the fence line without him becoming agitated. The next step was going to be getting closer to him. It was going so much slower than Julianna had thought it would.

The next Saturday was rainy, but that didn't stop Julianna. She had to spend time with Sahara, rain or shine. She put on her rain parka, which rustled when she moved, and he had not liked that at all. He was so nervous and high strung. Julianna was starting to doubt her own ability. Yes, she had been around horses all her life, but none were like this. Could she win the horse over with just love?   She had stood outside in the rain all day. Thankfully it wasn't too cold, but she was starting to get chilled. She ended up taking the parka off, so she was soaking wet. She had an old baseball cap on her head but that did little to keep her head dry after many hours. All day, she talked to Sahara, who seemed oblivious to the rain, eating contentedly all day. She walked all the way around on the inside of the field, and he ignored her. Maybe he was finally accepting that she was going to be in his space. She had taken a few steps in his general direction, not a direct line, but sort of round about. He had just trotted away to widen the distance. She was encouraged that he wasn't squealing his disapproval nor had he pawed the ground or run at her. Trotting away was much better than charging forward. She finally decided to call it a day and go home. What she needed now was a hot shower and something hot to eat. Daniel was going to throw a fit when he saw her.

Next morning she decided to try a different tactic. Thankfully, it wasn't raining and looked like it was going to be a nice day. She used to draw and sketch when she was younger, and still had some art materials lying around. She was going to take her tablet and sit inside the fence and try to capture Sahara on paper, maybe a nice charcoal of him.

She also had another idea to try. She stopped at the market on her way to the farm and bought some apples. The old saying about the way to a man's heart was through his stomach was about to be tested on horses!

After she let Sahara out and cleaned his stall, she went put her chair and sketch pad on the inside of the fence. She then went and got a bucket and put some sweet feed in it, her bait, along with the apples. She put the bucket of sweet feed a few feet away from her chair and told Sahara she had something good for him to eat. She made a big deal out of taking a bite of the crisp apple. It was good! She had Sahara's attention; he loved to eat! She knew he smelled both the feed and the apple because she could see his nostrils testing the smells. He opened his mouth and almost made a smacking sound. Oh, he wanted that sweet feed. She tossed a piece of the apple toward him. He leaned forward with his neck to reach out to the apple but couldn't reach it.

She went on eating her apple and telling him how good and sweet and juicy it was. Again, a little lip action from Sahara.

She finished off her apple and started sketching, just glancing up now and then to look at him. She saw him walk back and forth as if weighing his options here. He walked in a circle, tail swishing, trying to decide what to do. He finally took a few steps forward, closer to the apple piece she had thrown on the ground. He looked up to see if she had moved. She pretended to ignore him, sneaking peeks to see what he was doing. He finally walked over and snatched the apple up and ran away. She got another apple out and tossed him another piece. It didn't take him nearly as long this time to decide she wasn't going to grab him if he went after the apple. She cut the apple in slices and got up and put them in the bucket with the corn. When she got up, he immediately ran away, but he saw and heard her toss the apple in with the sweet feed. She went back to her chair and once again took out her sketch pad.

She had been mostly doodling on the pad, drawing the outline of his body, trying to get the proportions right. She started again to try to get down the shape of his head and his eyes. She sensed he was moving and didn't want to startle him by jerking her head.

He was really struggling with what to do about that food bucket. She kept her head down and scarcely breathed as he came all the way to the bucket. Every muscle was tensed on him, his ears pricked, alert for any motion. He eased his head in the bucket and jerked it out quickly, looking to make sure she had not moved. She started talking to him, telling him it was okay, he was a good boy, and he could he could trust her. A bird flew overhead and spooked him, and he took off running, bucking and prancing. She eased up while he was running in the opposite direction and moved the bucket closer to her chair.

He followed the same procedure on his approach to the bucket, slow and cautious, stopping to watch for any movement at all from Julianna, ears pricked. Slowly he made his way to the prize awaiting him, sweet feed. The bucket was scarcely two feet from Julianna's chair. He again ducked his head in the bucket for a nibble of the feed, knocking the bucket over in doing so. Julianna again was talking to him the whole time. He looked up at her, and she offered her hand with a big slice of apple on it to him. She could see he wanted the apple and was working his mouth with anticipation of the taste of the apple. He leaned in as far as he could without taking a step and stuck his neck out as far as it would reach, but he was a little bit short of the apple. She slowly moved her hand toward him, palm side up, completely flat, the apple sitting on her outstretched hand. She could see the battle in his eyes, wanting the apple, but not sure he could trust her. Again, she talked to him in soothing, loving tones. He looked at her, and she could see his eyes soften just a little as he curled back his lips and quickly snatched the apple from her hand. He took off with back legs kicking and ran tossing his head as he went. This was much different than before. His moves and kicks weren't threatening, they were happy. He was so proud of himself, strutting almost, like a huge weight had been lifted. Julianna had tears in her eyes. She knew they had just crossed a big barrier. To some it might not seem like much of a big deal, but to her it was major progress. The end of week two was definitely good!

CHAPTER 9

Wanda Hamilton sat with her arms crossed as she listened to her parents, in the back seat, talking about how worried they were that Victoria had not shown up for dinner. It was always Victoria. It had always been all Victoria. Never mind that it was Wanda's birthday, and she was supposed to be the one celebrated. Her birthday had been ruined because Victoria had not been there.

Victoria had always been the perfect one, the pretty one, the one who got all the attention. When Victoria was born she had been a perfect baby; she never cried, was always happy, never sick. Jim and Betty Trent had been so happy with their new baby. Neither Jim nor Betty was particularly good looking. To say they were average would have been kind. Every now and then you see average looking people have beautiful children, and Victoria was one. With her golden hair and blue eyes, she looked like an angel. Both parents doted on her. Betty entered her in baby contests and, later, every beauty contest she could find. Victoria was always a winner. She had gone all the way to Miss Illinois before she had failed to take first place. The only thing that kept her from winning that was her lack of any real talent. She had won the swimsuit division and Miss Congeniality but she didn't have the talent to win the title.

Wanda had lived in Victoria's shadow all her life. She both loved and hated her sister. Jim and Betty were blue collar workers; Betty worked in the local bakery and Jim was the manager of an auto parts store. Victoria's contests expenses and needs were always put before anything that Wanda wanted. "Victoria wants to take gymnastics classes so she can be a cheerleader.

We can't afford whatever it is you want, Wanda." "Victoria needs a new dress and new shoes." It was always Victoria. Wanda resented her sister and her beauty and her perfection.

Wanda was the opposite of Victoria in every way. Wanda was born four years after Victoria. She wasn't a pretty baby, nor a good baby. She was whiny, had colic and was forever sick. Where Victoria had been a beautiful blue-eyed blonde, Wanda had mousy brown hair and hazel eyes. Her hair was thin and oily. Where Victoria had been a cheerful outgoing child, Wanda was sullen and reserved. Wanda was pudgy whereas Victoria had a perfect body. Victoria had full, pouty lips and straight white teeth that never needed braces. Wanda had thin lips and a downturned mouth, and her teeth were too big for her mouth. Wanda grew up very self-conscious of her crooked teeth and always hid her mouth with her hand when she smiled, which wasn't very often.

Victoria loved her little sister and tried to be her best friend, always giving her tips on makeup and hair styles. This only made Wanda have even less self-esteem and feel even uglier. She had long ago gotten sick of people exclaiming, "You're Victoria Trent's sister?"—as if no way it could be true. Wanda had escaped into the world of books. She read all the time as a child. She went to the library in town and at school and kept a steady stack of books to read.

When Victoria married Hayward, Wanda was working part-time at the library and taking college classes as she could afford them. Victoria had come home to visit and told her sister she wanted her to do two things. The first was to enroll in school full time, and the second was to make an appointment with an orthodontist. Victoria knew how self-conscious Wanda had always been about her crooked teeth. She told Wanda that Hayward was paying for everything. Her college expenses would be paid in full as would her dental bills. Wanda refused at first and told Victoria that she couldn't buy her love. Victoria had looked like she'd been slapped, and tears streamed down her face, "I'm not trying to buy your love, I just want you to be happy." Wanda felt like a total jerk for hurting Victoria. No matter how mean and nasty Wanda had been to Victoria over the years, Victoria had always been loving and kind. Now, Victoria had not come for her birthday dinner and even though she probably had a good reason, or may be at the house waiting for them when they got home, Wanda was annoyed.

Victoria wasn't home when they got there. The beautifully decorated birthday cake Betty had made for Wanda's birthday was left uncut. No one was in the mood to celebrate when no one knew where Victoria was. They had hoped there would be a message on the answering machine explaining her delay but there wasn't. No one answered her home phone and her cell phone went immediately to voice mail, indicating it was turned off. That was very unusual because Victoria never turned her phone off, especially when Hayward was out of town. Victoria had told them Hayward was on a business golf trip and would not be able to come with her to the birthday dinner. Now Wanda, her parents, and her husband Andrew started worrying something had happened to Hayward. After all he was in his 60's; actually he was the same age as Jim. They had no idea how to get in touch with Hayward. They would just have to wait until Victoria called and told them what had happened.

Sunday brought only more worry. No news from Victoria, and no phones being answered. Finally about 7:00 the phone rang. "Hi Wanda," Hayward said, "Sorry I missed your birthday dinner last night. Is Victoria still there? I can't get her on her cell phone, and she's not home yet."

Wanda for the first time began to feel afraid. "Hayward," she said, "Thank God you've called. We are all worried sick. Mom and Dad are still here. Both are too upset to drive back to Chicago until we know something. Victoria never arrived yesterday. We thought something might have happened to you. We haven't been able to get her at home or to answer her cell phone."

Wanda could hear the panic in Hayward voice as he said, "When was the last time you talked to her?"

Wanda replied, "She called yesterday morning to say she would be leaving in the early afternoon to drive down. She had a nail appointment and was taking Precious to be groomed and then she would be leaving. "Hayward, what do you think has happened? What should we do? It is not like Victoria to go off and not tell anyone."

Hayward's heart was beating so hard he could barely think. God, if anything had happened to Victoria he simply could not live through it. She was his life. Hayward tried to keep his voice calm as he told Wanda, "I'm going to call the police and report her missing. I know they usually require 48 hours before they start an official search for a missing person, but I'm going to call in every favor I have to get her found. I will not leave a stone unturned until she is home. I will call you all as soon as I find out something. Tell your parents to stay there with you."

Hayward got on the phone and started calling in favors. He didn't want to hear the usual bullshit about 48 hours, and maybe she just went off for some quiet time. He practically exploded when the desk sergeant suggested maybe they were having marital problems or she had someone else and had run off. Hayward called the police chief, the mayor and the governor. He was a powerful man with a lot of contacts. Within an hour of his call there was an

APB out for Victoria and her license plate number, car make and model had been given to every state and local police agency in the state.

Within an hour, a state police vehicle reported finding the Porsche at a rest area on Interstate 55. The officer told dispatch the car was jacked up and the right rear wheel was gone. The car was locked and there was no sign of disturbance around the vehicle. The car was parked in the area designated for walking dogs. The officer further reported that he had gone into the rest facility to inquire if anyone knew how long the car had been there. The cleaning staff was all that was there on that Sunday, and they reported the car had been there all day. They could contact the cleaning crew from Saturday to see if they had noticed anything.

The officer asked for the number of one of the Saturday cleaning crew. He called and asked for Mr. Jensen. He identified himself as Officer Davis with the Illinois State Police and then asked him if he had noticed the Porsche at the rest area any time on Saturday. "Well, yes sir, I did. I saw the car parked out back around five o'clock. A woman, blonde, a real looker, too, I might add was holding a little white dog and talking to a man who was jacking up the rear wheel. The tire looked flat. Next time I looked out the car was out there but the van was gone. Did I mention the van? No, don't believe I did. There was a white utility van parked a couple spaces from the car. I assumed the woman had called someone to come help her with tire. When I looked back out, the woman and the van was gone. They never came back for the car. Can't say as I would leave a car like that sitting all night, I would have had it towed in." The officer thanked him and hung up.

As soon as the officer reported this to his superiors, the call was made to Hayward. "Surely Victoria would not get in a van with a complete stranger," he thought. He was always telling her to be careful. Victoria was always smiling, the old cheerleader in her, she never saw a stranger. Yes, he knew if the person had acted sincerely and offered help, she would have gone with him to get the tire fixed. This was not good news. Maybe the whole thing was set up, he thought. Maybe Victoria had been followed and kidnapped. Hayward's mind was racing, and he felt sick to his stomach. Whoever had her could have every dime Hayward had. "Just please," he thought, "don't hurt her."

Hayward personally called the FBI; he wanted federal help looking for Victoria. The agent he got when he was finally connected to a live person was Special Agent Maggie May.

* * * * * *

Victoria had just about convinced herself that Aaron and Elvis were going to ransom her and not hurt her. After all, they had let her take a shower and had fixed her something to eat, treating her like a guest. About the time she started feeling better about the situation Elvis had tossed her purse to her and said, "Well, Vickie, put some lipstick on, it's time for the party to start."

Her stomach had turned a flip-flop. Lipstick party—what was he talking about? "Let's all go on in the bedroom," Aaron said, "I have everything ready."

What was he talking about, Victoria thought. She didn't want be in the bedroom with these two.

"Vickie," Aaron said, "Can you dance?"

Dance, she thought, they want to dance? This kept getting weirder...

Elvis came over to the chair in the living room where she had been sitting and pulled her up roughly by the arm. "Put that lipstick on, red if you have it. I've been looking at your lips all evening. You've got the kind of mouth every man dreams about, you know it?"

Another stomach flip for Victoria. She didn't like the sound of his voice nor the look in his eyes, and she cringed just thinking about that toe thing on his thumb. It was disgusting. Elvis caught the look that crossed her face and saw her glance at his two thumbs. "You don't like my thumbs do you? You'll like it before the night is over. You'd be surprised at how many woman love what my thumb can do." He laughed a laugh that made a shiver go up Victoria's spine.

When they got to the bedroom, she saw the light was very dim, just one small watt bulb on the stand beside the bed. The rest of the room was so dark she could hardly see anything. As her eyes adjusted to the darkness she saw two chairs sitting on the other side of the room. Aaron was already sitting in one of them. Elvis said, "Vickie, did you ever see the movie True Lies that had Arnold Schwarzenegger and Jamie Lee Curtis in it?"

What was this about she wondered? Yes, she nodded. She had seen the movie when it had first come out but that had been a long time ago.

Elvis continued, "Remember that scene where she was playing a hooker and she was supposed to plant a bug in the room?" Again, Victoria nodded she remembered. "Well, we don't want you to plant no bug, but we want you to do that scene. Me and Aaron are gonna sit over here like Arnold did and you are gonna strip down for us and dance us a striptease dance." She shook her head no in horror. No way she was going to strip for these two.

"Oh yes, you're gonna, too," said Aaron, "If you don't I'm gonna kill your little Precious here." She looked over to where Aaron was sitting. He had

Precious in his lap and a knife in his hand. "Don't think for a minute I won't do it," he said. She knew he meant it, and she heard Precious yelp.

"Don't hurt her!"

" I was just squeezing her a little," Aaron said. "Wish you had some high heels on. I love to see women dance in high heels and red lipstick. Come on Vickie, start dancing, I want to see you do that move where Jamie Lee turned her back and bent over and looked through her legs, and don't forget the part about licking your finger and humping on that bedpost. Hurry up, you're holding up the party."

Another yelp from Precious brought her into action. She could do this, she thought. She had taught aerobics classes for years and had hundreds of dance routines in her head. She didn't want to strip, but at least she had her underwear for what it was worth. She wished she hadn't worn a thong. The black lace push up bra was bad enough, but the thong might put these men over the edge. If one of them touched her she would die, she thought.

She slowly started one of her old dance routines and moving around the floor a little. She had been on stage and in front of crowds all her life between beauty contests and aerobics classes, but she had never felt more awkward and nervous than she did now. She tried to let her mind wander and her body move to a song she heard in her head. She finally took a deep breath and pulled her tank top over her head and let it drop. She heard one of the men say, "Look at those tits, brother, hot damn."

She danced around a bit more staying with her old dance routines from aerobics classes. She threw in a pelvis thrust every now and then, nothing too suggestive. She felt like she had been doing this for hours, but in fact it had only been a couple minutes. She turned her back and bent over like they wanted. She still had her skirt on, but as short as it was, they still saw plenty. She heard their sharp intake of breath. She put a couple of old cheerleading moves in her dance and kept going.

Finally, she heard one say, "Vickie, take off that skirt." Another yelp from Precious. She unzipped her skirt and worked it down her legs. It was a spandex miniskirt anyway so she had to wiggle out of it.

"Dear God," she thought, "let this end." With that over if she remembered the movie correctly, she was supposed to go lay down on the bed, but she didn't want to think about that, so she kept dancing.

One of the brothers, they sounded exactly alike, so she didn't know which one, said "Vickie, take off your underwear."

She shook her head and stammered, "Jamie Lee didn't take off her underwear in the movie."

"Well, I guess we just done changed the script then," the brothers both laughed. Again she shook her head no, and again she heard a slap and a loud cry from Precious. "Don't hurt her, I'll do it." She was in tears as she stepped out of her panties and unfastened the front of her bra and let it fall to the floor. She felt dirty and exposed. "How could women do this for a living?" she wondered.

"Lookie, there brother, all she's wearing is a smile and diamonds. I ain't never seen nothin' look so good. Are them real diamonds? They are aren't they, Vickie? Them diamonds are probably worth more money than we have made our entire lives or ever will make."

Victoria, nodded, "Take the diamonds and call my husband. He will give you anything you ask to return me safely. He won't file charges, I promise. Just let me go home, and you'll be rich for the rest of your lives."

"Hmm," one of them said, "We'll think about that. In the meantime let's get on with the movie, time to go lay on the bed and close you eyes. Remember that part?"

Victoria's knees were so weak she could barely walk to the bed, and she was so afraid her teeth were chattering. "Please, God," she prayed, "Don't let them rape me. No matter what I promise them if they rape me, Hayward will kill them."

She lay down on the bed and closed her eyes, shaking so badly she was making the bed move. She could hear a shuffling and footsteps coming close to the bed. She had her eyes shut tight. She could hardly breathe, tears oozing out of the corners of her eyes. She felt hot breath close to her ears and then one of them said, "How about giving me a kiss?" She kept her eyes shut and shook her head no. She felt movement and then felt his lips against hers.

"Open your eyes Vickie." When she did, she screamed. It wasn't his lips on hers at all. It was his penis. "NO!" She screamed and lunged like a lioness at him, trying to claw him. He slapped her hard across the face. "You bitch," he yelled, "You're going to pay for that". A red scratch was bleeding down his chest. It was Aaron. Those odd eyes were as cold as a lizard's as he held her down. "Elvis, grab her legs and tie her down."

She twisted and screamed and tried to hold her legs together, but Elvis pried them apart and tied them to each bedpost. "Now Elvis, come tie her arms." Again she was writhing and struggling with all her might. Elvis slapped her again, her ears ringing from the blow. Elvis tied her hands together over her head and to the bed. She was completely vulnerable, legs spread wide, arms tied tightly over her head. Still, she struggled against the ropes that bound her. "Now Vickie, like I said give me a little kiss." Aaron tried to shove himself into her mouth. Both brothers had a full erection, and both were huge.

"Open your mouth." She shook her head no. "Elvis, you know what to do."

When she looked up, Elvis was holding Precious. "You goin' to open your mouth now? No? I'm goin' to kill her." She could see him squeezing Precious' neck tighter and tighter.

"Please," she said, "Please no." Aaron took that opportunity to shove himself in her mouth. "Now," he said, "You're going to do me first, and then you're going to do Elvis. I've been waiting all day to have those lips on my dick." He started thrusting inside her mouth, so hard and so far she was gagging. Victoria thought she'd rather be dead than to be subjected to this. Little did she know this was just the beginning.

* * * * *

Special Agent Maggie May didn't mind working the phones on Sunday. The FBI office in Chicago was slow most weekends. Her phone shift was about to end when the call from Hayward Bentley came. She could tell the man was frantic with worry about his missing wife. He was demanding the FBI get involved. He was sure his wife had been kidnapped. He wanted to get his phone lines ready to trace calls so when the kidnappers called they could locate where Victoria was being held. Maggie tried to calm Hayward down. "Calm, down, sir," she said. "I need you to start at the beginning and tell me what has happened."

Hayward blustered, "We're wasting time here. Okay? Okay! My wife was supposed to drive down to Bloomington last night for her sister's birthday dinner. She never showed up. I was out of town on a golf outing with a couple of the partners in my law firm. Her sister tried calling our home and Victoria's cell phone and got no answer at either. They couldn't find my cell phone number so they had no way of contacting me to see if I knew where Victoria was. They actually thought something may have happened to me that kept Victoria from coming. Victoria always has her cell phone on; even when she is re-charging it she leaves it on. When you call her number it is going directly to voice mail, that means it's turned off, some thing is wrong here."

"When I got home this afternoon and saw Victoria wasn't home. I called her cell and got her voice mail so I called her sister to see if she was still there or what time she left. That's when I learned she had never arrived. I called the police and they wanted to wait 48 hours before they considered her officially missing. I'm a wealthy man, Agent May, and I have influential contacts in Chicago. I called everyone I knew from the chief of police to the governor to get the police to start looking for Victoria. A state police cruiser spotted the car at a rest area on Interstate 55. He questioned the Saturday maintenance staff, and one of them remembered seeing my wife talking to a man who was taking the back tire of her car off. The maintenance worker said the next time he looked out, the man, my wife, and the white van the man was driving was gone. The car has been sitting with the rear jacked up for over 24 hours. We're not talking some beat up Chevy here. She was driving a new Porsche Boxster convertible. Someone has kidnapped her. I'm sure of it."

Maggie listened to the very distraught husband tell his story. She had the same gut feeling he did. Something was very wrong here. Women like Victoria Bentley just didn't disappear. She hoped for Mr. Bentley's sake it was a kidnapping. Her suspicions were far more dark.

For months Maggie had been telling anyone who would listen she felt something very evil was out there. She just knew it. Although any policeman will tell you to follow your instincts, Maggie didn't have much to go on. It was more intuition than facts so no one was taking her seriously. They all thought she had an over active imagination. Anytime she was in the office and had spare time she was running different searches through the FBI's search engine for unsolved missing person's cases. She had found a large number of unsolved cases going back many years, which was not surprising. She kept narrowing her searches down and increasing the area to include states bordering Illinois. All the cases she was separating into a new file were people who not only were missing, but had also seemed to vanish from the face of the earth. The numbers were startling. Was it possible someone had been killing for years and had been able to go undetected, staying under police radar?

As she read through the case files, she thought the answer to that was yes. Many of these missing people were people that no one would bother looking for very long. A few were runaways, some prostitutes, hitchhikers, and people who lived on the fringe of being homeless. Some of these slept in shelters or at churches, etc. Some were alcoholics, and some were just down on their luck, needing a helping hand. All those who had been reported missing from agencies such as these were people who were straightening their lives out. They had jobs and were working towards getting a place of their own when they literally disappeared, never coming back even for their meager belongings. Most police departments were too over worked to look into cases like these. They didn't have the manpower and figured the people had just moved on or didn't want to be found.

But there were also a number of people who just plain left home one day or night and never came back. Some were salesman, some were college kids, and some were workers who worked shifts where they got off work at midnight or later. These included nurses and factory workers and employees of stores that were open extended hours. People just disappeared. No signs of struggle, just gone. There had been a couple missing person cases very similar to the story Hayward Bentley told. A car with a flat abandoned and the occupant never found. Maggie thought there was a predator out there, a predator who had been killing for many years. Victoria Bentley was just the first higher profile person who had been taken. Maggie would bet a month's pay there would never be a ransom call or note. She felt in her gut Victoria was either already dead or soon would be. Whichever the case may be, Maggie wanted on this case.

* * * * *

Victoria wished they would go ahead and kill her. She wanted to die. She didn't think she could live in so much pain another minute. Both men had forced themselves into her mouth, and her throat was so sore, her mouth swollen and throbbing. Her lips were dry and cracked. Her captors had slapped her so hard so many times she had lost count. She knew her face was swollen and bruised. She had always bruised easily. She was still tied with her hands above her head. Her arms ached and felt like they weren't getting enough circulation. Aaron and Elvis had left the room. She didn't know how long ago. It seemed like a long time, but she had no concept of time here. All she knew was she was in hell and these men were insane. Hayward would have them hunted down and killed for what they had done to her.

When they returned, they started on her again. They licked and bit her everywhere. She couldn't stand the thought of these men touching her. Her skin crawled and she gagged at their tongues licking her. When they bit her the first time, it literally took her breath. She felt like a wild animal had attacked her. Elvis kept promising her the thumb trick, and she didn't want to think what he was talking about. They had licked her nipples and then bit so hard she wasn't sure the nipples were still attached. They worked their way down her body this way and then started at her feet and licked and bit all the way up her inner thighs. The pain of their bites was about to make her pass out. She knew she couldn't take much more. Aaron leaned over and said, "Vickie, you wet yet? Elvis, see if she's slicked up for us."

My God, was this mauling some kind of morbid foreplay? Were they now going to rape her, too? She felt Elvis rake his finger across her, "Dry as a bone, Aaron. This bitch is one of those who look so hot and dress to get men to look at 'em then when you want some they turn into Ice Bitches. Get her slicked up Aaron."

Aaron roughly smashed his face into her crotch, humping her with his face, licking her. She struggled against her ropes.

"Hot damn Aaron, you got her hot now. She's bucking like a bronco. Let me at her. Vickie, dahlin', I'm going to give you my thumb trick first." She tried to scream but through the bites she had screamed so long and hard, she had lost of voice.

Elvis continued, "Feel when I put my thumb in you, like this," as he shoved inside her, "Well, now, when I turn my thumb just so. . . don't that just set your g-spot to twitching?"

She couldn't stand the thought of that thumb being inside her. It was gross. They were gross. This was a nightmare. She'd wake up and everything would be fine. This could not be happening to her. The next thing she felt was the searing pain of being raped. They took turns on her. At some point she passed out. They quit when she passed out. That's how evil they were. They wanted her to feel the pain. They splashed cold water on her to bring her to and told her they were going to untie her. They undid her arms and legs and turned her over. Blood came rushing back in her arms, and they hurt as badly as the bites pulsating all over her body. Just as she wondered what they were doing, they roughly grabbed her and told her to get on her knees. She was too weak, One of them bit her so hard on her butt she knew it had to have brought blood.

The next thing she knew she felt a pain searing through her like none other. Dear God in heaven, they were sodomizing her. She was trying to scream, but the sound that came out didn't even sound human. Her vision started going black, and finally Victoria Bentley was released from the pain of her hell.

They tortured Victoria most of the night Saturday and all day Sunday before they finally strangled what little life she had left out of her. Precious joined the dead, Aaron broke the little dog's neck with one twist. They wrapped the body in a sheet and took it out and put it in the freezer in the back of the van. Only one thing left to do, Victoria Bentley just as all the victims before her, was about to be rendered.

They took her to the slaughterhouse. It was dark and they used only a penlight to unlock the back door and carry the body in. Once in, they took the body into the butchering area and literally cut Victoria's and Precious' bodies into small pieces, crushing bones and skull into small, unrecognizable parts. They then transferred the pieces in tubs to the rendering area. All units had been emptied and cleaned on Friday after the end of the work day. After Monday's horses were slaughtered, the conveyor belts would empty the parts into the different boilers and steamers for the rendering processes to take place. By the time the end process was done, nothing would be identifiable. All that would be left would be bone meal and talon and dog food by products. Aaron and Elvis separated the parts into the designated boilers. They would not be checked in the morning since they had been cleaned on Friday. All of tomorrow's kill would just go down the belt and empty into the machines. Victoria would cease to be, without a trace and no evidence, the perfect murder, again.

They went back in to the butcher area and cleaned up all the mess, leaving it spotless. Within an hour of pulling behind the slaughterhouse, they were back in the van. No one came out here at night. Early tomorrow morning the trucks would be bringing the horses into the killer lots and it would be business as usual.

The only things they needed to get rid of were Victoria's purse and clothes and the tire from the Porsche. They would burn the clothes and purse, and next time they went for a drive to the river, they would sink the tire. The only other things they had, which they planned to keep, were the diamonds. They figured with the right contacts they could get a nice bit of money for them, but they would have to sit on them for a long time. Every pawn shop in the country would probably be alerted to look for them. What they needed was a jeweler to take the diamonds out of the mountings. Then they wouldn't be traceable. They were sure there were jewelers in Chicago would do this for a price, and even better, they could kill the man after they got the diamonds, so he couldn't talk. The men were on a killing high. This had been the ultimate kill. No one could top Vickie.

* * * * * *

The FBI and the Illinois police had not been able to locate a single lead or any trace of Victoria Bentley. Hayward had become an old man seemingly overnight. Special Agent Maggie May had seen the loss of loved ones affect loved ones, especially in a particularly tragic death. Hayward was grieving not only for the loss of Victoria, but not knowing what had happened to her was haunting him. He needed closure. Maggie had promised him she would do everything she could to find out what had happened to Victoria, no matter how long it took.

Maggie was supposed to go home to Brannon in a couple weeks for her parent's anniversary party. If she didn't come up with any new leads on the Bentley case she would go ahead and make the trip. She was anxious to see her parents and anxious to visit with her long time friend Jett. She knew Jett and Savannah had had a hard time adjusting to the death of Blake. Jett and she had exchanged emails almost every day for the past year. Jett had told Maggie about Savannah's imaginary horse, how he had "arrived" within a couple days after they had been notified of Blake's death. Jett had sought advice from Maggie on how to handle the horse. Should she go along with Savannah and humor her, let the horse be nature's way of helping heal her and adjust to the loss of her father? Should she be strict with Savannah and tell her there was no horse? She had been worried because Savannah insisted that Blake had sent Star to take care of her and her obsession about the horse had only gotten stronger as time had gone on. She asked Maggie her thoughts on this because she knew Maggie had minored in psychology in college and also being with the FBI had given her even more training in the way the mind works. Maggie was anxious to talk personally to Savannah and see how she seemed. A child having an imaginary playmate was very common, but if she was taking it to the extremes Jett had spoken about Savannah might need to see a child psychologist to cope with the loss of her father.

Maggie wasn't the only one planning to go to Brannon. Elvis and Aaron were going there as well. They had a cousin that had moved there from the mountains several years ago. Jimmy Dan had a son, Dalton, who worked at Ho Supawa, the Japanese auto plant. On a visit to Jimmy Dan a year ago they had gotten the idea to try to make some extra money by selling horsemeat to the Japanese manager who headed the Brannon plant. Aaron and Elvis knew Japan was one of the main importers of horsemeat. It was considered a delicacy, and only the wealthy could afford it. They even ate it raw. Sakuri, it was called.

Elvis called the plant and asked to make an appointment to see Mr. Yoshika. When his secretary asked the reason he told her it was a personal matter. He told her he and his brother wanted to honor Mr. Yoshika by bringing him a gift. The secretary told Elvis that Mr. Yoshika was a very busy man but did not want to be rude to his American friends, so he would see them. Elvis explained they were coming from out of state and asked if it would be possible to see Mr. Yoshika at the plant on Saturday morning. After conferring with her boss, the secretary came back and said although it was highly unusual, Mr. Yoshika would see them at 11:00 a.m. on Saturday morning.

When Elvis and Aaron met with Mr. Yoshika they were on their best manners. They were hoping this gift might bring some business their way. When Mr. Yoshika saw what they had brought him, he was very grateful. He questioned where they had gotten this meat and the legality of having it. Elvis told him they worked in a horsemeat processing plant. That sounded much better than slaughterhouse. He told them the workers at the plant were entitled to a certain amount of meat a week if they chose to take it. Since none of the other workers took their allotment, Elvis and Aaron could get more. Of course, this was all just a story they made up but they didn't think this guy knew the difference, and they were right. He told them that the head of the company from Japan was planning on making a visit to the Brannon plant to evaluate their production. Would it be possible for the brothers to provide enough meat for a small dinner party? His wife was going to host a dinner for Mr. Katto, and it would bring them much honor to serve such a delicacy to him.

Ah, yes, this was just what the brothers had hoped for. They arranged a price and agreed to deliver the fresh meat on the day before the dinner. It proved to be a great success and word had traveled in the Japanese business community about the Pucketts and their ability to provide such a treat for their dining pleasure. Soon several Japanese were quietly contacting the brothers as word got around, and they had a good income coming in from the black market meat. They warned their customers this had to be kept very discreet since it was not American custom to eat horsemeat. They assured them their meat was only from the finest horses and was so fresh it was still walking the day before. This attempt at humor brought smiles from the Japanese.

Mr. Katto was coming back for his yearly inspection of the plant, and Mr. Yoskika called Aaron and Elvis to see if they could once again deliver the meat. That put them in Brannon the same weekend Special Agent Maggie May was coming to visit her parents.

CHAPTER 10

▼

Jett was starting to worry about Savannah. She had thought in the beginning Savannah's imaginary horse friend was a child's way of coping with the death of her father. Savannah had seemed to take such comfort in Star, as she called her horse friend, that she didn't worry about it. She stopped crying and having bad nightmares when Star appeared. Savannah insisted her daddy had sent Star to watch over her. Jett assumed this was a phase and in time, when Savannah had come to terms with her father's, death, she would outgrow her imaginary horse. This was not what had happened. If anything, Savannah had become more obsessive about Star. She spent most of her time "talking" to him. She didn't care about going anywhere or playing with other children. When she was invited to one of her previously best friend's birthday party, she hadn't even wanted to go. Jett had to almost make her. She finally went but as Jett sat and watched her with the rest of the mothers at the party, she could tell Savannah couldn't wait to leave. As soon as the cake was cut and she'd eaten her piece, she'd come and asked if they could go home. Jett had smiled at that. She was her daughter after all. Don't ever turn down birthday cake!

Jett was beginning to wonder what would happen when it was time for school to start. She had been debating for a while about what to do about school. The over protective side of her wanted to keep Savannah at home and home school her. She was a smart little girl and already knew more than Jett had at that age. She had always read to Savannah and started at a very early age teaching her colors, how to count, and the alphabet. Savannah had every page of all of her story books memorized, and she could recite verbatim what was on every page. Jett had built upon that knowledge to help Savannah recognize the words she was seeing and saying. She could now pick out quite a few words no matter where they were and knew what they were. Jett had taught her how the different letters of the alphabet looked and how they sounded, and in doing so had given Savannah the basics of learning how to read by sounding out the words. She was reading phonetically. Kindergarten had already started this year but she could still enroll her. School only lasted half a day. Maybe it would be best if she went ahead and put Savannah in school. At least that way she would be interacting with other children her age and maybe, just maybe, that would help her outgrow Star.

Jett had also given thought to buying a horse or even a pony for Star. Here again the protective mom came out and she worried about Savannah getting hurt. Even a pony is heavy and could easily break a foot if it stepped on Savannah's. And of course at some time or other almost everyone has fallen or been thrown by a horse. Falling off a pony wouldn't be as far to fall as from a tall horse, but still it could result in serious injury. Thinking of her baby on a big horse, immediately brought the image of Christopher Reeves to mind. He was a perfect example of what she worried about. He was an experienced horseman, but accidents still happen even to the best of us. The thought of Savannah severely injured, paralyzed, was too much for her mind to even contemplate. Blake, however, had promised Savannah a horse from the time she was old enough to know what one was. He loved horses and wanted to pass on not only his love of them but also his knowledge of them to his little girl.

"If only Blake were here," Jett sighed to herself. She would trust Blake with Savannah on a horse. His grandfather had taught him how to ride almost before he could walk.

Maybe she could start by finding about some local riding schools. She wanted Savannah to know what she was doing before she bought her a horse. For that matter, maybe she would take lessons with Savannah. Now that, she thought was a great idea. Jett had always loved the idea of having and riding a horse, but never had the opportunity. If they took lessons together, they could learn together not only how to ride but the proper way to take care of a horse. She needed to know a lot more than just how to sit on a saddle. She needed to know how to handle a horse on the ground, the do's and don'ts. Common sense told her not to walk behind a horse, but would a child think of that unless she were taught? Savannah was fearless. She wouldn't think a horse would kick her.

Jett was glad to hear her friend Maggie was coming home for her parents' anniversary party. Maggie had taken a lot of psychology classes in college. Maybe she could offer some advice on the best way to handle Savannah. Jett could trust Maggie to tell her the truth. Maybe Savannah needed to see a child psychologist. Up to this point Jett had rejected that notion, but time had not made Savannah better. If anything, things were starting to get worse. Savannah was starting to have nightmares again. The first time Jett heard her scream out in her sleep it scared her half to death. With a pounding heart, she had run to check on her. Savannah didn't tell her what she dreamed and the first time she didn't ask, just told her it was just a bad dream and everything was okay. She had gotten her a drink of water and cooled her sweaty forehead with a damp cloth. Within a few minutes, Savannah had gone back to sleep. Jett didn't think too much about it, after all everyone has bad dreams.

But Savannah's dreams were continuing and becoming more frequent. In the mornings, she said she didn't remember what she'd dreamed. Jett thought Savannah wasn't telling her the whole truth. Savannah got so she didn't want to go to bed at night, afraid she'd have a nightmare. She used every excuse she could think of not to have to go to bed. When Jett finally got her to bed, she would ask for another story to be read to her after the first was finished. When that one was finished, she wanted a drink. Then she wanted to go to the bathroom. And so it went, night after night. Jett got so she dreaded bedtime as much as Savannah. Savannah now was starting to ask if she could sleep with her. Jett did not want to start that. She knew too many parents who had given in to let a child sleep with them just for one night, and it had turned into a regular thing. Savannah had a nightlight in her room so she wasn't in total darkness. Jett was staying firm on this point.

Jett was puzzled as to why the nightmares had begun. What had prompted them? Maybe Maggie could get Savannah to talk about her dreams. Jett certainly hoped so. Her sleep had been disrupted, too. She wasn't exactly having nightmares, but she certainly had been seeing something strange in her sleep. When she thought back, her dreams had started about the same time as Savannah's nightmares. Maybe she and Savannah both needed to rejoin the world.

Jett and Blake had discussed almost every thing while they were married. The subject of death had been one of the things they discussed. Like all new lovers, at first they had vowed never to love again if either of them died, but later they had talked about it again after Savannah was born. She didn't remember now how the subject had ever come up, but Blake had told her that if anything ever happened to him he would want her to go on with her life and be happy. He didn't want her to live her life in the past and if the right man came along, he wanted her to remarry. He said she was too vital, too loving to wither her life away. He also told her that he didn't want Savannah to grow up without a father. At first she protested, but after they talked awhile she agreed not to close her life off, and he promised the same if something happened to her. She was glad now they had had that conversation because she knew that if she ever did find a companion it would be with Blake's blessing. She loved him like she would never love another, but that didn't mean she couldn't love at all.

She thought maybe it was time for Savannah and her to stop being so reclusive. They needed to get out more, socialize more. She had been thinking of going back to work, too.

Every time she went in the bank they asked her when she was coming back. She realized she missed going to work, missed talking to people, having adult conversations. She missed having lunch with girlfriends or even skipping lunch to go her favorite store's sale. If she put Savannah in kindergarten, she could work while Savannah was in school. Then, next school year when Savannah would go all day to school, she could go back fulltime. She could adjust her schedule so she would be home when Savannah left for school and when she returned in the evening. She hadn't said anything to Savannah about this yet, but she was going to run it by Maggie to see what she thought.

CHAPTER 11

▼

Julianna felt like she was finally making some good progress in getting Sahara to accept her presence. She was now in week four and although she still had not touched him, she was very close to that achievement. If she were going to be riding him in eight weeks, she needed to move right along; she had no time to waste.

She had bought a couple books on natural horsemanship and even checked a DVD out from the library on how to train a wild mustang. In the end she decided what she was doing was the best way to handle Sahara. Take one little step at a time, praise every action, reward every positive thing. Sahara had responded to this system where all those fancy trainers had failed. She never yelled or raised her voice to him, she tried to stay calm and loving in every move she made. She talked to him constantly. They were bonding; he was waiting at the gate of his paddock every day when she got there. It was getting dark sooner now so she had portable lights brought in so she could light up a part of his field when she was there at night.

One day she was later than usual getting to the farm. The last appointment, which was at 6:00, was the part she hated most about being a veterinarian. A family was coming in to have their cat put to sleep. The cat was 20 years old, blind, deaf, diabetic and had somehow gotten outside and unable to see or hear, had been hit by a car a couple weeks ago. It hadn't killed the cat, but it had broken her leg and caused some internal bleeding. They had bought the cat in when it had been hit and wanted to try to save it. One of the other vets had put a cast on the leg and patched the cat up as much as possible; however, the cat was in pain, wouldn't eat and was now in kidney and liver failure. The family knew it was time to put Tootsie out of her pain, even though they were grieving about it. The couple's ten year old little boy Brent was taking it very badly. His eyes were red and swollen practically shut from crying. He had never known life without Tootsie. Julianna wanted to take the little boy in her arms and hold him tight and tell him everything would be okay.

She told the family to take all the time they needed to say goodbye to Tootsie. When they were finally ready, Brent said with a hoarse trembling voice he wanted to hold Tootsie. Julianna had to fight back tears herself. He was being so brave, she thought. She explained to the family how the procedure would go. First, she would give Tootsie a shot to relax her and let her go to sleep. After she fell asleep then Julianna would give her another shot that would end her pain forever. She told Brent to hold Tootsie and love her like he did every night when they went to bed, and to her it would be like she died in her sleep with him loving her. She then told Brent all about Rainbow Bridge where all our pets wait for us until we die, so we can go to heaven together. Brent had never heard the Rainbow Bridge story and it comforted him to know Tootsie would be waiting for him.

Explaining it all and taking the extra time with the family, made Julianna late getting to the barn.   She was still thinking about Brent when she got to the barn and walked right in the dark barn without thinking about closing the other entrance from the field first. She reached and turned the barn lights on and saw Sahara standing a few feet from her. Thank God she didn't react or jerk away. Instead, she walked on like this is what they did everyday. She talked to him the entire time, telling him the story about the little boy and the cat and how sad it was and how brave the little boy had been. She hadn't realized how much she had been holding in until she realized she was crying. She covered her face with her hands and just bawled, letting the emotion of the day drain away. She felt warm breath on her hand and then felt a nose on her shoulder.

Julianna lowered her hands from her face and looked right in to the big liquid eye of Sahara. Without thinking, she put her arms around his big neck and buried face into his tangled mane crying. She was acutely how tense his body was. This was the first time she had touched him, and he was giving her his trust. She dared not make a sudden move for fear of scaring him. Through her tears she started talking to him, and gradually she could feel the tenseness leave him as he relaxed and stood there with his back leg bent, the way horses do when they are relaxed. She stayed there with her head next to his, loving him, rubbing her hand down his long elegant neck. The tears of sadness over the day were now replaced with tears of happiness with finally having Sahara come to her, sensing her unhappiness and coming to her. His large soft eyes looked at her with no fear.

She felt now like she would be able to ride him. She was not going to rush anything. After all, she had two more months, but she thought if she built on the trust he had given her tonight she could meet her deadline. She talked to Sahara, telling him she was going to get his water and food ready and then proceeded to do so. He was a little startled when she turned the water hose on to fill his water, but he didn't run off or rear up. He cautiously followed her into the stall as she scooped his grain in his feed bucket. Her inner warning system was lecturing herself about letting him in the stall with her. He could easily pin her or knock her down and stomp her. Just because she had touched him she didn't want to be careless. Sahara had seriously injured people.

When she finally got home that night she was physically and emotionally exhausted. Daniel was waiting at the door when she walked in. She knew he was worried because she was late. She should have called him, she realized, but she been so upset about the little boy and his cat she didn't want to talk to anyone. Now as she saw the concern on Daniel's face she felt badly.

"You've been crying," he said, "Are you hurt? Are you okay? Did the horse hurt you? Let me look at you, not waiting for her to answer one question before asking another. Julianna finally shook her head. "I'm fine, long day, good and bad things happened. I'll tell you all about it." She recounted the appointment with the family and Toostie, how heartbroken but brave Brent had been, and how sad it had made her. She told him she had been late leaving the clinic because she didn't want to rush the family or Brent. She then told him about the wonderful breakthrough she had made with Sahara. She started by telling him she'd forgotten to close the barn door from the field side before going in, and right away Daniel started to interrupt her. She could tell he was getting ready to lecture her, so she stopped him. She went ahead and told him how she'd been so upset she had covered her face and started crying when Sahara had come up beside her. She started crying again just telling him about Sahara and how special he had been, sensing her unhappiness and offering comfort to her. She told him she knew it was a big break, and she felt so confident now that she would be able to ride him by the time the Prince came back.

Daniel told her how happy he was for her and how he knew how important this project had become to her and that she had fallen in love with Sahara. He had been worried about her obsession with Sahara. Julianna always gave 100%, and between working and Sahara he thought she was pushing herself too hard. She had lost weight, and she was already too thin. She assured him she felt just fine and in fact was starving. Daniel had cooking duties that night, and he already had dinner ready. Daniel had to admit she ate well and even had a bowl of ice cream afterwards. He had a fire going in the fireplace to take the chill out of the room, and they snuggled on the couch with only the fireplace giving light. In just a few minutes he could tell from Julianna's breathing she was asleep. He lay beside her, thinking how much he loved her and how lucky he was to have her for his wife. He couldn't wait to have children. He wanted a little girl that looked just like Julianna. Of course she wanted a little boy that looked just like him. Maybe before long they could start working on that family.

The next day when Julianna went to care for Sahara she wondered if the colt would revert to his skittish self or be trusting. She decided to play it cautious. She opened the barn door to his outside field from outside the fence like she always did. Even the tamest of horses were sometimes high spirited in the morning and would come running and bucking out of the barn after being enclosed. Sure enough he came charging out of the barn, tossing his head and kicking up his hind legs playfully. It wasn't done in a threatening way, more like he was feeling good. She closed the door behind him then went back around to the front of the barn and went in to muck his stall.

After she finished, she went back out and climbed over the fence to top off his water trough for the day. He was used to her doing this and had gotten used to her walking around the field while he was there. She called out to him, telling him she had an apple for him, and held her hand out to show him. Would he come? Yes, he came prancing over and took the apple from her outstretched hand. This would be the test, she thought, as she reached out to stoke his neck. Again he tensed, trying to decide if he wanted this, but soon relaxed and seemed to enjoy her touch. She decided every day she would lengthen the time she touched him and would start trying to make him comfortable with her touching him everywhere. Again she was going to be patient, take her time and let him determine how far each time she could go. She hoped to accomplish a lot this month. She wanted him to be comfortable being touched all over. She wanted to be able to pick up each of his legs and clean his hoofs, and she wanted to get him used to be groomed and bathed. That knotted mane was going to take some work. It was going to be like trying to unknot a thin gold chain. She wanted him to let her put a halter on and off him and to be able to cross tie him.

She was also going to start bomb proofing him. This meant she needed to introduce different sounds to him so he wouldn't get scared and take off at the slightest thing. Horses are prey animals, which means their first instinct when something scares them is to run for their life. If she was going to ride him he had to get used to all kinds of noises so he wouldn't get spooked and buck or take off on her.

The next visit she brought a halter, a brush, some baby oil and a lead rope. She didn't do anything with it, just brought it, let Sahara see, it smell it, and get used to it. The brush and oil she put away. The halter and rope she draped over the side of his stall. She took everything step by step, getting him used to one thing before introducing him to something else. By the end of that week, she was able to take a halter on and off him with no problem and she had rubbed the oil into his tangled mane. The oil would help loosen the knots and make it easier to brush his mane.

The next week she introduced him to the water hose. Of course, he had seen the water hose many times and in previous training attempts probably had been sprayed in an attempt to bathe him. She started like he'd never seen a hose before, letting him smell it and touch it. She rubbed in on him, and left him alone with it to explore. When she turned the water on, she kept the water hardly running at first and just wet his feet. When he was comfortable with that she moved on up and up until he stood to have his body completely wet. After a couple days of that she fully bathed him and he actually seemed to enjoy it. The water acting with the oil made it much easier to manage the knots in his mane. By the end of the weekend he was clean, shiny, and his mane and tail flowed gracefully. He was so beautiful all cleaned up.

She started taking him for walks along the farm's roads, getting him used to sounds of cars doors, honking horns, birds flying over and seeing other horses in the fields. He did call out to the other horses, but he didn't try to break away. She was able to calm him and keep him by her side. She walked him to a little creek that ran across the farm and showed him there was nothing to be afraid of in crossing the water. At first he balked, but she just turned him around, talked to him, reassured him and gently, ever so slowly one step forward, two steps back, got him finally to cross the creek. She was so proud of him; he was doing so well.

The next thing she did was to bring a saddle blanket and saddle into the barn. She again hung them over the stall and let him get used to the idea for a few days. Next, she just started putting the blanket on his back. When he seemed comfortable with that, she got the saddle. He snorted and backed away from the saddle. He had bad memories of saddles and his ears were alert, and he was swishing his tail back and forth. She knew by his body language he was agitated. She didn't push it any more that day. Very slowly, day by day, she finally got Sahara to accept the saddle. Next, she would try a bridle and bit. So far she had used only a halter and lead rope on him.

When she brought the bridle with bit into the barn, Sahara really reacted. He turned and ran out of the barn, clearly not interested in any part of it. She put it aside and went outside to calm him. Julianna bribed him with some apple slices, and he came over to She talked and petted him until he calmed down. She started looking at his mouth and put her thumb behind his teeth to see if he would open his mouth for her. When he did, she saw the reason he had reacted to the bit. She could see evidence of scarring on the inside of his mouth. Someone had been very rough and abusive, trying to train him into submission. Poor baby, she thought, no wonder he didn't trust men. She'd seen this type of red neck macho attitude all her life, and she detested it. She never wanted or intended to break Sahara's spirit. She wanted to be part of him not dominate him. She would forget about a bit. She would just attach reins on his halter to ride him when that time came.

The end of the second month came quickly. Sahara was very comfortable being touched all over, having his legs picked up, his hoofs cleaned, being saddled, and he was getting more comfortable and less spooked at different sights and sounds. Now when she took him for walks around the farm, she did so with his saddle on, letting him get used to the feel and weight of it. On one afternoon she had taken him all the way up to the main house. Mr. Martine had seen her and come out. He was amazed. The last time he had had a good look at Sahara he looked like a wild animal. Now he was walking quietly with full gear on a lead, and he was groomed, shiny and looked beautiful.

Julianna beamed with pleasure at all the compliments Mr. Martin gave. She could tell he was genuinely shocked she had gotten this far with Sahara. She told him he still had not been ridden but that would be next. She also told him as he approached that Sahara still had a trust issue with men and may not allow him to pet him. She knew any man that had ever attempted to work with Sahara would have a very hard time earning the horse's trust. Sahara had not forgotten the abuse he had endured at the hands of men.

Julianna's next project was to actually get on Sahara while saddled. She started this by just leaning her weight on him and the saddle, testing her foot in one of the stirrups, bearing a little weight on the stirrups, then letting go. When Sahara seemed comfortable with the idea, she talked to him the whole time and got on him. After all the time, patience and preparation she had put into it, he didn't do a thing. She was on cloud nine.

She rode him around his little field, letting him get used to her being on his back, letting her get used to working with the reins. She didn't want to jerk on the reins too much or he would over react. She knew she wouldn't have to give him much of a cue to get him to respond to what she wanted. The entire third month she proceeded very slowly, teaching him by the pressure on the reins and the position of her own body language what she wanted him to do. To anyone watching, it looked like she was doing nothing. She and Sahara were so in tune to one another she felt him responding almost as soon as she thought a command.

She let Daniel come out and watch her ride. He could only stand and stare in amazement as his wife and this once wild horse went around the field, stopping, going forward, back, trotting, switching leads, and doing it all without him being able to see Julianna giving a single cue. It was unbelievable. She even took the saddle and blanket off and rode him bareback. She told him that was the way she loved to ride him best, totally free, with just his halter and reins.

Sahara still did not like men, but she was trying to introduce him slowly to Daniel. If her dreams came true and she was able to get this horse from the Prince, she wanted Daniel to be able to be with him without fear.

It was Christmas Day when she was to ride the horse for the Prince. It was cold and was starting to snow a little when she and Daniel arrived at the farm. The Prince and Mr. Martin came out to greet them. Julianna told the Prince she would go get Sahara and bring him to the main house, to the field where she had first seen him. Daniel stayed with the men and Julianna walked on down to Sahara's barn. "This was it," she thought. "Oh Sahara, please be a good boy today." She talked to him the whole time she was getting his tack ready. She told him the Prince was out there and was waiting to see if she had been successful in breaking the horse to ride. She prayed that her riding him would be enough to save him. She knew the horse would go out of control if a man tried to ride him.

She didn't ride Sahara to the field and the main house. She walked beside him, talking softly and reassuring him. When she got to the field where the men stood watching, she opened the gate, led Sahara inside, and mounted him. He did everything she asked him! He was perfect. She glanced over at the Prince and could tell he was shocked. His jaw even dropped open. He wasn't believing what he was seeing. After she put Sahara through all the paces, she stopped, dismounted, took off his saddle and bridle and then rode him bareback, again doing everything perfectly, as one, with the horse. They were a striking sight, poetry in motion, a woman and a horse.

When she finished, she jumped down and walked over to the Prince. Her face was flushed red, both from excitement and the cold. She had never felt more alive than she did right now. The fate of Sahara now was in the Prince's hands. The Prince was so taken back by what he had witnessed he barely could speak. When he did, he told her he had not thought for an instant she would be able to ride the horse, not in 3 months or 3 years. What he had witnessed here was a magical thing, the stuff of desert legends, stories he had heard from olden time about the mysterious bond that happened to wild horses and certain women. It could not be understood by men and was not to be interfered with. And so, on that Christmas morning, he gave Sahara to Julianna, asking only that should she find a suitable mare he would have breeding rights. Julianna could hardly believe her ears, and Daniel was beaming with pride. Of course they agreed to anything the Prince wanted as long as Sahara was hers. This was the happiest day of her life.

When Julianna took Sahara back to the barn, she explained to him all that had happened, told him she loved him and laughed, and he nickered and nudged her with his nose. She told him she would come get him the next day because he was coming to live with her. He would be right outside her house now. He would have his own barn, and he would belong to her forever.

The next day Julianna was a little concerned Sahara would not get in the trailer. She had not worked with him on that. Like everything else she had done with him, she took her time, approaching the trailer slowly and walking him to it. He took one step in and stopped. She didn't try to force him in, just reassured him, brought him back around and approached again. This time he took two steps in before he stopped. The third time he went right on in the trailer. When they got him home, she slowly backed him out of the trailer and led him to his new home, his own barn and field. Now all she had to do was walk to the barn a few steps in the morning and Sahara was right there. Sometimes she wanted to pinch herself to make sure it was all true. No more driving long rides to and from the farm every morning and every night. She was going to finally get caught up on her rest. She wouldn't admit it to anyone else but she was exhausted from the pace she had kept and the stress she had been under for the last 3 months. She knew she'd lost weight and except when she was with Sahara, she felt tired all the time. He energized her. No matter how poorly she felt she could go in the barn and instantly all her problems disappeared. Daniel was happy, too. He finally had his wife back. He had been worried about Julianna. She looked worn out, and he could tell she was running on adrenaline most of the time. Now she could enjoy having Sahara at home, no pressure to meet any deadline, just enjoy having this beautiful horse.

At first Daniel had been worried even if Julianna managed to ride Sahara he may hurt her. Now, he didn't worry about that. He saw for himself the love the two had for one another. Sahara may hurt him, but he would never hurt Julianna.

The next couple of months passed by with no unusual occurrences. It had been a very mild winter, with more rain that snow, which suited Julianna just fine. She still didn't feel like her old self even though she was getting plenty of rest now. Her energy level was down, and she felt very lethargic most of the time. She was also feeling sick to her stomach a lot. The thought of eating or even the smell of food was nauseating to her. She realized it had been a couple months since her last period. Could she be pregnant? Oh, she hoped so. That would certainly explain her low energy level and nausea. She had stopped taking her birth control pills several months ago. She and Daniel hadn't been working hard at getting pregnant, but they had decided it was time to let nature take its course.

Now she was excited. A baby, yes, it all made sense. She wasn't going to say anything to Daniel yet. She would make an appointment with the doctor for her next day off and see if her hunch was correct. When she called the doctor they had an appointment available for the following Wednesday. That was perfect. She was off that afternoon, and Daniel was working. She wouldn't have to explain where she was going after work. This was going to be a good surprise. She could hardly wait to see the expression on his face when she announced the good news.

The week slowly passed by, even though Julianna was sick every day she hid it with enthusiasm. She kept crackers with her all the time and they seemed to help settle her stomach. She had already stopped all drinking anything with caffeine and hadn't so much as taken a Tylenol since she realized she could be pregnant. She started to confide in her mother and father, but she knew they'd be so excited they wouldn't be able to keep a secret and it would be all over the clinic. No, Daniel would be the first to know. Then maybe they'd invite both sets of parents out to dinner and break the big news.

Of course she told Sahara all about the baby as she fed and groomed him every night. She loved just spending time brushing him and talking to him. When she told him about the baby, he had shaken his big head and neighed. She laughed at him and told him she thought he was jealous. She told him he didn't need to be jealous she would always love him. Again he shook his head, pawed his front right hoof on the ground and neighed. Then he turned and laid his big head across her shoulders and nickered softly.

Daniel had walked by the barn and heard Julianna laughing and Sahara neighing. He could hear her talking to the horse, but not what she was saying. He opened the barn door and said, "Hey you, two, what's so funny?" Julianna laughed again and told him she and Sahara were sharing secrets.

Sahara had gotten used to Daniel and no longer was reacting to his presence. He wasn't friendly to him, and Daniel thought it was more that he tolerated him. He knew the horse's devotion laid totally with Julianna. She kept saying one day he'd be able to ride him, too, but he didn't think so. Those two had a special bond. He didn't think Sahara would ever let anyone else ride him, certainly not a man. That didn't bother Daniel at all. He was planning on getting a good horse of his own. He didn't want a high strung Arabian. He preferred a calm Tennessee Walker or quarter horse. He didn't want a stallion either. He preferred a gelding to ride, especially on the trail. Mares were moody no matter what breed, and stallions were always wanting to cause trouble with any other stallions or falling in love with some mare on the trail. He couldn't see he and Julianna ever being able to take Sahara on a trail ride with other horses. That would be a disaster in the making. He was thinking then they needed to get two horses, two geldings so they could ride together. He hadn't said anything to Julianna about it, but he thought she'd agree with his thinking. Right now it wasn't an issue because they weren't ready or financially able to buy two horses.

Wednesday afternoon finally came and Julianna went for her doctor appointment. She knew she was going to get a lecture about not coming in for her pap smear this year or last year. She had been so busy with finishing school and starting working and then Sahara she had kept putting it off.

Julianna had known Dr. Suzanne Davis for a long time. She was also her mom's ob/gyn doctor. She had been coming to Dr. Sue, as everyone called her, since she first started having her periods. She liked the doctor very much. She was a caring, gentle compassionate doctor. She felt at ease with her Dr. Sue.

Julianna signed in at the receptionist's desk, giving her new address, phone numbers and insurance information. She was about 15 minutes early for her appointment, so she had brought a book to read while she waited. She loved reading good murder mysteries and was getting really interested in the book when the nurse called her name. The nurse led her down the hallway, weighed her, measured her height, and then took her into the examining room. She took down the usual information, asking the reason for the visit, took Julianna's blood pressure, and asked if she was having any problems, or was on any medications. She then instructed Julianna to remove her clothes and put on the examining gown and told her that the doctor would be in shortly.

Julianna did as instructed and sat waiting, reading her book until Dr. Sue came in. Dr. Sue arrived a few minutes later, all smiles, smelling faintly of some subtle perfume. She gently chastised Julianna for missing her appointments then asked why she was here. She also told Julianna she looked like she'd lost weight and consulted the chart to see what Julianna had weighed on her last visit. Julianna told her she had lost weight and then proceeded to tell her that she had been feeling nauseous and extremely lethargic. She added that she'd missed a couple of periods, too, and so putting that all together, she hoped she might be pregnant. She had resisted the urge to buy one of those home pregnancy tests because she didn't want Daniel to know. She wanted to surprise him. As Julianna was telling her this Dr. Sue was doing the preliminary exam, looking in her eyes, feeling her neck lymph glands and listening to her heart beat. She asked Julie if her neck was tender and Julianna thought Dr. Sue looked a little concerned. Dr Sue asked her again in more detail how she'd been feeling and for how long. Julianna explained that she had been working very hard for several months and told her all about Sahara and the three months she spent trying to ride him. She admitted she'd been tired all the time but who wouldn't be. She was going to the farm every morning before work, then working a full day at the clinic, then back to the farm with Sahara, then home to do the usual house wife thing, cooking laundry, cleaning, etc. She had been under a lot of stress and attributed her feeling tired all the time to her schedule. Then she started getting a lot more nauseous and began losing more weight because she got sick every time she ate. Even when she didn't eat, the thought of food made her sick.

Dr. Sue listened thoughtfully and then said, "Okay, let's do your Pap smear and exam and see what's going on." After she finished she told Julianna she didn't think she was pregnant. The exam didn't show any evidence of pregnancy. She wanted to do a urinalysis and some blood work to see if anything showed up. She seemed concerned that all Julianna's lymph node areas, neck, groin and underarms seemed to be enlarged and tender. When Julianna saw the look of concern on Dr. Sue's face, she asked what she thought was wrong. Dr. Sue wasn't specific, just said she wanted to see the results of all her tests before they went any further. Dr. Sue said as soon as she got all the results in she would give her a call. The nurse then gave her a little cup and told her to go to the restroom down the hall, get a urine specimen and then come to the lab where they would draw the blood. Julianna was starting to feel a little scared. The lab technician had taken four vials of blood from her arm. Dr. Sue had looked worried, too. Surely there was nothing wrong with her. She'd always been the picture of good health. She'd just let herself get run down. She probably needed to eat better, sleep more and take a good vitamin supplement.

She decided not to say anything to Daniel about going to the doctor, no use to worry him. She felt a little down when she went home. She had been so sure she would have happy news to share. When she got home, she changed into jeans and her favorite raggedy sweatshirt and went out to see Sahara. She told him all about going to the doctor and how worried she was, and once again he laid his head across her shoulders. He seemed to be sad, too. She thought maybe taking a little ride on Sahara would cheer her up. Riding Sahara always made her feel magical. She put his halter and reins on and with the help of a stool got on his back. They went for a long, slow ride through the fields. This was exactly what she needed. By the time she got back to the barn with him she was in a much better frame of mind. She'd just been feeling sorry for herself, she thought. There wasn't a thing to worry about. She looked around and saw the first shoots of daffodils and crocus showing through the ground. Spring was nearly here, soon everything would be green, trees would be blooming and the gloom of winter would be gone.

That weekend she convinced herself she felt better. She made a point to eat well, no junk food and she went to bed early. She and Daniel had a wonderful weekend, planning where they were going to plant spring flowers and marking off areas of the lawn she wanted to turn into flowerbeds and her rose garden.

Monday she was having a hurried lunch with her mom at a little restaurant across from the clinic when her cell phone vibrated on her belt. The call was from Dr. Sue. "Julianna," Dr. Sue said, "I have the results of your tests back. I would like to go over them with you. Is there anyway you can come to my office at 5:30 today?" Julianna told Dr. Sue that she and Daniel had ridden to work together today and both were scheduled off at 5:00 so that should be no problem. "That's perfect," Dr. Sue said, "I'm glad Daniel is coming with you. I'll see you at 5:30."

Julianna's mom gave her a questioning look. "What's wrong, Julianna? Why is Dr. Sue calling you?" "Oh, Mom," Julianna said, "It's nothing. I've just been feeling tired and lost some weight so I went to see Dr. Sue. She did some blood work and has the results back. I'm probably anemic and need some iron supplements or vitamins."

Julianna's mom pursed her lips, "Well you do look pale. Your color is not good at all. You look sallow." Julianna rolled her eyes, "Mom, I'm not sallow, that's just the color my self- tanning lotion looks like when it's wearing off. I'm fine."

"You be sure to call me and tell me what Dr. Sue says," her mom said, adding, "Do you want me to go with you?"

"Really Mom, Daniel wouldn't be going with me if we weren't carpooling today. This is nothing. I promise I'll call you tonight."

Dr. Sue hung up the phone with a heavy sigh. She hoped she had sounded cheerful enough and had not said anything to scare Julianna. It was days like this that she did not like being a doctor. She got up from her desk, put on her white lab jacket with Dr. Sue embroidered above the pocket and went to see her next patient.

CHAPTER 12

▼

"Mommy," Savannah asked, "Do you ever dream about Daddy?" Jett turned back the quilt and Savannah got in bed." "Sometimes, I do," she answered, "Do you?" Jett hoped this conversation would be the start of Savannah telling her about her dreams.

Savannah said, " I used to dream about him a lot, and sometimes it was so real that even when I thought I was awake he would be here talking to me. Has that ever happened to you? Once when I woke up I could smell Daddy. You know how he smelled when he had just shaved and put the smelly stuff on his face? My room smelled just like Daddy."

Jett's eyes filled with tears. Yes, she knew exactly what Savannah was talking about. Several times since Blake died she had awakened after a dream only to see a sudden shadow and the lingering scent of him. It had not scared her. She had felt comforted that he was keeping an eye on her. She had not told anyone about this experience. She knew some people didn't believe in ghosts or spirits or being able to communicate with a passed love one. She had always kept an open mind about such things. Her family had a long history of people with "the sight" as they called it. Her grandmother had had a sixth sense or intuition or whatever one wanted to call it. Jett never understood it, but her grandmother had always been right in the things she saw or predicted would happen. Maybe Savannah had inherited this sixth sense.

"Yes Savannah," Jett replied, "I know how real dreams can seem, and I can smell Daddy sometimes, too. What else do you dream?"

Savannah's little face frowned and Jett could tell she was struggling with a decision. Finally, she started talking. She told Jett that sometimes she had good dreams, dreams about Daddy and dreams about being with Star. But sometimes she had bad dreams. The nightmare dreams she called them. She said she dreamed about men who killed people and they killed horses, too. Star had told her about these bad men too because he didn't want any more horses to die. I saw the faces of the bad men in my dream and something else. It's gross, and it scares me she'd said. He's a mean man and he has two thumbs on his hand, she went on. And he and the other man look exactly alike, except the other man doesn't have two thumbs, but his eyes are scary. They are different colors, she told Jett. She went on to tell Jett that sometimes she saw a woman in her dreams. And the woman was crying and looking for her little dog and the bad men were with her. The little dog was lying in the floor but its eyes were closed, like it was asleep or maybe dead. She was afraid the bad men were going to get her, too. Star said the bad men were coming here soon and I'm scared, she'd said.

Jett had gathered Savannah in her arms and held her closely to her as she had sobbed out this story. Good Lord, Jett thought. What an imagination! Why in the world would Savannah dream such horrible dreams—people and horses getting killed? She didn't know what to say. She was so glad Maggie was coming this weekend. Hopefully, Maggie would be able to help calm Savannah's fears.

Jett had held Savannah until she stopped crying and told her nothing would happen to her and the bad men were just dreams. Savannah had shaken her little head, eyes full of tears, "No, Mommy, that's why I hadn't told you before. I knew you wouldn't believe me. The bad men are real. I know they are. Star knows they are, too. And something else, Mommy," Savannah said, "I don't want to go to school. Please don't make me go to school."

Jett didn't know what to say. She had not said one word to Savannah about her thinking about putting her in school. She hadn't told anyone. She had planned to talk to Maggie about it when she came. She gently wiped Savannah's tears and, with a tissue held to her nose, told her to blow her nose. She then asked Savannah why had she thought she was going to school, who had said that to her. Savannah shrugged her little shoulders. Finally, she looked up and said, "Mommy, I heard you say it. Not out loud," she continued, "Sometimes I just hear things like you are talking to me but you really aren't talking. Like, one day you weren't talking, but I could hear you say in my mind that you wanted to go back to the bank to work and for me to go to school. "My God," Jett thought, "The child can read my thoughts."

"Does this 'hearing people thing' happen with a lot of people or just me?" she asked Savannah. "Mainly it's just you, mommy, but sometimes other people and sometimes other kids. That's why I like to play with Star. It's just me and him, and I don't have to listen to all those voices when other people are around."

"Dear Lord in heaven," Jett thought, "My baby is reading minds and clairvoyant. No wonder she likes to be alone and escapes with an imaginary horse friend." As if on cue, Savannah said, "Star is not imaginary, he is real!"

"Tell me about Star," Jett said. "What does he look like?" "Oh Mommy," Savannah said, "He's the prettiest horse in the whole world. He is black with a white star on his forehead. He has a long mane and tail and he has bangs that hang down to his eyes, just like mine! He wasn't born here. He was born across the ocean in a place where there is sand everywhere, and it is hot all the time. Soon he'll come to live with us. I'm sleepy now. Mommy, will you stay with me until I fall asleep?"

"Sure, Baby," Jett said, "I'll stay right here. You go to sleep now." Within a few minutes Savannah was sound asleep. Jett turned out the lamp and tiptoed out of the room.

* * * * * *

Maggie May had a pounding headache. She had been up since 5:00 this morning, and it was now close to midnight. She had gone over every word of every report from every person interviewed in connection with the disappearance of Victoria Bentley. The case haunted her day and night. She wanted so much to give Hayward Bentley some kind of closure about his wife's whereabouts. Hayward called her everyday to see if there were any leads or any tips called in to the case. He had put up a half a million dollar reward for information leading to the arrest of whoever had taken her. Of course a half million dollars brought out all kinds of tips from all over the country, not to mention the regulars who called after any major crime. Victoria had been seen from Maine to California and from North Dakota to Mexico. Everyone who saw a blonde woman with a dog must be calling she thought. None of the so-called tips or leads had turned up a thing. No one had seen Victoria since the maintenance man at the rest stop had seen her talking to the man driving the white van. You couldn't get any more anonymous vehicle than a white van. There must be thousands of them out there. Maggie felt in her heart Victoria was dead, but she wanted to solve this case.

Another blonde woman had disappeared. She was 22 years old and had worked at a diner just outside Chicago. Actually, the diner was off the interstate at a truck stop. It was one of those places where long haul truckers could park, eat a meal, and even have a shower for those who wanted to use the facility. Mandy Gillespie worked the 3:00–11:00 p.m. shift at the restaurant part of the truck stop. A couple nights ago, she had clocked out at 11:20 and left work. She lived in a small apartment about a ten minute drive away. She had a boyfriend named Barry who sometimes picked her up from work if they were planning to go out. If that was the case and she stayed the night with him, he always brought her back to get her car when he went to work in the morning. The next morning when Mandy's car was still in the parking lot, no one thought anything about it, thinking she was with Barry.

Mandy didn't show up for work at three. She didn't show up at all, and her car was still at the parking lot. Unable to get Mandy on the phone and driving by her apartment and seeing her not there, Barry came by the truck stop to see her. That's when people started worrying. Mandy was rarely late for work and when she was, she always called saying so. No one had seen or heard from her since she walked out the door that night. Barry had called all their mutual friends and no one had seen or heard from Mandy. He called the police and reported her missing. The police had taken a statement but really could do nothing because there was no evidence of a crime. She hadn't officially been missing 48 hours anyway, so there wasn't much they could do. Mandy's disappearance had only come to Mandy's attention because she had notified all the state and local agencies to notify her about any missing persons. Ordinarily a case such as this would never make a blip in the news or the FBI. Maggie wondered how many "Mandys" there were out there, the thought of it made her head pound harder. She had a gut feeling whoever had taken Victoria Bentley also had taken Mandy Gillespie. She hadn't said anything about that to anyone in the office. They'd think she was letting her imagination get the best of her. She had called and talked to the officer who took Barry's statement and told him to please let her know if there were any developments in the case.

Maggie was correct in her thinking. Aaron and Elvis had taken Mandy. They had stopped at the truck stop before to get gas traveling to Chicago and had noticed the blonde. After they killed Victoria, they were in a wild state. Now they wanted only to kill another Vickie. She had been the ultimate. They thought about her all the time. They had decided to do a kill. The truck stop was perfect, not so far away they couldn't get there and be back way before work time in the morning, but not so close that anyone in town would think anything about a missing waitress almost to the city.

They remembered talking to her before when they were there, and she had told them she worked the 3:00–11:00 shift. They hoped she still worked there and that she was working that night. Their luck held because they could see her from where they were parked in the dark lot. They saw her walk out the door and head toward the back parking lot. They didn't know who else might be getting off at this time, too, so they knew they would have to be quick. There was no one else coming out of the restaurant and from this angle, no one from inside could see past the line of tractor trailers parked. Elvis slipped out of the van and hid in the shadows. Aaron drove the van up right beside Mandy, rolled the window down and said, "Excuse me, ma'am" like he was going to ask for a direction. Elvis came up from behind her, stuck a knife in her back and told her if she screamed he'd slit her throat. He then opened the back of the van and made her get in. He got in, and Aaron took off. The whole thing transpired in less that a minute. Within 5 minutes they were back on the interstate with a gagged and bound Mandy in the freezer. Mandy had fought Elvis in the back of the van. In the struggle, one of her earrings had come off and slid under the front seat. Of course it was dark so no one noticed, least of all Mandy who knew she was going to die if she couldn't get away. When he finally got her tied and gagged he told Aaron, "Got us another hellcat here, brother, we're gonna have some fun tonight." The violence had excited Elvis.

Aaron laughing said, "You already got a boner brother." "Well, you know," he said, "I had to hit her a couple times, and that turns me on."

Yes, violence begets violence. They had come from a violent upbringing. They could well remember their father's drunken rages and the beatings. They remembered the cries of their mother and then the grunts of their father and the old squeaky sounds of the bedsprings. He always screwed her after he beat her. Maybe that was the only way he could get it up, too. It was true with them. Many nights as young boys they had masturbated to the sound of those grunts and the screams of their mother and the old bed springs.

When they got home Aaron tossed Mandy over his shoulders like a sack of potatoes and took her to the bedroom. She fought like a wild woman and the harder she fought, the more violent and more aroused they became. They beat, raped, and strangled her just as they had Victoria Bentley. Mandy realized in her semi state of consciousness right before she died that they both were calling her Vickie.

In all it hadn't taken very long. They had her at the slaughterhouse and in the rendering pots and back home by 4:30a.m. There was no use to try to sleep. They were on a high from the kill. They threw Mandy's clothes, shoes and purse in a garbage bag which they threw in the dumpster at work. The dumpster would be emptied today, which made it all neat and convenient. Another perfect murder; another victim rendered.

CHAPTER 13

▼

Daniel sat in the den holding a tumbler of bourbon in his hand. The house was dark. The TV was on, the only illumination in the house, just as it was every night. Like every night he had no idea what was on. It was just noise to fill an empty, lonely house. He kept recalling the events of last year and a half over and over. Julianna and he had driven in to work together that terrible day. When they got off at 5:00, she asked him if he minded going by Dr. Sue's with him. She told him she gone to the doctor last week because she thought she might be pregnant. "Pregnant," he had said, "Are we pregnant??"

" No," Julianna said, "at least I don't think so. I went because I thought I might be. You know I've been so tired lately and nauseated and I have missed a couple periods, so I thought maybe I was. I didn't want to tell you until I was sure. When I went to see Dr. Sue she said my exam didn't show any evidence of pregnancy, but she wanted to do a pap smear and run some blood work and a urinalysis to see if she could find why I was feeling so badly. She called today and said the tests were back and asked if I could come in at 5:30. I told her you would have to bring me since we rode together and she said fine. She was glad you would be coming. That's all she said so that's all I know."

The office was empty when Julianna and Daniel entered Dr. Sue's waiting area. Dr. Sue came out to greet them and ushered them to her office. She asked if they wanted something to drink. Neither did. She took a deep breath and started talking.

"Daniel, I hope Julianna has told you she came to see me last week, thinking she might be pregnant." Daniel nodded that she had. "Because she was feeling badly and missing periods I ran some blood tests." Again, both Julianna and Daniel nodded. "I want to order some more tests. I want to Julianna to have both a CT scan and PET scan."

Dr. Sue had gotten up from her desk and had walked around to face them. Julianna thought she looked much older than she had ever remembered, and her eyes looked very sad. She took Julianna's hands in hers and said, "I don't know how else to say it, so I'll just say it. You have cancer. Are you familiar with PET scan?" PET stands for positron emission tomography. It is very similar to an MRI, in that it gives us a three-dimensional look at your body. With a PET scan you are injected with a radio isotope along with a glucose solution. We generally do the scan about an hour later. The isotope causes a fluorescent effect so we can see more clearly what areas of the body are infected by cancer. Like an MRI you don't have to change positions, and it is not painful."

Daniel had never been more stunned in his life. "No," he'd yelled, "That can't be. There has to be some mistake. Julianna is a little tired, but she's fine." His face was blood red, a vein throbbing in his temple, his hands clenched.

Dr. Sue, quietly said, "Daniel, please, sit down, I know this is a shock." All the color had drained out of Julianna's face the minute she heard the word cancer. She sat in the chair, her lips trembling. Daniel looked at her and his heart broke. He knelt in front of her and held her in his arms.

Dr. Sue continued, "Her pap smear showed advanced stage cervical cancer. Her blood cell counts are way out of proportion. Both her liver and kidney functions are highly elevated. When I examined her all her lymph areas were swollen and tender. We need to get these other tests done as soon as possible. We need to know exactly how far the cancer has spread, if at all. The sooner we find out, the sooner we will be able to get treatment started. I have her scheduled for both tests in the morning in Lexington. Dr. Nile, one of the best oncologists in the state is in Lexington. I have already called him and he has agreed to review her tests and see her as soon as the CT and PET scans are in. I feel it imperative we don't waste any time here."

Julianna and Daniel were nodding in agreement, both numb and in shock. Dr. Sue continued, "I will be there with you in the hospital tomorrow morning, Julianna. You will need to be there by 5:30 a.m. Go to the outpatient area on the second floor. I pulled some strings. You are going to be the first patient. The radiologist has already agreed to be standing by to read your films and get his observations to Dr. Nile. Dr Nile will see you in his office Tuesday morning at 8:00 with your results and recommendations."

She gave them copies of the lab work. She knew being doctors themselves, they would understand the severity of the blood work results. She also gave them a copy of the results from the lab on the pap smear. She asked them if they had any questions, but she knew they were too shell shocked to ask anything. She saw them to the door and told them she'd see them at the hospital in the morning. When she closed the door behind them, she covered her face with her hands and cried. They were so young, she thought.

Daniel and Julianna had driven home in silence. Both were trying to digest what Dr. Sue had said. Both had seen the tests results, and both knew they were facing something very serious. When they got home, neither felt like eating although both made a half attempt at some soup. Before Julianna had eaten a couple bites, she had run to the bathroom and thrown up. Daniel had run after her. She had told him she was okay. She felt fine. It was just her nerves. He had nodded that he understood and had held her. He told he loved her and they would get through this, no matter what. She smiled. She loved him so much.

She told him she needed to see Sahara, needed some time with him and asked Daniel if while she was at the barn he would call her parents and his and tell them what they knew. They would need to have their schedules changed at the clinic to cover the next couple days while they were having the tests done. They knew that wouldn't be a problem. The other doctors would gladly take on the extra load so they could be off. She didn't think she could talk to her parents tonight, and she hoped they would understand. She was barely hanging on to her composure now, and she knew she would break down completely if she talked to them. Daniel wasn't looking forward to making the calls but understood what Julianna was doing. He would also tell them not to come running over here tonight. He knew they would want to. He and Julianna needed time to be alone and she needed to get some rest.

She went on to the barn and fed and got Sahara settled for the night. She told him all about what had happened while she brushed him, and finally she put her arms around his neck and cried. What would happen to Sahara if something happened to her? She loved him, she didn't want to die and leave him. Sahara nudged her with his velvet nose and gave her horse kisses, nibbling on her neck with his lips. She cried even harder.

The next two days were a blur of tests, more blood and more tests. The news they got Tuesday morning was bleak. The cancer had metastasized, spreading already to her lymphatic system and liver. She was terminally ill. Both sets of parents had been with them when they went in to see Dr. Nile. He had told them the cancer might be slowed by chemotherapy and radiation, but only slowed. There was no cure for Julianna. The type cancer she had was fast growing. She had at most six months, he thought, maybe longer if her body could stand the chemo. He told them to go home and talk it over and decide what method of treatment they wanted. Everyone was crying except Dr. Nile.

When they got home, Reverend Jenkins was waiting for them. Julianna suspected her mom had called him. She was glad she had. He came in and had prayer with them and told them he was there to help in any way he could. They could call on him day or night. Julianna had felt a peace come over her when Rev. Jenkins prayed. She would listen to what Daniel and their parents had to say, but she thought she had already made up her mind about her treatment.

Julianna and Daniel, as well as their two fathers, were well aware of both the advantages and disadvantages of chemotherapy. Like in humans, if caught early enough, cancer cells can be destroyed by chemo. The negative part of chemo is that since it is toxic enough to kill cancer cells, it also kills healthy cells. The impact of the treatment alone can cause additional problems to vital organs. Looking at the case from a purely medical stand point, all of them could see that chemo would not cure Julianna and depending on how her body reacted may not even give her more time or quality of life for the time she had.

Of course looking at it from a husband's, father's, and father's-in-law point of view, they all wanted her to fight for all the time she had. The mothers, too, just wanted Julianna to be with them as long as she could.

It was a very emotional issue. Julianna listened to everyone's opinion. She and Daniel talked about it at length. In the end everyone said ultimately the decision should be left to Julianna. She was a doctor. She knew as well as any of them what the stakes were. Her decision surprised no one. She was rejecting treatment. She wanted to live out her life, however long she left, to the fullest. She didn't want to spend her days going in and out of hospitals, having chemo treatments and then being sick and weak form the treatments, especially knowing they weren't going to cure her. She wanted only to be made comfortable—for now that meant some medication for the nausea she was having. She would add medications for discomfort and pain when those conditions arrived. She didn't want to be in a hospital. She wanted to stay home. When her care required it, they would call Hospice in to help. She would live and die with dignity.

Her and Daniel's parents were ready to do whatever they could to make Julianna's last months good ones. Did she want to travel while she was still feeling good; if so, they would pay all the expenses so that she and Daniel could go anywhere in the world. It was like her own Make A Wish Foundation. Anything that was in their means to grant her, they would. They would also keep Daniel's part of the practice going so he could be with her.

She had been touched at their love and generosity. She had declined. She wanted to stay right at home with the people she loved and with Sahara. She wanted to spend as much time as she could with the horse she loved so much. She had a lot to explain to him, a lot to try to make him understand.

Daniel was going to have to promise her he would keep and care for Sahara. She would never leave this world in peace until she knew Sahara's future and well being was secured. She would have Daniel start working with him more and more so he would be at ease and trust Daniel after she was gone.

She did cut her schedule at the clinic to 3 mornings a week. She wanted to work as long as possible. She didn't think every other day would be too much for her. She wanted to stay busy. She loved being a veterinarian. She wanted to keep helping make a difference in helping animals for as long as she could. There was nothing as rewarding to her than to know she was able to make someone's sick cat or dog well again.

The cancer took a toll on her strength and energy. She eventually cut her work to two days, then one. Finally she had to stop altogether. She spent her days at home, organizing picture albums and other things she never had time to do before. She wrote letters to all the people closest to her to read after she was gone.

At least one morning a week, Reverend Jenkins stopped by. She looked forward to his visits. They had lively engaging conversations about religion, faith and love. She felt at peace with her life and her death. Unknown to even Daniel until after her death, Julianna had asked Reverend Jenkins to take her to the funeral home. There she had made all her own arrangements, choosing her own casket and all the other grim details that so overwhelm loved ones when death comes knocking on the door. She told Reverend Jenkins what scriptures she wanted read and what songs she wanted played or sung at her funeral. She had the clothes picked out she would wear. She had left no detail unarranged. She had told Dr Jenkins instead of flowers being sent to her funeral, she wanted a scholarship fund opened in her name. She wanted the scholarship to go to a girl who wanted to be a veterinarian and needed financial help.

She spent a lot of time with Sahara. Sometimes she took her sketch pad out with her to try to capture a bit of his pride and spirit. Sometimes she just sat and talked to him and let the warm sun shine on her face.

Her mom and Daniel's mother, plus the women from church kept a steady stream of meals coming for Daniel and her. Everyone was so thoughtful and caring. When she reached month three, she was very weak. Most days she was too weak to walk the distance to the barn or the field where Sahara was. Daniel got her a motorized scooter, like she'd seen elderly people use in grocery stores so she could go to the barn. Her dad and Daniel had built a wheelchair ramp so she could get off the porch. It gave her a lot of freedom, especially enabling her to spend time with Sahara. She could easily open his gate and maneuver in his field with her scooter. She wanted so badly for Sahara to understand what was happening to her. She didn't want, when she died, for him to think she had abandoned him. She talked to him all the time and only hoped he understood. She thought he did. She knew his sense of smell was very keen. She thought he would be able to smell and know something was wrong with her. He was always very gentle with her. He would come and stand beside her, nudging her with his head to be petted. She loved him so much, loved to breathe in the smell of him and feel the velvet softness of his nose.

One day she had wanted to ride him or really just to sit on him a while as he grazed. She didn't even have a halter with her, and she didn't have the strength to try to jump or climb on his back. She led him to the fence and tried to get up that way, but she was too weak to climb the fence. That's when she knew Sahara understood. The big stallion knelt down beside her so she could get on his back. When she was safely on and had her arms around his neck, he got up. She laid on him, arms around his neck, whispering love to him. When Daniel came home, the sight of her on the horse she loved so much, without so much as a rope brought him to tears. She loved Sahara so much. To think he had once been so wild no one could touch him. Now here he was, with a sick woman lying on him, arms draped around his neck while he grazed contentedly. Sometimes, Daniel almost felt jealous of Sahara, jealous of the bond and love she had for the horse. How would he ever live without her? He had known her all his life. The only real girlfriend he had had, the only woman he had ever made love to. She was so damn brave, comforting everyone when she was the sick one, the one dying.

One weekend she hosted a pajama party for all her girlfriends, inviting some of her sorority sisters from Ohio State to come too. The house had been full of women laughing and giggling like little girls. Julianna had a great time reminiscing about fun she'd had. Before the girls left, she told them to go to her closet. Everyone was welcome to take anything they could wear or knew anyone could wear. It was the most unselfish thing Daniel had ever seen, and he knew she was doing it not only because she wanted to but because it would save him and her mother from having to pack up and give away her things. She was always thinking of them.

She lived almost five months. Hospice made her as comfortable as possible. Her pain level was managed and although she slept much of the time, at least she wasn't suffering. No matter how bad a day she had, she always had a smile for Daniel and insisted every day going out to see Sahara. Finally she was no longer able to eat or drink. All of them knew it was just a matter of time then. Hospice told then usually in three of four days after she stopped eating she would be gone. Her parents had been staying with them. They wanted to be with her at the end. The last day Julianna had been in a semi-comatose state. She would briefly open her eyes at times, attempt to smile, but was too weak to talk. She could understand and would gently squeeze your hand when they talked to her or asked her something. Several times they thought she had died. She would stop breathing or so it seemed, only to gasp a couple seconds later. Her breathing was so shallow you couldn't see her chest move. Reverend Jenkins had come by and said a prayer for all of them, and she had squeezed his hand to let him know she heard him and knew he was there. Could anything be worse than watching the woman you love die? Daniel didn't think so. Every time she seemed to stop breathing he would hold his own breath.

Suddenly her eyes opened, and her voice was strong. "Daniel, I have to see Sahara, I have to tell him something. Please, now."

He didn't argue, just picked her up in his arms and carried her outside to the barn. Her parents came, too. Inside the barn, the big stallion was pacing and squealing, clearly upset. When Daniel came in carrying Julianna, Sahara immediately quieted down and came walking over.

"Let me down, Daniel, I need to talk to Sahara," she whispered. "Help me, stand." He steadied her and she put her arms around Sahara's neck, and he immediately lay down so she could lean across his back. She stroked his neck and whispered to him and he nickered back to her as if he understood everything she was saying to him. When she finished, she looked up and Daniel knelt beside her. "Daniel, I am sending someone to take care of you and Sahara. Promise me you will keep him and wait for the sign."

He didn't understand what she was talking about, but he agreed. She then leaned over and put one arm around Sahara and one on Daniel and said, "I love you." She closed her eyes, and she was gone.

The next few days passed in a daze for Daniel. He didn't know how he'd gotten through it, but somehow he had. Now, here he sat, over a year later, swishing bourbon in a tumbler, sitting in the dark, feeling sorry for himself. He was disgusted with himself. Julianna had been tough, and brave and courageous. He had buried himself in work during the day and with self-pity at night. This had to end. He had to get on with his life. Julianna would never want him to be this way.

Daniel got up walked to the kitchen and poured the glass of bourbon down the drain. Tomorrow would be the first day of the rest of his life. He had fulfilled his promise and kept Sahara. He would never forget the look in the horse's eyes when Julianna died. He knew those big eyes reflected the same sorrow and heartbreak he felt. He had been afraid Sahara would literally grieve to death after Julianna died. He had heard of animals refusing to eat and drink, wasting away after the death of a longtime companion. He had never heard of a horse doing it, but he had never seen a bond like Sahara and Julianna had either. He was also afraid Sahara would revert to the wild horse he was before Julianna had worked her magic with him.

Sahara was still not friendly towards Daniel, but he tolerated his feeding and caring for him. He seemed to be in another world most of the time, staring toward the driveway as if he had understood Julianna saying she was sending someone for them, and he was watching for them to arrive. Daniel felt as sorry for Sahara as he did for himself. Julianna had certainly been devoted to the horse. One of the first things she had done when she got him was to find a female farrier to trim his feet. Female farriers are not unheard of, but they aren't easy to find. Shoeing a horse is hard work. Julianna had finally located a female farrier in the southern part of the state who agreed to take Sahara as a client. It took some persuading on both Julianna's and Betty Jo's part, but Sahara finally let her work on his feet. She had been very patient and good to him. He trusted her to a point. That was the only way his feet would ever get trimmed. He still would not let a man anywhere near him except to be fed by Daniel. After her cancer was diagnosed, Julianna also had introduced her mother into Sahara's life. Grace had been a horsewoman her whole life. She had taught Julianna to ride. Julianna thought at least her mom could come over after her death and groom Sahara and talk to him. Mother and daughter had almost the same voice, and she hoped Sahara would bond with her mother. Grace had been very patient and kind to Sahara, and he had accepted her presence although clearly he preferred Julianna to groom him. Grace had never attempted to ride Sahara, nor did she want to. Julianna didn't encourage her mother to ride him. She only wanted him cared for. She couldn't bear the thought he would ever look as unkempt as he had when she had first seen him with that terribly tangled mane.

After that night Daniel, made a real effort to get on with his life. He joined a health club instead of going home and drinking. The exercise helped him not only work out the year of drinking, but also helped him feel better. He renewed old friendships and made new ones. He knew there would never be another Julianna, but he did want to find someone he could share his life with. He wanted kids and the sound of laughter and dogs in the house. The hard part was getting back into the dating scene. He felt awkward asking someone out. He and Julianna had always been a couple. He didn't know how to date, and he felt too old to be playing the field and the dating game.

Gradually he did have a few dates, dinner and a movie, that kind of thing. He enjoyed the companionship, but he didn't feel the chemistry with anyone. He wondered when or if that would ever happen. Of course, once his friends realized he wanted to date, everyone wanted to be a matchmaker. He didn't know which was worse, being lonely or having every woman from 18–50 years old being pushed his way!

Chapter 14

▼

Aaron and Elvis were not having a good week. Killing that truck stop waitress had not done anything to ease the haunting they felt. Everywhere they looked they saw someone who reminded them of Victoria. They were starting to lose their grip on their own sanity. They were finding it hard to concentrate when people at work spoke to them, and their tempers were short with everyone. They were glad they were going to Brannon this weekend to see their cousin and to deliver the horsemeat to that Jap at the car plant.

They thought this would most likely be their last delivery of meat. Things were changing at the slaughterhouse and that was another reason the Pucketts were in such a foul mood.

Groups of damn animal lovers all over the country had organized and were pushing for laws to stop horse slaughter. Their plant was one of the last ones still open. The boss had called them in his office and talked to them about it. He thought the end of their jobs was coming. He had had death threats at home he said. Starting next week the company was hiring 24/7 security at the slaughterhouse. There had been anonymous calls made that maybe there might be an accident here, maybe a fire. The company was going to have to protect their property. He had even heard that starting next week there were going to be organized picket lines and the press from the three major networks, plus CNN and FOX were going to cover the protests. Even as Mr. Hardt was telling them all this, their minds were reeling. Shit, this was going to ruin everything. 24/7 security meant no sneaking out meat and even worse no way to dispose of bodies. What were they going to do now? They felt like going out to the truck and coming back in with an AK-

47 and just killing everyone in there, going out with a blaze of glory. They'd seen that one bitch that lived here in town on local TV always whining about the slaughterhouse, about pollution to the river from the plant, about horses having souls and not being livestock. Aaron and Elvis hated her. They'd wanted to kill her for a long time, shut her the fuck up. The only reason they hadn't killed her before now was because they knew the suspicion would come straight to the slaughterhouse, and they didn't want to spoil their perfect set-up. Now this bitch had gotten national attention with that group she belonged to. Seems no one much knew horses were still being slaughtered for human consumption until some damn race horse broke his leg and died and all the people who followed him starting being activists for everything connected with horses.

The Pucketts hated them all. Animals were animals, survival of the fittest. You kill it, you can eat it. They'd lived by hunting. The animal lovers didn't care, and they were going to send a lot of hard working taxpayers right to the unemployment line if the plant closed for good. Aaron and Elvis fantasized about bringing that loud-mouthed bitch in here some night, killing her just like they did the horses. They'd use the head bolt on her, course what only stuns a horse would kill her, but they'd still do it. She'd know what was coming next. Then, they'd hang her upside down on a hook and slit her throat, let all the blood drain out, butcher her up and render her. They'd be rid of her loud, whiny mouth for good. She's just sticking her nose where it don't belong. Still it would come right back on the slaughter house, so they hadn't done it...now though, if she was going to mess them up, they might just kill her and leave her out somewhere. Maybe they could arrange an accident for her, something to think about when they got back from Brannon.

Mr. Hardt paused and asked them something, but they been too lost in their own world to hear him. " Hey," he said, "Aren't you listening to a thing I've been saying? I'm asking you if you would be interested in working up in Canada with the company if the laws get passed down here. The company has asked me but I'm ready to retire anyway, so I thought you boys might want to move. I know you like to hunt, mighty fine hunting up in Canada. Why don't you all think about it? I told the company that I'd put a bug in your ear about it, see what you thought."

The Pucketts weren't really interested in moving to Canada. They didn't like foreigners of any kind. Hunting was good, but the weather was too damned cold all winter. No, unless they thought the law was closing in on them, they would stay right here in the good ol' USA. Of course they knew the law didn't have a thing on them, they'd been killing twenty years and had never gotten caught, never left a clue. They read somewhere some psychiatrist wrote all killers want the publicity and want to be caught. That was bullshit, showed what they knew. The Pucketts hated everyone. They had no feeling or conscience whatsoever about killing a person or an animal. They killed for their own blood lust and enjoyment, the thrill of the kill. They loved the power, the high they felt. They were in total control of whether someone lived or died. They only cared about each other. Everyone else could go to hell, and they'd help them get there. They were true sociopaths. They seemed like everyday people, held down jobs and interacted with people without anyone suspecting, killers they were.

Now their perfect murder method and ridding any evidence of the bodies was coming to an end, and their mental state was deteriorating every day. Not only that, they were haunted by Vickie. Everyone else they had killed hadn't been a blip on the screen, nobodies. The world was better off without the whores and druggies and homeless. They had done the taxpayers a service by ridding society of their like. Vickie had been the prettiest, most perfect woman they had known, but even she was stupid. Women were stupid most of the time in their opinion, only good for two things. . .screwing and killing. As pretty as Vickie had been, she'd been more worried about that damn dog of hers than her own hide. "Don't hurt Precious." How stupid was that? What had she thought, they were going to let her go?"

And then the waitress at the truck stop, had her iPod stuck in her ears from the minute she walked out the door, never saw or heard them coming. Stupid, yes she was probably a whore, too. They had all deserved to die.

* * * * * *

In Chicago, Maggie was still hitting a dead end on the investigation of Victoria Bentley's death and the unofficial investigation she was doing in the death of Mandy, the waitress from the truck stop. Both had vanished without a trace. How does that happen? How many more people had disappeared? Hayward Bentley still called her everyday, asking if there were any new developments. He had been sure the lure of a half a million dollars of reward money would bring some new leads. Human nature was that everyone told someone what they did or someone suspected them, and half a million dollars would go a long way toward making someone rat out a friend. In the city, he'd seen and read about people getting killed for $20.00.

Sure, they'd had a lot of so called leads since the reward money came out. None of them was valid. That's what concerned Maggie, the point she was getting at—no one knew anything and there were no clues and no body. It was commonly known in homicides if the killer wasn't found within 24–48 hours, there was an increasingly good chance he would never be caught— the colder the case, the colder the trail. Victoria's case was cold, and so was Mandy's. Other than the one man at the rest area saying he'd seen a white van and a man, no one had seen anything. How many white vans were there in the country? They didn't have a license plate number much less the state the plate was from or the make and model of the van itself. They had nothing.

Maybe going to Brannon to her parents' anniversary party would refresh her mind a little. She would discuss the case with her dad. If she were missing something, maybe something she had missed that was right in front of her, he would catch it.

She was also looking forward to seeing Jett and little Savannah. Jett was really worried about Savannah's imaginary horse friend and the nightmares she was having. Maggie thought having an imaginary horse for a friend was very cute. It showed Savannah's imagination was healthy and active. The nightmares were a little disturbing, but all children had bad dreams from time to time. Savannah had lost her father. War was hard to explain to a child, death was hard to accept. Maybe the nightmares were all part of the death of Blake and the fear Savannah has that something else bad will happen to her or her mom. She would talk to Jett and Savannah. Maybe she'd take Savannah out for a drive, just the two of them to talk. She might open up more about her fears, her horse friend and her dreams without Jett around. Jett was a protective mother, maybe overprotective, and maybe her insecurity was causing Savannah to react this way. Jett had mentioned wanting to talk to Maggie about some other things, too. Maggie hoped she could talk her friend into getting out more, and she really thought Savannah should be in school. That again was Jett trying to overprotect Savannah. Savannah needed to be with and play with children of her own age. Jett had kept a protective wall around her ever since Blake was killed. It had been over a year now, and Jett needed to loosen the hold on Savannah. She hoped the opportunity would come so she could gently tell this to her friend.

* * * * * *

Jett closed her eyes and rested her head on her elbow. She was exhausted from the previous night and there was no getting comfortable in this chair in the hospital waiting room. What a night it had been! It had started out normally. She had read Savannah a bedtime story and tucked her in, sitting quietly beside her until she fell asleep. She had then gone to bed herself, watched a movie on TV, and then read awhile before turning her light out. She awoke to Savannah running in the room at 3:00 a.m., telling her to wake up. Half asleep, she thought Savannah had had a nightmare. She was crying, "Hurry Mommy, hurry."

Jett finally got herself awake and asked Savannah what was wrong. Savannah said, "I was dreaming when Daddy came and told me papaw was sick and I needed to come wake you up to tell you to call that number. Daddy said, 'Tell Mommy to call 911 for Papaw right now.' I'm scared Mommy, Daddy said Papaw's heart was sick. Call now, Mommy, hurry, papaw is sick. I don't want Papaw to die like Daddy!" Then she had once again started sobbing.

Jett didn't know what to do. She believed in angels, and she believed the dream that both she and Savannah had when Blake died, telling them he would take care of them. She could call her parents and see if Dad was sick, but that might be wasting time. If nothing was wrong, she'd feel like a fool for calling 911, but if Dad was in trouble, then a phone call could save his life. She dialed 911. She believed in Blake, and she believed Savannah. She gave the 911 operator her parents' address and told them she suspected her father was having a heart attack. She did not tell the operator the details, that she hadn't even talked to her parents and this was all the result of a five-year-old child's dream.

* * * * * *

Nate Sizemore had awakened at 2:50 a.m. He had a bad case of indigestion, probably from the spaghetti Louise had fixed. He'd been having indigestion a lot lately, heartburn he called it. This was a bad case; his chest was on fire, and he felt sick to his stomach, too. He got up and went to the bathroom and was about to go to the kitchen to get some Maalox when Louise woke up and asked him what was wrong. He told her heartburn, and that he was going to get some Maalox to go back to sleep. He had raked leaves that afternoon and his left arm was hurting bad. "Getting old," he thought. Louise had gotten up anyway and was headed to the kitchen when they both saw flashing lights in the driveway.

"What in the world is that? Louise said, and looked back to see Nate clutch his arm to his chest. He was pale and had a fine sheen of sweat on his forehead. A knock on the door came and Louise, worried about Nate, went to answer the door. It was the paramedics! Who had called the paramedics? As soon as she opened the door they had rushed right in and with one look at Nate, had immediately gone into action. They gave him nitroglycerin, started an IV and took his blood pressure. Louise didn't understand any of what was happening, Nate had heartburn, surely nothing else. They wheeled in a stretcher and took Nate out before she could even gather her thoughts. She ran after them to the ambulance, and they told her they were taking him directly to Lexington to the Heart Institute. They hoped they'd stopped the heart attack in time. With that the ambulance had pulled out, and as soon as they got off her street, she could hear the siren on. Nate was having a heart attack? Who had called? As she was walking back in the house to change out of her nightgown and into some clothes the phone rang. "Good heavens," she thought, "What now? Who would be calling at this hour? It's 3:00 in the morning."

When she answered the phone, it was Jett. " Mom," Jett said. Before she could say another word Louise told her Dad was evidently having a heart attack, and the ambulance had just left. They were rushing Dad to Lexington. She was going as soon as she got dressed.

"I'm going, too, Mom. Do you want me to pick you up? I'm leaving in 5 minutes. You go get your clothes on and get your purse and dad's insurance information and be ready to go when I get there." With that, Jett hung up. Savannah had been right. Thank God she had listened to her. Pawpaw did have a sick heart. "Dear God," she prayed, "Let Dad be okay."

Hurriedly, she put on the same jeans and sweatshirt she had taken off the night before and told Savannah to get dressed, too, as quickly as she could. They rushed out of the house went to pick up her mom and rushed to the Heart Institute. They went directly to the ER and told them who they were. They had to give the receptionist at the ER all her Dad's information: name, address, social number, insurance, etc. Jett handled that part. Her mom was so badly shaken she could barely tell her own name. Savannah was sitting beside mamaw as she called her mom, holding her hand.

They sat for what seemed an eternity before a nurse finally came out to the waiting area at the ER and asked for the Sizemore family. They quickly stepped forward. The nurse said Nate had stabilized and they thought they had prevented any serious damage to his heart thanks to the paramedics arriving and taking action so soon. They had already scheduled him to have a heart catheterization at 7:00 a.m. and would be taking him to a room soon. It was nearly 5:00 then. The nurse let the three of them go to Nate's cubicle to see him. He smiled weakly at them when they walked in. Jett's eyes filled with tears. She had always been a daddy's girl. She couldn't imagine not having him. He had always been there for her. Now, for the first time, he looked old and pale, and it scared Jett to think she could lose him. Her mother was shaken, too, and worn out. She bent over and kissed Nate on the head and trying to make light of the situation said, "Heartburn, huh?"

He smiled and said, "Now don't lecture me, Louise." Ah, that was her dad, full of spirit. Savannah went over, kissed Nate's hand, and told him she loved him. The nurse came back in and said they could follow along because the aid was coming to take Nate to a room. One of them could stay in the room with him if they wanted, as long as they sat quietly and let him rest. The others could wait in the waiting room on the same floor where his room was.

Louise stayed in the room with Nate. There was a nice cushioned chair she could rest in herself. Nate had been given some medication and was sleepy, so Louise dozed in the chair beside him. Jett and Savannah headed to the waiting room. There were a couple of sofas done in a blue and mauve tweed fabric and several big cushioned matching chairs and some tables and magazines. Jett sat on one of the sofas. Savannah curled up beside her with her head in Jett's lap and fell asleep. Jett smiled; children could sleep anywhere.

Jett was too wired to sleep. She kept thinking about what had happened. Her mother had been too upset yet to ask why Jett had called and how the paramedics had known to come to the house when Nate himself thought he only had heartburn. "Wow," Jett thought, "Just wait until they hear the whole story." Savannah's dream about Blake telling her to wake mommy up had most likely saved her father's life. She had a very special little girl here.

She smiled as she saw Savannah was wearing her cowboy boots. Jett had bought her a little pair of pink cowboy boots when her friend, Star had first arrived. She had told Savannah if she was going to be a cowgirl, she needed boots. A year later she was in her second pair, having outgrown the first ones. She wore her boots everywhere and with every thing. Even this summer she wore her boots with her little shorts as well as to church with her dresses. Savannah flatly refused to wear anything but her boots.

At seven they had taken Nate to do the heart cath. Savannah and Jett stayed in her Dad's hospital room and waited. Jett sent her mom to the hospital cafeteria, insisting she go eat some breakfast. The nurse had told them Nate wouldn't be back in his room for at least an hour, possible longer. Jett didn't want to have two sick parents on her hands. She made her mom go eat. She told her as soon as she got back, she and Savannah would go eat, too.

All three felt much better after some breakfast. Jett and Savannah had barely gotten back to the room before the aid brought Nate back. The nurse told them the doctor would be in as soon as he could to tell them the results of his tests.

It was both good news and bad news. The bad news was Nate needed bypass surgery as soon as possible. He had three blockages in his arteries, all over 95% blocked. The worst one was 99% blocked. The doctor told them if the paramedics had not arrived and started treating Nate when they did and the heart attack had happened, Nate would have probably died. It was a good thing they had called when they did. Five minutes may have been too late. They were scheduling surgery for the next morning. His condition needed immediate attention. It was too life threatening to delay the surgery. The doctor was ordering a continuous IV with a slow drip of nitroglycerin to make sure they kept Nate's blood flow as good as possible to ward off any possible attack between now and the surgery. The nitro gave Nate a headache, which was normal. It dilates the blood vessels for maximum blood flow, which can also bring on a pounding headache. The nurse brought him a pain pill for the headache and told Jett and her mom he would probably go to sleep. They should take this opportunity to go home and get some rest themselves and come back later in the afternoon

As much as Jett wanted to stay with her dad, she knew the nurse was giving good advice. Her mom needed to get some sleep and rest. Jett, too, was tired. Savannah had been a little angel through all this. They all would need to rest, get something to eat and take a shower before coming back later in the afternoon.

Jett and her mother returned to the hospital that afternoon and stayed with her dad until visiting hours were over. While they were there, the surgeon who was going to do his surgery came in and talked with them, as did the anesthesiologist. Both seemed very confident and relaxed about the surgery. Jett felt much better after meeting the doctors, and she felt confident that her dad was going to be just fine. He had always been in good health and took care of himself. No one would have ever thought of Nate having a bad heart. It's hard to fight genetics. Sometimes no matter how hard you try to take care of yourself, your body works against you.

She knew the Heart Institute did open heart surgery everyday. To these doctors it was just another day in surgery. She thought sometimes doctors got so much in a routine they didn't realize anymore how traumatic something like this is to a family. The doctors face this everyday. A person however, usually faces open heart surgery just once, and often it is a life or death situation. Her mom was trying to be very brave, but Jett could tell she was scared to death. She kept looking at Nate and tears would well up in her eyes. They had been married a long time, and not only that, it had been a good marriage.

Nate insisted they go on home after visiting hours. They all needed to get a good night's sleep. Jett and Louise were coming back at 5:00 in the morning so they could see Nate before they took him off to surgery. Jett had left Savannah with one of her little girlfriends while she visited with her dad. Amy was a sweet little girl, and she and Savannah played well together.

She didn't know what to do with Savannah tomorrow. She hated to drag her out of bed so early in the morning. It was a half hour drive to Lexington from home. That meant in order to get her mom and get to the hospital on time for the surgery they needed to leave home by about 4:15 in the morning. She didn't know how long the surgery would last; however, she knew it would take several hours from the time they took her dad from his room until he was out of recovery.

As it worked out when she went by Janie's house to pick up Savannah, Janie offered to let Savannah spend the night. Savannah had never spent a night away from home and was all excited about having a pajama party with her friend Amy. Janie knew how early and how long Jett would be tomorrow and said she didn't mind in the least taking care of Savannah. She would even let Amy stay home from her half-day kindergarten to play with Savannah.

Jett agreed to let Savannah stay. It did make more sense and she knew Janie was an excellent mother, so she didn't have to worry. She sure hoped Savannah wouldn't have a nightmare. She didn't want to get into the kind of dreams Savannah had. She only told Janie sometimes Savannah had bad dreams and if she did tonight, just to sit with her a few minutes and generally she would go right back to sleep. Janie told her not to worry one bit. Amy had nightmares sometimes, too. Jett told Janie she would call her the next day after surgery as soon as she knew how her dad was, and she would be back to get Savannah as soon as she could.

The next morning she picked her mom up and they were able to spend a little time with her dad before they took him off to surgery. They had come in a few minutes before and had given him a light sedative, and already she could tell he was getting drowsy. She and her mom both told him how much they loved him and that they would be right here the whole time waiting for him. He told them he loved them too. After they wheeled him out, her mom broke down and had a little cry. Her nerves were pretty tense from the stress of the last couple days.

The nurse told them to go to the surgery waiting room and they would get updates from the volunteer who manned the desk there when information about her dad was available. So there she was, sitting in a too hard chair with her head doddling, thinking back on all that had happened. A pretty unbelievable thirty-six hours.

Finally they got an update. The surgery had been successful! Her dad was going to be fine. After recovery, they were taking him to the Cardiac Care Intensive Care Unit, where he would be for the next 24 hours. He would be on a ventilator when he came from recovery. How soon he was weaned from it and breathing on his own would determine how long he would be in CCICU. Visitors were only allowed for 10 minutes every 4 hours in CCICU. When they visited him at 8:00 pm, he was off the ventilator, his color looked great, and the nurses said there was no reason for them to stay at the hospital all night. By the next morning, the nurse thought they would be moving him to a regular room he was doing so well.

Jett and her mom went on home. They were both exhausted. If there was anything more stressful than sitting in a hospital all day Jett didn't know what it was. She asked her mom if she wanted to go home with her, but she said no, she'd sleep better in her own bed. Jett dropped her off, went by Janie's to pick up Savannah and went home.

Savannah had done great at Amy's. She hadn't had a nightmare and was quite pleased with herself for having been to a sleep over with her friend. She was talking a mile a minute, telling Jett all the games they had played and the movie they had watched. Star was there, too she told Jett. "He goes everywhere I go," she'd said. He liked Amy, too. Jett thought Savannah would never calm down enough to go to sleep, but she finally did.

Jett hadn't had dinner, but she was didn't feel hungry and was too tired to eat. All she wanted to do was take a nice hot shower and go to sleep. Tomorrow was Friday. Maggie would be coming in although Jett wouldn't see her until Saturday. She was really looking forward to a visit with her old friend. Since Monday was Veterans Day, Maggie had that day off, too. She wouldn't be leaving until late Monday afternoon to drive back to Chicago. Jett fell asleep almost as soon as her head hit the pillow.

Friday morning the phone ringing woke her up. Wow, she must have really been more tired than she realized, the clock beside her bed said 8:15. It was probably her mom calling. It was. Her mom said she had already called the hospital, and her dad had already been moved to a room. She was going to drive herself today. She thought Jett could come up later if she wanted and bring Savannah. That sounded great to Jett. When she got up and peeked in on Savannah, she was still sleeping. Jett was going to let her sleep as long as she wanted today.

Jett and Savannah went after lunch to see her dad. The hospital had rules about letting children visit the patients and, at first, didn't want to let Savannah see her grandfather. Jett told the nurse if it hadn't been for Savannah, her father might not have lived. She had not yet told her mother and father how the ambulance had arrived at their house before they realized that they needed one. The nurse, intrigued by the snippet of the story, agreed to let Savannah see her grandfather. The nurse followed also to hear the story. When they all got settled Jett asked her mom and dad if they knew how the ambulance got there so quickly. They said they didn't know and were completely bewildered and wondered why Jett herself had called so early, too.

Jett told Savannah to tell what had happened. Savannah told the group how she'd had a dream and her daddy had come and told her to wake up mommy really fast and tell her that papaw had a sick heart and for mommy to call that number they had taught her to call when something bad happened. "911," she said, "Daddy said tell mommy to call 911 for papaw."

Jett then took over for her part of the story. She told them how Savannah had come running into her bedroom telling her to wake up, papaw was sick and daddy said to call 911 right now. Jett said at first she thought Savannah had just had a bad dream, but when she heard what Savannah was saying, and how upset she was she knew this wasn't an ordinary dream. She knew she had two choices; ignore Savannah's dream and put her back in bed or do exactly what Savannah had said Daddy told her to do. She believed in angels, and she believed in Blake's promise to watch over them. If she ignored this, her father might pay with his life. So she had called 911 and given them her parents' address and the information that she thought her father was having a heart attack.

Jett's father then told them his story. He had woken up thinking he had heartburn because he'd been having indigestion a lot lately. He'd gotten up and gone to get some Maalox out of the kitchen, hoping not to wake Louise. She had awakened and followed him to the kitchen anyway, and he'd no more than got in the kitchen when his left arm started hurting worse than usual, and he and Louise had seen the lights from the ambulance in the driveway.

The EMT had come in and taken over, just in the nick of time. Nate was one very proud papaw to have Savannah for a granddaughter.

The nurse left the room with tears in her eyes. What a wonderful story! She couldn't wait to tell the other nurses on the floor about the miracle in room 555. Soon the whole floor was buzzing about the little girl whose dream had saved her grandfather's life.

Reverend Jenkins was at the hospital visiting Mrs. Riley from the church on the 5th floor when he heard the story, too. After hearing it, he went to room 555 to see if the little girl was still there. He wanted to hear her story first hand.

Savannah and Jett were just getting ready to leave when Reverend Jenkins came in. He told them he was at the hospital visiting one of his parishioners and had heard about Savannah's dream. He asked her if she'd tell him what happened that night. Savannah looked at Jett and she nodded it was okay to talk to Rev. Jenkins.

Savannah re-told her story, telling Rev, Jenkins how scared she'd been, not of Daddy or the dream but scared she wouldn't get mommy to call 911 in time. She was afraid mommy wouldn't believe her. She knew Daddy was an angel now and in heaven and she knew if he told her something it was true, even if it was in a dream. She told Rev. Jenkins how she and her mommy had both had a dream the night Daddy had died telling them he would always love them and he would send someone to take care of them. She then started talking about Star and that's when Jett gently stopped her, telling her Rev Jenkins was too busy to hear about all that and they needed to go.

Reverend Jenkins was rapt with attention while the little girl told her story. Her big blue eyes were as wide and innocent as a summer's sky. She had heard and she had believed with no hesitation what her dead father had told her to do. Yes, this was a miracle story, and it was also going to be the subject matter for this Sunday's sermon. He would call his sermon," The Faith of a Child." He had been a little amused when the mother had hushed her talking about Star, whoever that was. He bet this little girl had a lot of stories she could tell. He hoped he would get to talk to her again, soon. She was a special child there was no doubting that.

CHAPTER 15

▼

The Hawkins sisters had not seen each other for four years. They talked on the phone nearly every day, but health conditions had kept either of them from traveling to see the other.

Maci and Hailey Hawkins were as close as two sisters could be. The girls had been raised in the rural hills and hollows of eastern Kentucky in the same vicinity as the Pucketts. Their parents had let them have a long leash growing up. They didn't have a lot of supervision. In the late 50's and early 60's when they were children, it was a far different time than now. There were no internet, no cable TV, no cell phones and text messaging, no DVDs, nor iPod or MP3 players. Television reception was limited to only the local channels and even getting that took a huge antenna placed on top of the house or wired and run to the top of the hill for reception. Even then there was only black and white TV, the reception so snowy you'd be lucky to get two channels. No boom boxes in that time either. The best you might have was a transistor radio but because of the mountains, only one or two AM stations could be picked up. Sometimes at night if you were really lucky, you could pick up a Chicago station.

In the hollow where the Hawkins lived, almost everyone was related to everyone in one way or another. There was no fear some sexual predator would grab your child. Everyone knew everyone, and children were safe to go unsupervised. Of course, every community had some shady characters, but everyone knew who they were and stayed away from them. Cars and houses were usually left unlocked. No one around had anything worth stealing anyway.

The Hawkins family was not related to anyone in the hollow where they lived. They had moved there because Cy Hawkins, the father, had been transferred from his job to a location there. Mountain people are very leery of newcomers and compared with their neighbors, the Hawkins were like alien city slickers. Most of the community was made up of Pentecostal Baptists who did not believe in having much fun doing anything. Girls wore dresses or skirts year round, and mothers wore no make up or jewelry or pants. Some women had never cut their hair. Church was an all day affair, and there was a lot of talking in tongues and preaching hell and damnation to sinners.

The Hawkins family was Methodist. Elizabeth Hawkins was a pretty woman who wore both make up and jewelry. She wore her hair coiffed and fashionably short and wore shorts in the summer and pants anytime she pleased. Maci and Hailey wore shorts and sleeveless tops and were even known to play outside in bathing suits with a water hose. They rode bikes everywhere, something usually only the boys in that area did. The Hawkins were very much outsiders. However, Cy Hawkins was a man who loved everyone and got along with everyone. Once people met him, they soon also accepted his wife and two girls and the way they were. Not only that, it wasn't long before the influence of the Hawkins girls could be seen in the community. Other girls their ages started wearing shorts and playing outside instead of sitting primly in dresses on the swing of the front porch.

Maci was the older by three and a half years. In the summer when school was out, the girls explored the hills. Cy taught Maci how to use a snake bite kit and that being done, the girls were pretty much turned loose. They had their grandfather's old army belt complete with canteen and bayonet. What kept the girls from spearing themselves climbing those hills is a miracle in itself.

Cy also taught the girls how to shoot and how to fish. They spent many hours shooting with their dad at target on the hillside and many lazy days fishing with him on area lakes. Both girls were daddy's girls and somewhat tomboys. Maci was the prissier of the two, who always looked neat and wanted all her outfits to match, her hair, although a long mass of curls, was always in place. Hailey, no matter how hard she tried, looked like she'd just crawled out of bed. Her shirttail was always hanging out, and her hair never looked combed, partly because she had a habit of twisting it in her fingers. Her clothes always looked rumpled. The sisters were loyal to one another and that carried on throughout adulthood. So did their appreciation for guns that they had learned at the knee of their father.

Both left the hills of eastern Kentucky as soon as they were of age. Now Hailey, aged 55 lived in Brannon, Kentucky. She and her husband

Mick McGuire had moved from Lexington to Brannon a couple years back. They had bought a little farm where they had some horses and were both enjoying living in the quiet of the country. Mick was originally from Brannon, so moving from Lexington where they both worked to Brannon was like moving home to him. Mick was one of those guys who never meets a stranger, always has a smile and knows everyone. Hailey was more of a loner, preferring the company of her horses or her dog, Boo, to most people. She was friendly enough when people spoke to her, but she didn't invite company or conversation. Hailey also had a tendency to dress unusually, or at least to other people it seemed so. Hailey loved the clothing of the old west and the time of the singing cowboys like Roy and Dale Evans. Hailey had a closet full of western shirts lavishly embroidered with floral patterns, longhorns, and smiley arrows above the front pockets. She wore split western skirts, like the old time cowgirls wore and had a collection of over 50 pair of cowgirl boots. Some of her shirts and skirts had fringes, too. No one around Brannon dressed like Hailey. But Hailey didn't care; she didn't dress that way to get attention, she dressed to please herself. She had seen the stares and giggles, but she didn't give a damn. She loved her cowgirl clothes and they were both comfortable and functional.

Maci had left the Lexington area twenty years ago for a better job in North Carolina. She and her husband lived on the outskirts of Raleigh. Maci had injured her back a few years ago and was now on pain medication all the time and walked with the aid of a cane. Because most of her work was done by computer, her employer allowed her to work from home. Maci was still a prissy dresser as Hailey put it and loved jewelry.

When states started issuing permits for people to carry concealed weapons, both Hailey and Maci had been among the first women to become licensed. Getting a license to carry a concealed deadly weapon required training and testing. Maci completed her course in North Carolina, and shortly thereafter Hailey completed hers in Kentucky. They were both excellent marksmen, having learned respect and use of firearms from their father at early ages. Both sisters liked to target practice and went to local indoor shooting ranges to sharpen their skills. Both sisters had quite a selection of semi automatic handguns. They firmly believed in their rights to own and bear arms. They did not believe stopping the sale of guns would reduce deaths from gunshots. It was their belief most of the crimes committed with guns were illegally bought to begin with. That would never stop. Bad guys would always find guns.

Anyone who saw Boo with Hailey would never think she needed a gun. Boo went everywhere with Hailey. He rode in the passenger front seat if no one else was with Hailey. If they had a passenger, then Boo rode in the back of Hailey's jeep. She always kept the back seats folded down to give Boo more room. Boo was an enormous Rottweiler. He weighed 185 pounds. He had a huge head and large muscular chest and a thick, massive neck. He was, to say the least, a very intimidating dog. He looked like a black bear riding in Hailey's jeep.

Hailey and Mick got Boo from a friend when he was 5 weeks old. From a puppy, Boo was mean. He would attack Hailey's legs and growl if anyone picked him up. If you tried to pet him he would growl. Hailey, fearing he was sick, took him to the vet. The vet examined the growling dog and pronounced him physically fine although he warned Hailey he thought she should get rid of the puppy. The vet said he was going to be a mean dog, and she should put him down. Hailey could not accept that. She looked at the little black ball of fur, and no way she was going to kill him. The vet was wrong. She would love the puppy, and he would respond to that love and not be mean.

Both Hailey and the vet were correct. The puppy that grew to be the huge dog did respond to love and was devoted to Hailey, however, he was a vicious dog. The only way Hailey and Mick had been able to keep him was through a lot of love and a lot of training. Boo was a little psycho, but a brilliant dog. The only thing the trainers agreed upon was that Boo was smart but they didn't know, even with training if he could ever truly be trusted. Hailey would not give up on Boo. Eventually it was decided to train Boo to attack, but only on command, like a police dog. Controlling his natural disposition would be the key to keeping him. Boo had a little problem with the release command, but finally understood. He was trained with both verbal and hand signals. No one could be really sure if Boo could be trusted 100%. Hailey and Mick were very careful about who they let around him and never let him out unattended, even at home on their farm.

The local bank and drive thru fast food restaurants became accustomed to seeing the big dog. He always loved to go through the bank drive-through because the tellers always had dog biscuits for him. Even at some of the drive-through lanes at fast food restaurants, when Hailey would stop to buy herself a cup of coffee and a hamburger for Boo, the employees were known to slip him something extra. Boo loved to eat, and that's another way they were successful in training him. Good behavior was rewarded with good things to eat.

Hailey was sure this weekend while Maci was visiting they would be going to one of Boo's favorite places, The Custard Stand. The Custard Stand had been on the road leading to the river outside Brannon for 50 years. The sign outside was faded and the building was outdated and nothing much to look at, but The Custard Stand had been a hometown favorite for a couple of generations.

The Custard Stand, that's all it was ever called, was one of those old 1950 drive-in ice cream stands. It sold frozen custard in sugar cones or waffle cones, plain or dipped in chocolate. It also had chocolate soft serve ice cream or mixed swirl of vanilla and chocolate. It was the plain vanilla custard that kept people coming back. It was a closely guarded recipe. It wasn't exactly as smooth in texture as what you get from a Dairy Queen, but the taste was a cross between whole milk custard and old fashioned snow cream. It was wonderful with just a hint of vanilla. None of the name brand franchise places could touch the flavor of The Custard Stand. The building was originally just a two window walk-up. You placed your order through a little sliding window and received it through the same window. The building itself was small with just enough room for the ice cream makers and equipment and a little room for storage and supplies in the back. The Custard Stand sold sundaes and banana splits as well as milkshakes. They also had hot dogs on steamed buns and chili dogs. They sold chips, coffee and soft drinks as well.

Over the years they stayed with this simple menu, and it was enough. Business was still good after over 50 years. The business had changed ownership a couple times, but the atmosphere, menu and recipes stayed the same. The only thing the latest owners had changed was a new addition, so that people could come inside to order if they wished. It also had a few tables and chairs for those who wanted to eat there. The owners usually shut down for a couple months if the winter was bad, but stayed open, weather permitting until almost Christmas. Loyal customers would buy gallon containers of custard to last them until the stand re-opened.

Hailey and Maci both loved the frozen custard, and so did Boo. Boo also loved the chili dogs. If anyone even mentioned "the Custard Stand" Boo would jump up and bark, wagging his little stub of a tail. He would even go get his leash and bring it to you.

Maci had a history of migraine headaches, and airplane travel and the sudden change of air altitude and air pressure were about 100% sure to bring one on. When Hailey picked her up at the airport, she only had to take one look at Maci's face to know she had a bad migraine. Maci went straight to bed when Hailey got her home. She figured a little later in the afternoon, Maci would want some frozen custard. She'd been talking about it for days every time they talked.

CHAPTER 16

▼

Aaron and Elvis had left after work on their trip to Kentucky to deliver the horsemeat to Mr. Yoshika. As they left the slaughterhouse, Aaron nudged Elvis and said, "Look, Elvis, that damn bitch that started all this stink in town about horse slaughter is across the road with a fucking reporter." Elvis looked across the road, just as they saw the woman pointing their way and talking to another woman holding a microphone. A Chicago TV news van was parked next to them.

Elvis said, "Keep your head down and walk straight o the van. We don't want no attention and we sure as hell don't want our faces on TV."

Aaron was mad, ""We're gonna have to kill that bitch. She's ruining our life. As soon as we get back, we're going to have to arrange an accident for that nosy bitch."

Elvis said, " Just get in the van, and let's go, we'll talk about that later."

They were driving the van to Brannon for the convenience of having the freezer to pack ice for the meat and also for taking the Porsche wheel to dump in the river while they were in Brannon. The Kentucky River was just a short drive from Brannon, and they knew just the spot to take the wheel to sink it. Too bad they couldn't sell it to a junkyard, but it was too risky.

On the drive down, they started talking about what they would do if the laws were passed to halt all horse slaughter, not just a temporary injunction like was happening now. Aaron was still in a sour mood over the woman at the plant so he wasn't talking very much. Elvis kept throwing out suggestions and getting nothing but a shrug or a grunt from Aaron. Finally, he came up with an idea that got Aaron's attention.

"You know," Elvis said, "Maybe we could buy the plant from the company. We've saved a lot of money over the years, and we've got those diamonds we could sell off. We could buy the plant. Because it's owned by foreigners, maybe they'd sell it cheaper to us since they can't do their business there anymore."

"Why the hell would we want to buy it if we can't do business?" Aaron asked.

"We could still do business," Elvis said. "We could turn it into a beef processing plant. It's got to be basically the same thing, killing animals is killing whether it's a horse or a cow. They use the head stun bolt in cattle killing, too, not that it works any better than with horses." Half the time it didn't work, and Aaron and Elvis didn't care; they just slit the horses' throats or gutted them right there on the hook while they were still alive. "Besides, there's a need for the rendering plant to stay in business. It's the only one around here. Where are people going to dispose of their horses, cows, etc. that turn up dead? Not to mention all the ruined meat that gets brought in from all the grocery stores that doesn't sell and all the road kill and animals from vets that we dispose. There's still work that can be done here. If we can get our own business, all our killing problems will be solved and we can still make money. What do you say Aaron? Don't you think it's worth checking into?"

Aaron liked the idea, and the trip to Brannon went smoothly as they made big plans to buy out the slaughter plant and make it into a legitimate meat processor. They would call Mr. Hardt as soon as they got back in town and see what he thought their chances would be of getting the whole set-up at a decent price.

They got to Brannon late in the night and stayed at a motel instead of waking up their cousins in the middle of the night. They were meeting with Yoshika first thing in the morning anyway. This would make everything a lot easier.

As planned, they met Yoshika at the parking lot in the plant and unloaded the meat from the freezer into the coolers Yoshika had in his van. His wife and kids were there, too. Yoshika was working a few hours today to make sure everything was in top shape for the special people flying in to inspect the plant for Japan's main office of Ho Supawa, located in Tokyo. Yoshika's wife was taking the meat on home and starting her preparations for the dinner party they were hosting that evening. This was a very big honor for Yoshika and his wife.

After they left the auto plant, the brothers went on over to visit their cousins. They hung around for a while and then about noon told them they had some errands to run and would be back later. They wanted to drive on down to the river and ditch that wheel. It made both of them skittish, knowing that kind of evidence was in their van. When they got rid of it, they would be in the clear. They had been paranoid driving down, careful not to go over the speed limit and to use their turn signals, etc. The last thing they needed was to be stopped by some cop for a traffic violation who might ask them to open the back of the van. That would be their worst nightmare.

* * * * * *

Maggie May had gotten in late the previous night to Brannon also. She still had the Victoria Bentley case and the Mandy Gillespie case on her heart and mind. She felt driven to try to solve these cases. Hayward Bentley still called her every day. She dreaded the calls, but wouldn't refuse to take them. She knew he needed closure, even if it was the body of the woman he loved. He also wanted justice served for whoever had taken her. He knew in his heart she was dead even though Victoria's' mother and father still had hopes she was alive somewhere. Victoria's sister had taken Victoria's disappearance very badly. At first she had seemed miffed about the whole thing, like she was jealous of Victoria having all the attention when it was her birthday. But as the days and weeks passed and she realized her sister was most likely dead, she was overcome by a deep guilt for all the mean things she'd said to her sister over the years and how unappreciated she had been all the times Victoria had helped her. She wanted so badly to apologize to her sister for being so rude all those years. Now, she knew she'd have to live with those guilty feelings forever. The thing that had hurt her most was when Hayward had brought the gift Victoria had bought her for her birthday. When the police released the Porsche, he had found the gift in the car.

Victoria had known how much her sister loved books. She had found some very old and very valuable works of Shakespeare for her. Maggie could see the pain in the sister's eyes when she told Maggie about the books. She knew Victoria had searched a long time and put a lot of thought in to the perfect gift for her. She would cherish the books forever. She confided in Maggie that she felt guilty for Victoria's probable death. If it hadn't been her birthday, she wouldn't have been driving to Bloomington, she wouldn't have had the flat or whatever happened to make her pull in to the rest area. None of this would have happened. Maggie felt so badly for Wanda; however, it was somewhat normal for family or friends to feel guilty after a death. She had read many stories after the 9-11 disaster of survivors from the Twin Towers feeling guilty. Why had they lived when their friends or co-workers had perished? This was especially true for those people who missed being at work that fateful day because of missing a bus or taking a sick child to the doctor, little things that made the difference between them living or dying like the ones who were at work on time that day. Maggie tried to reassure Wanda that she was not responsible for whatever had happened to Victoria and that she would do everything in her power to find out exactly what had happened to her sister and why.

Hayward knew Victoria was dead. His only concern was that she didn't suffer. He couldn't stand to think what may have happened to her before she died. Were the killer or killers quick to kill her, or did they torture her? Was she kept alive for days being tortured and had they done unspeakable things to her? What about Precious? What had happened to her? Did they kill her, too? Hayward's mind would not shut down from thoughts like this. He had spent too many years as a criminal attorney. He knew only too well the horrible things people did to one another. He had seen too many crime photos, too much blood, too many autopsy photos of victims of violence. He had looked in the eyes of too many killer sand seen the blackness, the evil that dwelled within them.

The last time Maggie had seen Hayward she had been shocked at his appearance. When she first met him he was a 65 year old man who looked 55 at the most. Now he looked 75. He had aged from the stress and loss of Victoria. He tried to attack his work to take his mind off things but found it impossible to concentrate. Maggie felt the weight of his despair on her own shoulders. She felt like she was the only law enforcement officer to really care.

There were murders every day, fresh cases to be worked and solved. Victoria's case was not only cold, there wasn't anything to investigate. There was no trace. She had simply disappeared, just like Mandy at the truck stop.

Maggie's dad and she had talked a long time about the case when Maggie got in Friday night. She knew if she were missing something, her dad would help her find it. When she had told him everything she had and everything she'd done, Wyatt had sadly shaken his head. He had nothing to offer her, no suggestions. He told her as bad as it was some cases never get solved. Some bodies are never found. Maggie was not giving up. She would keep that file on her desk the rest of her career if necessary.

Even though she'd not gotten much sleep after arriving late and talking to her dad, she was still up 9:00 Saturday morning. She called Jett while she was having coffee to see how Jett's father was doing and to see what would be a good time to come and visit a little. Jett told her it would be a huge favor if she could come over and keep Savannah for an hour or so while she went to Lexington to see her dad. This would give her time to talk to Savannah without her mom around. Maybe she would talk more freely about her dreams if Jett weren't listening. After Jett returned from the hospital they'd have time for girl talk between the two of them.

Maggie liked the idea of spending some one on one time with Savannah. That's exactly what she'd been hoping for. She didn't want Jett prompting Savannah or interrupting in any way when she talked to her. She was going to go over to Jett's about noon. She was thinking of taking Savannah out for a drive. Fall had been late this year and even though this was the second week of November, the leaves and foliage were beautiful. The countryside was ablaze with color: rich reds, dark rust, bright yellow, and orange. It was beautiful. Some of the leaves were starting to fall, sprinkling the green lawns with splashes of color. Fall had always been one of her favorite seasons. She loved the crisp cool mornings and nights and the mild days of autumn. It was perfect jeans and sweater or sweatshirt weather. Today the sun was shining brightly, promising to be a beautiful day.

Jett told Savannah that Aunt Maggie was coming at noon to see her and would be staying with her for an hour or so while mommy went to check on papaw in the hospital. Savannah was excited and hurried off to get dressed and to tell Star they were having a visitor. She'd come back downstairs soon afterwards dressed in jeans and a sweater Jett had gotten her with a horse embroidered on it. It was Savannah's favorite sweater. The sweater horse even had a mane and tail made of yarn. The sweater was pink, Savannah's favorite color. Of course she was also wearing her ever present pink cowgirl boots. At least today her boots matched her outfit. She wore those pink boots no matter what she was wearing.

As soon as Maggie arrived, Savannah, for lack of a better word, galloped outside to meet her. Jett hugged her old friend and left almost immediately to go to Lexington, promising to be back as soon as possible. After she left, Maggie asked Savannah how she'd like to go for a drive in the country. "That would be fun, Aunt Maggie," Savannah said, "I'll go tell Star where we're going!"

"Okay", Maggie said, I want to hear all about Star while we ride." She watched as Savannah ran outside and went over to a tree in the yard. She was talking to her horse, even petting the imaginary friend, Maggie observed from the hand movements. She smiled. Savannah was a sure a cute thing with her little pink boots and horse sweater. Savannah ran back and got in Maggie 's car. " Aunt Maggie, Savannah said, " Star said to take me to the Custard Stand for ice cream, can we go there?"

Maggie laughed, " Oh, Star told you to get ice cream, huh? He's a smart horse and you're a lucky little girl to have him. I think having ice cream at the Custard Stand is a great idea. I always try to go there every time I'm home. No one has better ice cream. My mom and dad took me there when I was your age." Maggie smiled to herself. Yes, Savannah was a smart little girl to think of saying Star suggested going for ice cream. No wonder Jett had to keep on her toes all the time.

"Tell me about Star," Maggie said to Savannah.

"Oh, Aunt Maggie, he's the most 'beautifulest' horse in the whole wide world. He's black and he's got a white star on his forehead. That's why I call him Star. He's got a big long name, but I like Star better." She went on to tell Maggie the same story she'd told Jett. Star had been born far away in a place where it was hot and sandy. He had been abused and mistreated by mean men and finally had come over here in a big airplane. He didn't like men or trust men because they hurt him. Maggie listened carefully to this. She knew sometimes children transferred their own feelings to some other person. Was Savannah really saying she had been treated badly by a man and was afraid of men? She knew Blake would have never hurt her and Jett certainly wouldn't. She would have to ask Jett if Savannah had ever shown any fear around men or had any scary confrontation with any men that she knew of.

She was still thinking about that when Savannah told her there was more about Star that she hadn't told anyone, not even mommy, but Star said it was okay to tell Maggie. Savannah told Maggie she had told Star how Maggie was a policewoman and Star said to tell her everything, even about the dreams. At the mention of dreams, Maggie's attention picked up. "What about the dreams?"

"I'll tell you about Star first, and then after we get ice cream I'll tell you about the dreams. You see Star was afraid of men and everyone that tried to ride him was a man and treated him bad. Finally, one day a woman came to where Star was and started talking to him. At first he was afraid of her, too, but she wasn't like everyone else. She wanted to be his friend. She came every day to see him and she took good care of him and finally he let her pet him and after a long time she got to ride him. She even took him home with her after the man that owned him saw how good Star was with her. After that, Star and the woman were really happy. They loved each other. Star still doesn't like men, but he said the woman's husband was okay. He would never let him ride him though. Anyway, Aunt Maggie, the woman got sick and she and Star were very sad because they knew she was going to die. And, guess what? Aunt Maggie, she did die, and she died the very same night my daddy did. Star told me the woman was so sick, and her husband carried her out to the barn to so she could tell Star she loved him. Star said she whispered in his ear so no one else could hear and told him she'd just met someone that was getting ready to be an angel, too. And that was my daddy. She told Star that my daddy was sad that he had to leave me and mommy and the woman was sad she had to leave her husband and Star. She told my daddy she had just the answer. Star would take care of his little girl, that's me. And maybe someday, her husband and my mommy would meet and we would all take care of each other. Star came to be with me the day after daddy died, and we've been together ever since. Star says very soon we will meet in real person, then everyone can see him."

Maggie was listening intently to Savannah's story. She wanted to stop the car, hold Savannah in her arms and hug her tightly. This precious child had more than an active imagination; she was trying to take care of everyone. She had put a lot of thought in to who Star was and why he'd come. The story was so bittersweet. She wanted to cry. She saw why Jett was so concerned about her. She also knew sometimes things couldn't be explained logically. How had both Jett and Savannah dreamed the night Blake died that he loved them and would send someone to take care of them? Why had Savannah dreamed her daddy had come and told her to wake mommy up and call 911 about Jett's father? That itself was an amazing story. Jett had told her all about it and how the doctors agreed the early phone call may very well have saved Nate's life. Maggie had always believed in gut feelings, intuition, and a sixth sense, whatever one chose to call it. Savannah may not be a psychic, but she certainly was showing signs of being highly aware and intuitive to what was happening around her. Did she herself believe in angels? Yes she did.

About that time while Maggie was thinking all this, Savannah said, "Turn the radio up Aunt Maggie, your song is on. Mommy told me about your song even though she said you really weren't named for a song but you were named after your great-grandmother. Mommy always says when that song comes on the radio, that's Aunt Maggie's song."

Maggie was dumbfounded. The radio wasn't on. She had turned it off when Savannah started talking about Star so there would be no distractions. Instead of telling Savannah the radio was off, she quickly clicked it on. Rod

Stewart and Maggie May came blaring out of the speakers. She was so shocked she almost ran off the road. This was incredible. How could Savannah had possibly known what was on the radio? She now had to rethink the whole Star story. Was it possible? Could it be true??

When they got to the Custard Stand, business was brisk. They went to the inside area to order and Maggie chatted with a number of other people waiting in line to place their orders. Savannah asked Maggie if she could go outside and wait for her. She had seen the Custard Stand's resident stray cat outside and wanted to go out to pet it. Maggie nodded okay.

When Savannah walked outside, she was looking everywhere for the cat and wasn't paying attention to where she was walking. She walked right into two men walking towards the outside window to place their order. Savannah had been taught her manners so she automatically started to say, "Excuse me."

A rough voice said, "Watch out kid," before she had time to say anything. When she looked up at the two men to apologize, her breath caught in her throat. It was THEM, the bad men from her nightmares. She was so scared it seemed like time was standing still although just a second had passed. In that second she saw the two thumbs on one of the hands, and saw the other man's two colored eyes.

These were the bad men who killed horses and killed people too. She should run, she thought, but then the bad men would get away. Instead of running she screamed. When she screamed everyone in the parking lot turned to see what the problem was.

Inside, Maggie heard the scream, too. She looked outside to see Savannah, facing two men, and screaming at the top of her lungs. "Oh my God," she thought, "What is happening? Who are those men? Are they trying to hurt Savannah?" Forgetting all about the ice cream, she ran outside.

The two men were equally shocked as to why this little girl was screaming. Aaron said, "Shut up, kid. What the hell is the matter with you? We didn't do nothin' to you." Savannah started kicking the men with her little pink boot as hard as she could and hitting both men with her fists. She yelled at them. "You are mean! You are bad men. You kill horses! I hate you!! I hate you!! You kill people too. You killed that pretty woman!"

When they heard Savannah say that, they grabbed her. They didn't know who this kid was, or how she knew them, but she was going to have to disappear. People were staring and listening. No one seemed to be with the little girl. They would shove her in the van and take off.

At the same time they grabbed Savannah, Maggie came running out of the Custard Stand yelling, "Let go of her, now!" When the men looked up, they thought they were seeing a ghost. The way the sun was shining all they could see was a blonde woman who looked from a distance just like Victoria Bentley. For a second they lost all sense of sanity.

Elvis said, " NO, you're dead." You're not Vickie, you're dead!" All this time Savannah was still hitting, kicking and struggling to get away from the men.

When Maggie ran out and said, "Let go of her now," Savannah yelled at her. "It's them, Aunt Maggie, the bad men. They killed the horses and the pretty woman."

Maggie didn't know what Savannah was taking about, what horses, what pretty woman? In a reflex action, she reached behind her where she normally kept her gun in the small of her back. Both men recognized the move and immediately both, holding on to Savannah with one arm, pulled six inch hunting knives from hidden sheaths in their boots. Now they had knives on either side of Savannah's neck.

Maggie came up empty handed. She wasn't carrying a gun. She didn't usually when she was off duty. She did have one locked in the glove box in her car, but that was not going to do her any good. She yelled to the people in the parking lot, "Someone call 911!"

To Aaron and Elvis, she said, "Let the girl go, now." Savannah started yelling again. "Aunt Maggie, these are the bad men. They killed the pretty woman and her little dog. They killed Precious!"

CHAPTER 17

▼

Hailey got up early Saturday morning. Mick had left early to go eat breakfast with some friends, a Saturday morning ritual he'd had for twenty years. Hailey wanted to get the horses fed, be out of the barn into the field and finished with her barn chores by the time Maci got up.

Boo and Hailey had gone to the barn, gotten all the horses out and the barn mucked. When they came back to the house, Hailey went ahead and got in the shower and dressed. Today she was wearing one of her classic Scully embroidered cowgirl blouses. This one was green and had lavish embroidery of red and pink roses on the yoke both on the front and back of the blouse as well as matching embroidery on the cuffs of the sleeves. With it she was wearing a split skirt of denim and some light brown leather cowboy boots with the shafts of the boots inlaid in blue and green floral leather patterns, which really went well with the blouse. As soon as Maci got up, they needed to head in to Brannon. She wanted to stop at the feed store and pick up a couple bags of sweet feed and a bag of apple treats the horses loved so much. First, they'd go by the Custard Stand.

Maci came in the kitchen still wearing her pajamas. At least Hailey assumed they were pajamas. The top was a camisole style, pale lavender with birds of paradise intricately embroidered on it. The pants were of the same material with the same embroidered bird of paradise flowers. They were Capri style pants with ruffles at the ends of the legs of the pajamas. The pale lavender was a perfect contrast for the deep green and purple stems of the flowers and then the deep coral of the plumage of the exotic tropical flower. Maci had always loved bird of paradise; she must have searched a long time for these pajamas.

Hailey could only imagine what Maci paid for pajamas like this, but then laughed to herself. They were probably about as much as one of her Scully blouses. She and her sister were obsessive compulsive about some things, for sure. Because her sister's health was bad, she spent most of her time in pajamas. Maci spent as much money on comfortable pajamas with matching accessories as most people did for the clothes they worked in. She had on a pair of house shoes with birds of paradise on them, too, of course. The Hawkins sister had to have everything to match.

Maci was still nursing a little but of a headache, although it was now not in the migraine stage. When Hailey told her she needed to go to Brannon she said she was ready to go. "Do you care if I wear my pajamas? I'm not planning on getting out. You know how long it takes me to get dressed."

Yes, Hailey, sighed, she did know how long it took Maci to get dressed. Hailey could be in and out of the shower, dressed with hair dry and makeup on and out the door in half an hour tops. With Maci, it was at least a two hour ordeal. If she had to wait for Maci to really get ready, the feed store would be closed. It closed at 2:00 on Saturday and it was going on noon now.

Hailey, nodded and said, "Sure, you can wear you pajamas. You can sit in the Jeep with Boo while I get the feed and I can order our stuff at the Custard Stand and carry it out for you." At the sound of the Custard Stand, Boo barked and started wagging his stub of a tail. He ran over, got his leash, and now was prancing back and forth waiting for Hailey to put it on. " Okay, Boo, hold still. I can't get your leash hooked to your collar with you jumping around." She finally got it on and said to Maci, "It's a little cool for just a camisole top. Why don't you grab a jacket out of the closet?"

Maci opened the hall closet and picked out one of Mick's beaded Indian western fringed jackets. It was big on her, but who cared? No one was going to see her. She loved this jacket. The beadwork was great, and it looked like something out of a Buffalo Bill Wild West Show. Hailey turned to see what she had on, laughed and said, "Cute".

They got in Hailey's jeep, Boo in the back, and headed to the Custard Stand, their first stop. Sometimes your whole life seems to have happened for one particular place and time. This is what Hailey and Maci felt as they pulled in to the Custard Stand. What they saw in that instant was two men holding knives to the throat of a struggling little girl. They also saw a woman who appeared to be having a confrontation with them. Hailey recognized her. The woman was Maggie May, Sheriff Wyatt May's daughter. She had read an article about her in paper along with her picture when she had graduated from the FBI training camp at Quantico a couple years ago.

Boo began growling in the backseat. Even he saw something bad was going on. Hailey silenced Boo with a hand command. "Sister", Hailey said, "Get my gun out of my purse and hand it to me." Since they were little, the girls had called one another Sister instead of their real names. Maci took in the situation and saw the same thing and drew the same conclusion Hailey had without a word passing between them. She got Hailey's compact 9mm Sig out of the purse and handed it to her. She didn't have to ask if it was loaded. She knew it was not only loaded but already had one in the chamber, the same way she kept her guns.

"There's another gun in the glove box. You use it."

Maci opened the glove box and saw the Sig .380 laying there with an extra clip beside it. She took both the gun and the clip. All this happened in the mere seconds it took for Hailey to pull in directly in front of the van the men had been trying to get the little girl in.

Hailey and Maci got out of the car, guns drawn, in time to hear Savannah telling Maggie these were the mean bad men who had killed the horses, the pretty woman and the little dog, Precious. They didn't know what this was about, but from the look that passed over Maggie's face they knew this was big trouble. The men had not seen the two sisters and had no idea there were two guns aimed at their backs, but Maggie did see. It was some sight, one woman dressed like Annie Oakley and the other in what looked like pajamas with a Buffalo Bill Wild West jacket on! "What the hell," she thought. She felt like she was in the Twilight Zone.

When Savannah had screamed Maggie had reacted purely on police instinct. Then when she heard what Savannah was saying, she didn't understand. When the realization hit her what Savannah was saying about the pretty woman being killed and the dog, and when Maggie heard Savannah say, "They killed Precious," she had that instant clarity. One of the men had said, "You're dead, you're not Vickie." Savannah was right these were very bad men.

She didn't understand yet how Savannah knew, but she was ready to stake her whole reputation and career that this child was telling the truth. She knew her papaw was having a heart attack, she knew a song was on the radio, and Maggie believed her when she said these were the bad men that had killed the pretty woman, meaning Victoria Bentley and Precious, the dog.

The Pucketts realizing Maggie was not armed, started again dragging the struggling Savannah to the van. Maggie, yelled, "Stop, I'm the FBI, let go of that child this instant!" The Pucketts just kept on. She couldn't do a thing.

There were two of them, and she wasn't armed. "You can't stop us," Aaron said, "You're not armed."

That's when Hailey said, "She may not be, but we are." Aaron and Elvis turned to see the same strange sight Maggie had seen. One woman dressed like frigging Annie Oakley holding a 9mm Sig in her hand and the other in a damned jacket that looked like Buffalo Bill might have owned it with a Sig .380 in her hand.

"You two old woman aren't going to shoot us. You look like you just escaped from a Wild West Show." Still with the knives at Savannah's neck, they headed to the van door.

That's when Hailey gave the hand command and 180 lbs of Rottweiler came out of the Jeep and with two leaps attacked Elvis. In the surprise of the attack, Elvis had dropped his knife. Elvis was a wiry man, but his strength was no match for a trained attack dog weighing 180 lbs. Boo had launched himself midair and knocked Elvis to the ground and now had his neck in the clutches of his big jaw. He was snarling and growling, waiting for the "kill" command or "release" command from Hailey. Elvis was trying to push the dog off. Anytime he moved, Boo clamped with a little more pressure on Elvis' neck.

At the sight of Elvis under attack by the vicious dog Aaron had gone berserk. The only person in the world he cared or believed in was his brother. He would kill that damned dog. Still holding Savannah, he raised the knife getting ready to stab Boo, when a shot rang out. Without hesitation, Hailey shot Aaron in the upper arm that was holding the knife. Onlookers and Maggie could hardly believe what they had seen. Annie Oakley, as Hailey, had not aimed. She simply brought her gun up and fired, hitting Aaron exactly where she wanted. Maggie took that opportunity to run to her car and get her gun out of the glove box. She popped the trunk and got handcuffs.

When Aaron was shot he had let go of Savannah from the force of the impact and the pain. Hailey had simply looked at him and said, "No one hurts my dog. The next shot won't be your arm. You'll be dead."

Elvis had managed to get his hands around Boo's neck and was trying to choke him. Hailey could hear the Boo's raspy breathing and knew she had to stop Elvis. Maci saw and heard the same thing. She said, "Take your hands off the dog's neck, now."

"Go to hell, bitch," Elvis gasped. He was now bleeding from the canine teeth clamped around his neck. He gave more pressure to the choke. Maci fired, hitting Elvis in the knee. With both brothers now wounded and Maggie now armed, the brothers realized that without guns they weren't going to win. They had no doubt in their mind these two crazy women would shoot them, and now the FBI bitch had her gun. Maggie cuffed Elvis, with a snarling Boo still at his neck. As soon as he was cuffed, Hailey gave the release and guard command. Boo immediately released Elvis's neck and stood back, ever ready to launch another attack if given the okay.

Hailey and Maci stood by while Maggie cuffed the two men. When Hailey looked at the two, a realization came to her. She said, " I think I know these men, Sister," looking at Maci. Remember the twins that were born when we lived up the hollow? Let's see, Puckett was their name. Are you two the Puckett twins?"

After nearly being eaten alive by a dog and with blood oozing from gunshot wounds, Elvis rasped, "Who the hell are you? How do you know our name? "

Maci said, " Sister, you're right. I remember when they were born. One of them had two colored eyes and one had three thumbs. People were afraid of them, thought they were cursed. Their daddy was mean drunken son of a bitch who used to beat the shit out of the mother. We must have been about between 10-12 when they were born."

Elvis looked over at Aaron, with disbelief on his face, "Who the hell are these two crazy women? Shot us and now they're talking about us like nothing happened. We'll kill you, you sluts!"

Yes, Hailey said, "got to be the Pucketts. You can never quite lose the accent of the holler. We're the Hawkins sisters. You don't remember us because we're older than you, but I remember our momma talking about you two. She taught down at the school. Did you all even go to fifth grade? Momma taught fifth grade."

By this time a couple officers were helping take the Pucketts to the ambulances to be taken to the hospital. The Pucketts were still conversing with the two women. "Hell, I remember your momma. She was our favorite teacher, the only one that treated us good."

"Small world," said Maci.

"Small world?!" thought Maggie, "This has got to be the craziest day I've ever spent. Who are these people?" She'd heard of strange people coming out of the mountains, and if these four were any indication, the stories were true. She shook her head in disbelief at the discussion she'd just overheard.

With both women now with guns aimed on Aaron and Elvis on the ground, cuffed and shot in the knee, Maggie moved to cuff Aaron. About the time she got the cuffs on, they heard the siren and saw the police cars pulling into the parking lot. Maggie told the brothers they were under arrest for the attempted kidnapping of a child and suspicion of the murder of Victoria Bentley. She read them their Miranda rights, so that everything would be legally done. She wanted everything done by the book. She didn't want some legal technicality getting these guys off if they had done what she thought they'd done.

The police who answered the 911 call were better late than never. There had been a bad accident on the other side of town, and that's why it had taken so long to respond. Wyatt May was one of the first out of his car, gun drawn, running to his daughter.

"Everything's fine," Dad, she said. An ambulance pulled in the lot, too. "These men are going to need to go to the hospital. Both are shot and bleeding. These are dangerous men. Dad, do not un-cuff them, even at the hospital, and don't take your gun off them for a minute. Have a deputy on each one at all times. I need to take Savannah back safely to Jett, and then I want to interrogate these two. After you get them treated at the hospital, if they are able to released, take them to jail. Keep them separated. I don't want them to be able to see or talk to one another. Dad, these are the men who killed Victoria Bentley and most likely Mandy Gillespie. I want to call my office and have the FBI process this scene. I want the van impounded and not touched until our crime forensics unit goes over it with a fine-tooth comb. I am going to get on the phone and have surveillance put on their house. Their drivers' licenses have an Illinois address, and I'm running the Illinois plates on the van, too. If what I think is true, this case needs to go to Illinois. The murder charges, if that's what we find, are more pressing than the attempted kidnapping of Savannah. We'll extradite them to Illinois to face charges. I want the death penalty for these two. If I can find any connection with Victoria and Mandy, the death penalty can apply. I need a couple of your men to take statements from those two women, and I want to talk to them as well. If they had not shown up when they did, those men would have taken Savannah and gotten away."

Wyatt said, "I know one of the women, the one in the cowgirl outfit. That's Mick McGuire's wife. I think her name is Hailey. I don't know who the other one is."

"Okay Dad, good, at least you know one of them. We need statements from everyone here. This is a crime scene."

All the patrons and workers at the Custard Stand readily agreed to give statements. This was the biggest thing to ever hit Brannon. A shoot-out at the Custard Stand! The phones were going to be ringing off the hooks tonight. Everyone was given free coffee, soft drinks and ice cream while waiting to give their statements. People were told not to discuss what they'd seen with each other until after everyone had given their statements. They didn't want other people's versions of what they'd seen to affect what each person saw for himself.

Maggie called the Chicago office, and after some persuasion, got the desk to agree to call her boss at home and have him call her back. Her phone rang about 5 minutes later.

"Agent May, this had better be important. Gerard Jamison was the head man in Chicago's FBI office. "Yes, sir, it is. I'm down here in Brannon, Kentucky, sir and I think I have just apprehended the murderers of Victoria Bentley and possibly Mandy Gillespie, the young girl who disappeared from an interstate truck stop last week. It's a long difficult story to explain, but sir, I need your co-operation on this. If I'm not right, I'll turn in my badge and quit. I'm riding my whole career on this. The two I have in custody are Aaron Puckett and Elvis Puckett, white males, twins, born 8 January 1967. Their address is 66 Elm Lane, Parkland, IL. I want you to authorize agents to go to that address and secure the site. I want the forensics team down here to process the car for fingerprints, fibers, blood, hair, anything and everything we can find. My dad is the sheriff here. Sir, he is willing to turn the whole investigation over to us because of the nature of the case."

Jamison knew who Maggie May was and knew she was a conscientious agent. However, she sounded a bit over the edge on this one. She had told him the two had tried to abduct a child in the parking lot of an ice cream stand. He could not make the leap she had to tie that in any way with the missing women in Illinois. The only connection he saw was they were driving a white van that had Illinois plates. Hard to pull out the manpower Agent May was wanting with no more than that.

"Agent May," he said, "I'm not inclined to grant you all you want based on a white van with Illinois plates. What possible connection does that have to give us grounds to go forward? You said it's a long story, I think I need to hear it."

Briefly, she told him the story of Savannah, her dreams about the bad men, the killing of the pretty woman and the little dog named Precious. She told him also about Savannah waking her mother about her grandfather's heart and about earlier in the day when she had told Maggie her song was on the radio. "The only thing she has said that I don't understand is that these men kill horses. I don't know what that means, but I'd stake my career it will pan out, too. Another thing, when I came out of the ice cream stand to tell them to release Savannah, one of the men's blood literally drained from his face and he yelled to me, 'No, you're dead, you' re not Vickie, you're dead.' Sir, I am the same size Victoria Bentley was, and I have the same length blonde hair. When I walked out there, I think it freaked them out. They killed Victoria Bentley. The one who said it looked like he'd just seen a ghost. Savannah was kicking and hitting them, telling them they were bad men, and that they killed the pretty woman and they killed horses and they killed the little dog, Precious. Precious was Victoria's Maltese dog that disappeared when she did."

"Agent May, am I hearing you correctly? You want to risk your career as well as mine on the dreams of a five-year-old child who has an imaginary horse that tells her things? Listen, I've heard the talk around the office. I know you took the Bentley case particularly hard. I know you've kept the file on your desk and work it in all the spare time you have. Don't you think you have been obsessing too much on this one?"

Maggie struggled to keep her composure. She knew to anyone else the whole story would sound crazy. She also knew she wouldn't be at the Custard Stand right now if Savannah hadn't said Star the imaginary horse had said to take her there. Was Savannah clairvoyant as a result of the trauma suffered from the death of her father? She didn't know what the whole picture was, but she did know the child was correct in every thing she had said thus far and Maggie's gut, her own intuition, said to believe everything she said.

"Tell me," Agent May, "Were you armed? How were you able to take custody of these two men? Did they just give up and hand the child over?"

"Oh, shit" Maggie thought, "Now he's going to hear the rest of this crazy story." 'No, sir, I wasn't armed. I had my weapon locked in the glove box of my car. When I saw the two men trying to get the child in the van, I acted on instinct. Sir, the child was with me. I was responsible for her. She had gone outside while I was getting us ice cream. When I saw the two men, I ran out and told them to release her and by instinct reached for my gun, but had none. The men recognized the move and both drew hunting knives from their boots and had the child at knifepoint. About the time all that happened and they yelled about me not being Vickie, two women pulled up, blocking the van with their jeep. The women came out with guns drawn. When the men realized I wasn't armed they proceeded to try to take the child. One woman's dog attacked one of the men. The other man started to stab the dog, and the woman shot him in the arm. When the man under attack tried to strangle the dog, the other woman shot him in the knee. While this was happening, I got to the car and got my weapon. We then handcuffed the men, and the police and ambulance arrived. I had yelled as soon as I saw what was happening for someone to call 911."

"Agent May you're giving me a headache. Are you telling me two civilians were armed and shot the men, and where did the dog come from? This is the wildest story I have ever heard."

Sir," Maggie said,"The dog is a 180 pound massive Rottweiler named Boo. I have never seen anything like what he did. He's a hero dog. If it hadn't been for those two women and the dog, the men would have very likely gotten away with the child. And the women, well, I've never seen anyone shoot like they did. They just brought up their weapons and fired, no aiming, no hesitation. They both took incredible shots and stopped the men without loss of life. Believe me, sir, if they had wanted to kill the men, I'd have them in body bags right now. They only used the necessary force to stop them. I am getting ready to take their statements as soon as we hang up. I have secured the site. My father and his men are taking statements from everyone here. No one has been allowed to leave. This is a small town, sir, nothing has ever happened like this here."

"Agent May," Jamison said, "I doubt what you have described has ever happened anywhere before. I may regret this for the rest of my life and end up in a field office in Alaska, but I'm going to go along with you to a point. I will authorize and get the necessary warrants and paperwork to process the van and send our techs down to do it. I will run back ground information on the two men and find out all I can. When we get the forensics from the van, we'll go to the next step. Where are the men now?"

"Sir, I read them their Miranda rights, told them they were under arrest for the attempted kidnapping of Savannah Edwards and for questioning in the disappearance of Victoria Bentley. The men are currently being treated for gunshot wounds at the hospital. Then, they will be taken to the jail here. I have ordered they be separated where they cannot see or talk to one another at least until they are interrogated."

"Okay, Agent May, proceed on your end and I will get going on this end. Do not let anyone touch that car until we get there."

"Yes, Sir, and thank you sir," Maggie added.

When Maggie looked to see where Savannah was, she found her petting the big dog that had attacked Elvis. The two women were with Savannah and the dog. She walked over to them. The woman in the cowgirl outfit introduced herself. " Hello, I'm Hailey McGuire, and this is my sister, Maci Joseph. She's visiting me from Raleigh this weekend. And this big guy here, is Boo. Boo shake hands with Maggie May." Boo sat obediently and lifted his paw to Maggie.

Maggie shook it and laughed. "That's some dog you have there!"

"Thank you," Hailey said, "I think so. I've had him since he was 5 weeks old. I promised him a chili dog." At the mention of chili dog, Boo barked and started drooling.

Maggie laughed. "I'll go get the hero a chili dog. Do either of you want anything?"

Maci wanted ice cream, as did Savannah, who seemed to have shaken off the scare of the whole ordeal. Hailey wanted coffee. In a few minutes Maggie came back with a helper carrying their orders.

Boo literally inhaled his chili dog much to the delight of Savannah, and then came over with big sad eyes, begging for Savannah's ice cream. Hailey said, " Boo, be a good boy and let Savannah eat her ice cream. She'll save you some." Boo sat down never taking his eyes off Savannah's ice cream, saliva dripping from his massive mouth. Next thing you know, dog and child were trading licks on the ice cream cone. All of them laughed.

With all that out of the way, Maggie said she really needed to talk to both of them. She suggested they get Hailey's jeep so they could all be comfortable. Hailey agreed. Boo and Savannah got in the main back. Hailey opened the back hatch up so they would have fresh air and have more leg room. Savannah and Boo were sitting side by side, Savannah's legs hanging down, pink boots hitting the license plate. Hailey and Maggie sat in the front seat. Maci was in the back seat.

Maggie said, "First of all I want to thank you what you did here. You all are heroines, you know. I have to say, in all my years I've never seen better shooting and more calm attitudes under pressure than the two of you displayed. Both of you have missed your calling in law enforcement. Where and how did you both learn to shoot and how did you both happen to be carrying guns today?"

Hailey replied, "First of all, let me tell you that both Maci and I are licensed concealed weapon carriers. I know that will make you feel a little better. Maci's license was issued in North Carolina. Both of us learned to shoot and appreciate and respect guns from an early age from our father. We lived and were raised in rural eastern Kentucky. He taught us not only to target shoot but to draw and shoot, like we did today without seemingly aiming. It's all aiming, just a different way. You shoot where your eye is. Your arm is an extension of your eyes. We practiced as youngsters, walking along and shooting things on the ground and gradually over the years progressed to what you saw today. I carry a gun in my purse all the time. Maci was not carrying a weapon, but I had a gun in my glove box. She has the same gun at home so she was comfortable shooting the .380 Sig. Sigs are our favorites. We like the balance and weight of them, never much cared for Glocks. I've shot them, but I don't own one." Maci was nodding in agreement with all Hailey said.

Maci then said, "Guess you're wondering about how we're dressed or not dressed as in my case. I have a long history of bad migraine headaches, I've been plagued by them since I was a child. One of the things that will trigger a migraine almost every time for me is change in weather or air pressure. I flew in yesterday. By the time my plane landed in Lexington, I had a bad migraine. Sister took me home and put me to bed. This morning when I got up she was needing to come to Brannon to get some things and asked if I wanted to ride along. Since I take a long time getting ready and still had a touch of a headache and wasn't planning on getting out of the car anyway, I just came in my pajamas. I grabbed one of Mick's jackets on the way out of the house to knock off the chill. That's my story. I'll let Sister tell you her dress excuse," said Maci, laughing.

"Gee," Hailey said, "I dress like this all the time. Sister and I have always dressed in themes. When Mick and I decided to buy a farm and move to the country with the horses, it was only natural that I start dressing like a cowgirl."

Maci said, " I've been all over the country have seen some of the largest horse farms in the area, but I haven't seen anyone dress like you do, Hailey, straight out of a Wild West show!"

Maggie laughed, too. "I have to admit you two are quite the pair! I don't care how you dress. You saved the day." Looking toward the back of the jeep, Maggie said, "Is it safe for Savannah to be back there with Boo?"

"Yes," Hailey said, "Boo will not hurt her. He's a gentle giant as long as I don't give him the attack signals." They could hear giggling from the back of the jeep where Boo and Savannah were sitting. They couldn't make out what Savannah was saying, but she was having a talk with her new friend.

"I need to get her back to her mother," Maggie said. "She is going to have a fit if she hears what happened here before I tell her first hand. I think before we go any further I will call and let her come get Savannah. Jett should be back from the hospital by now. She went to Lexington to check on her father." Maggie took out her cell phone and dialed Jett's number.

She answered, "Hello."

"Jett, it's Maggie. Savannah and I ran in to a little problem at the Custard Stand. We're both fine, but I have some police work to do, and I was wondering if you could come get her. I'm going to be here for a long time and I know she'll get tired."

"Sure," Jett said, "What happened? Are you sure Savannah is okay?"

"Yes, Jett, Savannah is fine but we've had a very unusual day, to say the least. Come on to the Custard Stand and I'll explain everything."

Maggie continued taking the statements from Hailey and Maci while she waited for Jett. Both women agreed they had taken in the situation as they turned in to the parking lot, saw the child was being held at knifepoint, and realized no one was going to be able to stop the men from taking the child. Hailey had recognized Maggie, knew she was with the FBI, and saw she had a situation on her hands and was obviously unarmed. According to the women, they did what anyone would have done in the same situation. Both Hailey and Maci said they in no way jeopardized the safety of Savannah with their shots. They knew exactly where the bullet was going. They could just as easily have killed the men, and would have if the conditions warranted. They went on to explain to Maggie they believed in their constitutional rights to bear arms and always believed that guns saved more lives than cost lives. Bad men and law breakers will always find a way to get weapons, they said. When you take away a person's right to bear arms you take away their right to defend themselves or others from harm. They thought today's actions were a perfect example of how their lawful use of guns had saved Savannah from being abducted or worse.

Maggie told the women if her hunch was correct, the men they had shot were killers. Hailey and Maci didn't seem fazed by that statement. Hailey did say if either one of them had been successful in stabbing Boo she would have killed him. "No one hurts my horses or dogs," she said.

Things had gotten very quiet in the back of the jeep. When Jett pulled up, Maggie, Maci and Hailey got out of the Jeep. They walked around back where they found Savannah sound asleep and the huge dog curled around her protectively. Maggie gave Jett a quick run down of the events, stopping every now and then to answer a question from Jett. It was a pretty unbelievable story. Jett could only shake her head in amazement at what had happened. She found it incredible that her Savannah had confronted two men about hurting the pretty woman and the little dog named Precious. This was what the nightmares had been about. She had been terrified of the nightmares. It must have scared her to death to look up and see the two men she'd been seeing in her sleep right before her. Jett couldn't bear to think what might have happened here today if it hadn't been for the quick thinking and actions of the sisters, Maci and Hailey. If she had lost

Savannah, she would have never recovered. She looked like a little angel sleeping beside the big dog. The dog looked like a bear. His head was huge. Jett was afraid to startle the dog so she let Hailey wake him up so she could get Savannah.

Savannah woke up with a big yawn and surprised to see her mother. "Mommy," Savannah said, "Did Aunt Maggie tell you we caught the bad men? They were the bad men from my nightmares, Mommy. I knew I had to stop them or they would get away. They were creepy, Mommy, just like in my nightmares. Boo attacked them and then these women shot them, and Aunt Maggie put handcuffs on them. The police got here and we got free ice cream and Boo ate a chili dog."

At the mention of a "chili dog" Boo once again let out a bark, making them all laugh. "Boo said I could come visit him, Mommy, and he said they have horses where he lives, too. Can we go see Boo and the horses some time, Mommy?"

"Sure, Baby," Jett said, "As long as Hailey doesn't mind, we can go see Boo and the horses sometime soon." Hailey assured them they would be most welcome to come visit anytime they wanted.

By this time, the local and Lexington news had picked up the story about the shoot out at the Custard Stand. Area TV trucks and cameras and microphones were everywhere. Pictures were being taken and people were being interviewed. This was the biggest thing to happen in Brannon in a long time. Maggie had crime scene tape around the perimeter of the van and had two officers making sure no one touched it. She wanted to make sure no one bothered the van until the FBI crime tech came and bagged every piece of evidence that could be found. Maggie hoped there would be something, anything, in the van to tie the two men to Victoria Bentley or Mandy Gillespie.

Maci and Hailey found themselves on the front page of the Sunday newspaper. Maci, in lavender pajamas with bird of paradise flowers embroidered on them, topped off with a beaded fringed suede jacket and Hailey with her western shirt, split skirt and cowboy boots, both holding guns were a sight to behold. Maci wanted to go buy several copies of the paper to take back to Raleigh with her to show her husband and co-workers. No one was going to believe this story!

* * * * *

Reverend Jenkins saw the article in the Lexington Sunday paper and recognized the little girl in the picture as the same one he had spoken to in the hospital earlier in the week, the same little girl who had alerted her mother that her grandfather was having a heart attack. His sermon this morning was about faith and the inspiration for his sermon was this little girl and her faith that her daddy came to her in a dream and told her to do something and she did it without question or hesitation because of her faith in her father. Her father would never tell her anything wrong. She accepted his appearance in her dream and did exactly what he told her. His sermon was going to be about how if we had the same faith in our heavenly father that this child had, the world would be a much better place. If we only did what our Father commanded instead of doubting His word or trying to question Him, our lives would be blessed. He didn't have time to read the article now, but he was going to read it as soon as he got home from church. It appeared Savannah had been the target of an attempted kidnapping by two men. The two oddly dressed women in the picture had stopped the men and had shot them in doing so.

Jett, too, opened the morning paper to find her daughter front page news. She scanned the article quickly. She was relieved to read there was no mention of Savannah's dreams or anything about why the men had tried to kidnap her. Thank goodness no one had the whole story except a few, and they had been told to keep it to themselves. Jett didn't want people to think Savannah was some kind of psychic freak. Her life had been stressful enough so far without people picking up that bit of gossip. A lot of people already thought Savannah weird because she talked to an imaginary horse.

Maggie had come by late the night before after Savannah had gone to bed. She told Jett in more detail what had happened at the Custard Stand. She also told her about Savannah telling her to turn up the radio on the way over there to hear her song, *Maggie May*, and the fact the radio was not on at the time. She asked Jett how many more things Savannah had done like that. Jett told her Savannah was always telling her things Star said, which turned out to be true and then of course the story about her father and the heart attack which Maggie already knew. "Maggie, do you really think those men are the ones who took those two women whose cases you are working on?" Jett asked.

Maggie told her yes, she not only believed it, she was staking her whole career on the line, largely because of Savannah's dreams and the fact that one of the men had said "You're dead. You're not Vickie." She hoped when the crime lab got through with the van there would be enough evidence to arrest them for murder and move the cases to Illinois. If nothing was found in the van, chances are the men would only face attempted kidnapping charges for Savannah, and Maggie would be the laughing stock of the FBI.

The two men, Aaron and Elvis Puckett, were being held in Brannon's jail. They had been treated for their wounds and transferred to jail. Maggie had ordered them separated, so they could not see, hear or talk to one another. She didn't know if she could turn one brother against the other or not, but she sure didn't want them concocting some story together.

By the time Maggie finally got to her parent's house that night and got in bed, she was exhausted. It had been some day. She kept going over and over the events of the day to see if there was anything she missed or should have done differently. All in all, she thought everything was fine. Legally, the arrest was good. The Pucketts had been read their rights and had been treated for their wounds. They had been given the opportunity to make a phone call but had declined. Tomorrow the tech boys would be here and the van would be examined, vacuumed, dusted for prints, and gone over inch by inch. She prayed that they would come up with something, anything, to tie them to Victoria Bentley and Mandy Gillespie.

Sunday morning Maggie went to jail to check on the Pucketts. They were not in a good mood. Both demanded to be turned loose, and both demanded to see each other. The men had never been separated, and already it was starting to bother them. "Good," Maggie, thought, "Let them stay away from each other, see what happens." She told them they would go before the judge on Monday, and he would decide about bail or whether to hold them, and they were entitled to a court appointed attorney if they wanted. Each brother wanted to know where the other was and whether he wanted an attorney. Both were told they had to make their minds up individually. They seemed unable to make a decision on their own.

The crime van arrived and Maggie was there when they opened the back doors of the van. The first thing she saw was the tire and wheel from a Porsche. She could hardly contain herself. She would bet anything this was the tire from Victoria's Porsche. She called her boss and told him about the Porsche tire. "Could just be a co-incidence, Agent May. There's no law against having a Porsche tire," Jamison had said.

"Yes sir," Maggie said, "but Victoria had custom wheels on her Porsche and this is the same wheel. Don't worry, if there's anything to be found, these guys will find it," Maggie continued.

The van supplied them with a virtual gold mine of evidence. They had hair and fiber samples, numerous fingerprints to analyze, dirt, blood, and more.

When one tech bagged and brought out an earring from under the front seat, Maggie could hardly believe her eyes. Through the plastic she looked at the earring. She knew she was seeing the earring worn by Mandy Gillespie on the night she disappeared. Her coworkers had described the earrings she had on because Mandy had made them herself. She always showed the girls her new earring when she made a new style. She was planning to start selling some of her jewelry on EBay. She had a real eye for beads and color combinations. The earrings she had worn the night she disappeared were silver fishhook style with deep blue and green Czech glass beads and a peacock feather dangling from the end. Maggie wondered if there would be enough DNA on an earring wire to match to Mandy. She hoped so.

She knew the police had Mandy's fingerprints and hair samples they had taken from her apartment. They also had Victoria's fingerprints and hair from her brush at home. They even had hair from Precious' brush and bed. If they could get one match on anything, Maggie knew they could get warrants to go in their house and search. There was an old freezer in the back of the van. It was wet inside with a few pieces of ice still melting. Maggie wondered what had been in the freezer or whom. Just being around the van made the hair on the back of her neck stand up. It just felt evil.

They had already run their drivers license through DMV and found neither brother had any traffic violations. The address listed on their licenses was the same as listed with the plates on the van. Taxes on that property were paid and there were no outstanding warrants against either brother.

The police and FBI had a lot of Victoria's information on computer files, including her fingerprints. Maggie had her laptop there at the van and every time they lifted a set of prints, a preliminary comparison was made. The tech said there was no doubt about it. They had Victoria's prints on the tire, a thumb and index finger, very plain. In addition to that, there were fingerprints on the underside of the handle of the passenger's door in the front seat that looked like a match to Victoria, even though they weren't as clear as the tire.

They had a couple strands of long blonde hair, short white hair, and brown hair, along with hair the techs said looked like animal hair, maybe deer. Other hair samples he wasn't sure about, but there were plenty of them. Thinking back to Savannah saying the bad men killed horses, Maggie suggested the techs try matching the hair samples to horse hair. "Horse hair?" Dirk, one of the techs asked. "We got a couple of cowboys here? There's a lot of hair whatever it is, can't imagine this much hair falling off a saddle or a blanket? What makes you think it could be horse hair?"

" Oh", Maggie, said, "Just a hunch."

The match of Victoria's fingerprint on the tire and door handle of the van was enough for an Illinois judge to issue a search warrant of the home of the Pucketts. Maggie gave her apologies to her parents for having to miss their anniversary party, but she felt she had to be on site when the search was made on the Puckett home. Both parents, but especially Wyatt, understood. This was certainly a case that could make or break their daughter's career with the FBI. The FBI information searches went to work. By the time Maggie reached 66 Elm Road and accessed her email, she had a better idea of the life of the Pucketts. They were born in Eastern Kentucky, joined the Marine Corp, served their 4 years, and both were honorably discharged with medals for marksmanship. They had been employed for the past 20 years at BFI right here in town. Bank records showed a considerable balance in their accounts. They had joint checking and savings accounts. The home was in their joint names and appeared to be paid. On paper, the Pucketts looked like law abiding citizens.

The gate across the drive at 66 Elm Drive was padlocked with a NO TRESPASSING sign on the fence. "Gee," Maggie thought, "Guess the boys didn't like drop in company."

After cutting through the chains on the lock, the little convoy made its way to the house. In the convoy were Maggie, the local sheriff and deputy, the crime tech van, and the homicide officer in Chicago who had originally investigated the disappearance of Victoria Bentley. Another FBI co-worker, Van Drury, had also driven down with all the proper paperwork and warrants. Maggie had called Detective Newman after the positive ID of the fingerprints in the van and on the tire had been found. Maggie believed in full co-operation whenever possible with local authorities. She had never understood the territorial posturing done by the feds and locals. She felt the objective was to solve the crime, no matter who closed the case. Unfortunately, not everyone felt the way Maggie did. Most local and state authorities resented when the FBI came into the case. They felt it made them look inefficient and incapable of doing their jobs.

After the gate was opened, the motorcade made its way to the house. Maggie did a quick look around to get a first impression. What she saw was a white clapboard frame house with a full front porch. There were a couple of lawn chairs on the porch. Other than that, the porch was bare except for a rug at the door. Outside there was an out building. It looked in need of repair; the wood was rotten in places and the roof was sagging. Maggie guessed they didn't use this for much more than a storage shed. The yard looked neat. In back, Maggie could see the remnants of the summer's garden, dry cornstalks still standing in the ground. Nothing out of the ordinary at all, Maggie noted, a typical Midwestern rural home.

Everyone got out of their vehicles, and introductions were made all around. The local sheriff Andy Heiler was a red-faced pot-bellied man who had the look of a man who liked his beer. Maggie asked him if he knew what kind of business BFI was. "Sure do," Andy said, "No secret. Everybody around these parts knows what BFI does. It's been in the local news a lot lately, a lot of people looking to see it closed down."

"Really", Maggie inquired, "What does BFI do, and why do people want it shut down?"

"Well," Andy said, "BFI is a horse slaughter and rendering facility."

Horse slaughter…Maggie felt like she'd been slapped across the face. Savannah had said the bad men killed horses. "What do you mean horse slaughter and rendering facility? Why are horses being slaughtered? "

Andy continued, "Horses used to be slaughtered all over the country. Some were sick or old, some were just unwanted or wild, and some were just healthy young horses. What a lot of people don't know is that the US exports horsemeat for human consumption."

"What!" Maggie gasped. "People eat horses, our horses?"

"Yes, Ma'am," Andy said. "Over in France, Belgium, and Japan, among others, horsemeat is considered a delicacy. Long time ago horsemeat was used for dog food, but that pretty much stopped in the 70's. There are some zoos that still use horsemeat for some of their feed, but the main product of this plant is horsemeat for human consumption. At the present time the plant is under a temporary injunction to stop processing, but we've been through this before and usually the plant is granted a temporary order to continue business. In most states horse slaughter for human consumption is illegal, however, in Illinois, it's still legal although there is a bill before the governor to make it illegal. I'm surprised you don't know about it. Locally, it's a big deal. The plant here employs over a hundred people. Some, like the Pucketts, have worked there for years. Others work there because there aren't any other jobs to be found. A man does what he has to do to provide for his family. Not a lot of work to be found here locally, just farming and retail. To get a good job you have to commute to the city. Might not be tasteful work, but the pay is good. I've heard complaints of a few illegals working here from time to time, but overall, I think the manager, Cole Hardt, runs a straight business. He's been the manager here for years. BFI is owned by some Belgian-French conglomerate. They have fought tooth and nail to keep this plant open. It's the last one they have operational in the U.S."

Maggie asked, "Sheriff, what do you know about the Pucketts?"

" Well, ma'am, been sheriff here a long time, and the Pucketts have been here I'm guessing 20 years. When they came to town they'd just got out of the Marines. They came up to visit their cousin, liked the area, I guess, got a job at the slaughter plant and stayed. They bought this house not long afterwards. Can't say I know much about them. They keep to themselves, a little peculiar. People don't much like to be around them, say they feel uncomfortable. Me, I never had any problem with them. "

By this time the front door to the house had been unlocked and the group was ready to go in. Actually, the crime techs were going in to start bagging and dusting for prints and evidence. No one else was coming in until after they were done; they just looked through the door. They didn't want the scene contaminated in the event this was a crime scene.

"Sweet Jesus," Maggie muttered under her breath. Animal hides or trophy kills hung on every visible wall and almost every surface hung. A huge bear head hung on one wall, a huge elk on another. On others were deer heads, massive with racks of antlers. These guys were serious hunters if they had killed these animals. What made Maggie mutter was not the deer, elk and bear, but the horse hides. Beautiful hides with manes and tails still attached lay across the sofa and chairs. There were paints, and palominos, bays and buckskins. There were skins on the walls and on the floors. How could anyone skin a horse? It had taken a steady hand and skill with a knife to skin a horse in such a way to have the mane and tails intact. She couldn't get over it. These were the same men who had held knives to little Savannah's neck. If this was insight to their personality it's a wonder they hadn't slit her throat right there in the parking lot of the Custard Stand. She gave another silent thanks to Maci and Hailey for coming to the rescue, another pair of eccentric siblings, but the good kind.

The house yielded a wealth of evidence. There were clear fingerprints of both Mandy and Victoria in the bedroom. Victoria's prints were also found in the kitchen and the bathroom. There was again blonde and brown hair found as well as some white hair consistent with what a white Maltese might have. A sheet stuffed in the laundry had bloodstains on it. In one room there were gun safes, all locked. The safes were top of the line and were almost impossible to break into. The serial numbers were taken off the safes and the manufacturer had been notified to give the police the lock combination numbers. This would keep them from having to drill into the safes. No one even wanted to guess what might be inside those safes.

Back down in Kentucky the Pucketts were brought before the judge. The two gave a not guilty plea when asked about the charges. Their court appointed attorney spoke for them. The attorney later said he had been unable to get the two to speak to him at all about the charges. Each only wanted to see and talk to the other brother. The judge agreed to extradite the two to Chicago to be held on the charges of murder for the deaths of Mandy Gillespie and Victoria Bentley. They would be booked into the Cook County jail as soon as they arrived.

The safes were finally opened and those present were in awe at the arsenal of weapons the Pucketts had in their possession. Also found in the safes were the diamonds Victoria Bentley was wearing when she disappeared. Maggie almost wept when she saw them. No one had any idea where the bodies of Mandy and Victoria were, but everyone believed the Pucketts had killed them. Also found in the safe was a card with the name Geno and a phone number. Could it be possible these two knew or worked for Geno Giocamo? Was the mob somehow involved in the death of Victoria Bentley? This put a whole new spin on things. Hayward Bentley was a well-known criminal attorney. None of the police knew of any particular grudge Geno had with Mr. Bentley. The word would go on the streets tonight, anyone with any information about any connection between Hayward Bentley, the Pucketts and Geno Giacamo needed to be known. Known informants were to be questioned.

CHAPTER 18

▼

Maggie had made the phone call to Hayward Bentley as soon as the first set of fingerprints lifted from the tire matched Victoria's. She wanted to keep him abreast of the latest developments. She knew he had given up hope of finding Victoria alive. He now only wanted closure on what had happened to her and to bring her body home for a proper burial. He also wanted to see justice served to whomever had killed her. Victoria didn't know where the body was, but she did think the evidence against the brothers Puckett was adding up enough to convict them.

The Pucketts had remained apart and silent even after being moved to Cook County jail in Chicago. She had questioned them and got nowhere. She could feel the hate coming off them. She also felt their mental state was deteriorating. The last thing she wanted was for them to appear to be insane. She wanted the death penalty for these two. She didn't want them judged insane and not competent to stand trial.

She gave Hayward an up to date briefing daily on the evidence they were finding. She told him about the findings in the gun safes. She asked him if he knew any reason Geno Giacomo might have a grudge against him bad enough for him to hire these two to kill Victoria. The phone number had proven to be a phone number that was on file for Geno in police records. Hayward seemed completely at a loss on any connection between himself and Geno. As a matter of fact, he told Maggie only a couple months ago he and Victoria had gone to Mama Rosa's for dinner and Geno had sent champagne to their table. They'd exchanged pleasantries before leaving the restaurant. Geno had seemed to take a liking to Victoria and said they would always have a table there, and they would always be safe. It didn't make any sense at all to Hayward that Geno or the mob would be involved with Victoria's death. Victoria told him an informal request was being made to Geno through contacts concerning his connection to the Pucketts. She hoped Geno would agree to answer questions, especially if he was not involved in any way with the Pucketts or the deaths of Victoria and Mandy.

The safes held a couple of more puzzling pieces to the mystery of the Puckett brothers. There was a list with dates and dollar amounts due them by Mr. Yoshika. Beside Mr. Yoshika's name was Ho Supawa and a Kentucky area code matching Brannon's area code. The number was the number for the Ho Supawa auto assembly plant located there.

All the money was accounted for except for the amount indicated for the past weekend's entry. Interesting enough, when the Pucketts were arrested they had a considerable amount of cash on them, more than the amount indicated on this list. The money was bundled with the list in the safe. Were the Pucketts involved in some blackmailing scheme?

Maggie called her father, Sheriff Wyatt May of Brannon and told him about the money and notations in the safe. He agreed to go first thing the next morning to the auto plant and ask Mr. Yoshika just what his involvement was with Aaron and Elvis Puckett. Wyatt could not imagine under any circumstances what the Pucketts and Mr. Yoshika would have in common.

Also found in the safe was some kind of list with years listed, and after each year slash marks were recorded. The first year only had one mark but every year after that, the number of marks seemed to increase. Maggie had a gut feeling she knew exactly what the marks meant, but she hadn't voiced it to anyone.

The Pucketts had enough guns and ammunition in the house to start a small war. With as much ammo as they had on hand if the place had ever caught fire, the blast would have been heard for miles. One room in the house had reloading equipment. Apparently, the Pucketts loaded their own shells. They were serious gunmen.

In a side room back of the kitchen was a room filled with home canned fruits and vegetables. It also had a chest freezer. Maggie literally held her breath when the freezer was opened, preparing herself for some ghastly frozen body parts of Mandy or Victoria

Thankfully, that was not found. The freezer was full of meat and frozen corn and beans.

Maggie could not picture the Pucketts canning and freezing. She wondered who had done this work. All the neighbors were being questioned about their interactions and opinions of the Pucketts. It would be interesting to see what was learned.

Even though the slaughterhouse and rendering plant were not operating due to the injunction, workers were told to report to work as usual. There was always maintenance and cleaning to be done on equipment. Today was a no-kill day but still a working day.

When workers clocked in, they were met by Mr. Hardt, the plant manager, and told the FBI were there and would be questioning all workers. No one had any idea what any of this was about. Some of the illegal workers quickly ducked out and left, thinking it was an illegal worker round –up. Several officers were present and the questions were pretty routine. What did they think about the Pucketts? Had they ever noticed any unusual behavior from them? Had they ever seen the men violent? Did any of them have social contact with them? Know who their friends were? By the end of the questioning, they hadn't learned much about the Pucketts. They were loners, kept to themselves, did not socialize with the workers, and ran a strict operation. They weren't friendly and told no one about their private lives or what they did on their time off. Several of the workers admitted to seeing short tempers from the Pucketts and a violent streak in them. Pressing further, they heard stories of how the Pucketts seemed to actually enjoy killing. They would smile as they slit the throats of the horses and the spray of blood would hit them. No one ever complained to Mr. Hardt, but many thought the Pucketts were unnecessarily cruel to the horses. They had been seen killing them without the use of the head bolt.

As talks continued and more workers opened up, they admitted they were afraid of the Pucketts. One long time worker told of a day one worker was seen in an apparent argument with the Pucketts. The worker didn't come to work the next day and was never seen again. Many of them knew the Pucketts loved to hunt and were excellent marksmen. Those who had seen them kill the horses said they were swift and deadly with knives. The one interesting thing that came out was that several of the workers going home late at night from bars, dates, etc. had seen the Pucketts' van parked behind the plant. One said he had seen the van there just a couple weeks ago late one night or early one morning depending on how you looked at it. He had been coming in from a night of partying and spotted the van behind the plant. He never mentioned it to anyone. No one had because frankly no one wanted to mess with the Pucketts. It was common knowledge the Pucketts had keys to the building. Generally, they were the first ones there in the morning and usually the last to leave.

The search of the plant itself yielded no evidence. The employees had lockers and Aaron's and Elvis's were searched. Nothing incriminating was found. The interviews with the manager Mr. Hardt revealed little that had not already been known. He had given the Pucketts management positions and let them do their jobs. Mr. Hardt rarely went on the killing floor. He stayed in his office and attended to paperwork most of the time. He agreed the Pucketts had full run of the facility and had worked every part and every job. He did tell the agents he had spoken to the Pucketts last week about the possibility of moving to Canada to work at BFI plants there if the courts were successful in closing down US operations. He noted the brothers seemed agitated and angry, and he said several times he repeated things to them because it appeared they weren't really listening to him. He thought their behavior very strange. He said they had left right after work saying they were going to Kentucky to visit their cousins. When the agents questioned if he had known the Pucketts' van had been spotted at the plant late at night Mr. Hardt said he had been unaware of this and could not offer an explanation as to why the men would be here after hours, especially in the middle of the night. He claimed to have no knowledge of the horse hides the FBI had found in the Puckett home. He did agree it was possible they had picked out pretty horses from the kill pen over the years and skinned them after their death. He really didn't see a problem with them doing that because all waste generally was rendered anyway. The agents tried to hide their distaste for the thought of this and their revulsion that horses were killed in this manner and actually eaten in foreign markets. None of them had any idea this was going on in the U.S.

Further search of the Puckett property revealed nothing else. The out building held the usual assortment of lawn mowers, tillers and gardening tools, also what looked to be stretching racks for a crude hide tanning process. It seemed the Pucketts tanned their own hides from game they killed and the horses they had taken from the plant as well. Cadaver dogs had been brought in to search the property in hopes of locating graves, but there was no disturbance of ground anywhere on the property, and the dogs did not alert them to any find. Still no clue to where the bodies of Victoria and Mandy might be.

The hair samples from the house and van were sent out for DNA analysis as were the bloodstains on the sheet found in the laundry room. The ashes in the fireplace had been carefully sifted, and a heat warped blackened dog tag had been found with Precious' name. The case was certainly building against the Pucketts, except they had no bodies.

Maggie was sitting in her office reading through all the information on the case when her phone rang. When she answered, she was surprised when the caller identified himself as Geno Giacomo himself. He told her he had heard through sources there were some questions the authorities had about any involvement he might have with the men being held in the Victoria Bentley case. He told Maggie to bring Hayward Bentley and meet him for dinner at Mama Rosa's at nine that night, and he would tell them what they wanted to know. He assured Maggie, gave his word, that he had no involvement and that she could trust him to meet him for dinner. Maggie called Hayward with this development, and he agreed to meet Geno. He, too, believed when Geno gave his word, it could be trusted.

Maggie and Hayward decided to go together to Mama Rosa's. Maggie drove to the Bentley residence, and Hayward drove his car to the restaurant. Maggie had dressed with care for this meeting. She didn't own a large wardrobe, but she did have every woman's stand-by, the little black dress. It was hard to go wrong with the little black dress concept when you were unsure what to wear. She wore a simple strand of pearls and earrings and matching black heels and purse. She had even applied makeup and took pains with her hair. While on the job, she normally wore little or no makeup and left her near should length blonde hair straight or pulled back in a barrette. She felt good about the way she looked tonight. Meeting a man with the reputation of Geno Giacomo had given her a little case of nerves. It was not everyday a FBI agent was given an audience by a Mafia legend.

Hayward had also dressed for dinner even though his expensive suit hung on him, and his color looked pale. Dark circles were under his eyes, and lines etched his handsome face. Losing Victoria had taken such a toll on him, Maggie hoped tonight's meeting would help them bring new information to the case.

Geno and his entourage were already at Mama Rosa's when Maggie and Hayward arrived. Geno occupied the same table he had the night Hayward and Victoria had seen him there. To Hayward it seemed like a lifetime ago. Geno was dressed in a handmade suit that Maggie knew cost more than several months pay for her. He was not a big man, but he had an air of power and authority about him. He wore his still thick hair combed straight back. His hair was gray and had a slight wave to it. Dark brown eyes looked intelligently at her and his dominant Roman nose looked like it may have been broken at some point of his life. His olive complexion made his perfectly porcelain capped teeth gleam in the candlelight of their table. He had a coarse raspy voice, one that spoke of smoking and alcohol. She knew Geno had to be near seventy years old, but he looked fit. He had on a blue shirt to match the slight stripes in his suit and gold cufflinks glistened at his wrists. He wore a diamond ring on his right hand and a Rolex watch on his wrist. Everything about his dress exuded money, power, and old world tradition. Introductions were made and wine was served.

Maggie knew this was likely to be a long dinner. She knew better than to launch into a series of questions. She knew Geno would be the perfect host for dinner, and they would enjoy their dinner and after dinner drinks before business would ever be discussed. She would be patient.

They were never asked for an order but courses of meals came and were cleared for more. Dinner was long and delicious. Maggie knew Mama Rosa's was legendary for serving the best Italian food in Chicago. After eating, Maggie knew the praise was deserved. She had grown up eating Franco American spaghetti in a can. She smiled at the thought of the food she now enjoyed.

Geno had been quietly accessing the young FBI agent all evening. He found her charming and her slight country accent endearing. She was an easy conversationalist and was intelligent. He liked the way she looked him directly in the eyes when she spoke to him. He thought this young woman would be going places in her future. He had asked her about her upbringing, and she had joked that she had done the same thing he had, carried on in the family tradition. When he looked puzzled, she told him her father was in law enforcement and she had always wanted to be like him. Geno then laughed at his little pun, he liked her sense of humor.

At last while the men enjoyed after dinner drinks and Maggie had coffee, the subject turned to Aaron and Elvis Puckett. Geno told Hayward and Maggie he had many years ago gone to Canada on a big game hunt. He had taken his bodyguard, Vinnie, with him and there were three other men on this chartered hunt. One was a banker and the other two were the Puckett twins. Geno told them of the extraordinary shots the two brothers had made killing the elk and deer. He related Vinnie had actually become jealous of the shooting ability of the two. Geno himself was very impressed with the two strange young men and had taken them to dinner the last night of the hunt.

He had questioned the men about their abilities and where they had learned to shoot. The Pucketts told him they had learned to hunt at the knee of their father in rural Kentucky. They told of a rather impoverished life where they grew or killed every thing they ate. They learned patience and were natural shooters. They had run away from home and joined the Marine Corp where they further honed their skills with knife and guns.

Geno said he remembered well the skill he witnessed as they skinned the bear. These were serious hunters who knew what they were doing. As he remembered, they were going to tan the bearskin themselves and have both the elk head and bear head professionally mounted. They had gotten the money for the trip from using some of the money from the inheritance of the sale of land after their parents died. Geno continued, "They told me they worked in a horse slaughter plant and rendering facility. I admit I thought their skill as marksmen might be interesting to pursue. They were odd men. They had the killer instinct, no doubt about that. The thing that struck me oddest is that they seemed to enjoy their work killing those poor horses. I found it rather distasteful. They said they had a perfect set up for them and smiled about it. I never quite understood. I told them if they ever chose to leave the slaughterhouse I could always use a couple men with their skills and gave them the card you found with a contact number for me. I never saw or heard from them again after that night. I was surprised to learn they had kept the card all these years.

"I am telling both of you on my oath that I had no knowledge or nothing to do with the disappearance of Victoria. I was quite impressed with your wife, Mr. Bentley, the night we met here at Mama Rosa's" Geno said. "So many times as we men get older we are attracted to the youth and beauty of young women. Alas, often they are only attracted to us for the money and power we have. It was so clearly evident that was not the case with your Victoria. I can feel these things. Your wife was a passionate woman, and it was obvious by her every look and touch that she was deeply in love with you. I envied you that night, and I share your despair over her loss.

"Do I think these two men, the Pucketts capable of murder? Yes, I know men who can kill with little emotion. These men, even years ago showed no feeling for loss of life. The one thing I observed was that they were completely devoted to one another as twins often are. I have put the word on the streets, Mr. Bentley. No one is responsible for your wife's death except these two. I think perhaps it was a terrible chance of bad timing that she happened along that rest area at the same time they were there. I think they saw her and took her. I say this now not to bring you more pain but telling you what I think. I think they killed her and then used their place of employment to dispose of her body.

"The other young woman, I think, met the same fate. That is why there has been no body found and why you won't find a trace of one. Long ago when they said they had the perfect set-up, I think they had already committed the perfect murder. I deplore what they have done, and I hope they burn in eternal hell."

Maggie watched Hayward's face as Geno said this. Hayward slumped in his chair and looked totally shaken. Maggie told Geno the Pucketts had indeed had the elk and bear mounted. They were both on their wall at home and the bearskin rug was on the floor. She was impressed with Geno's memory and observations made so many years ago and told him so. She also told him she agreed with what he thought had happened to Victoria and Mandy. The thought had been so ghastly she had not said it aloud before then, but she had come to the same conclusion as Geno. It had all started to come together for her when some of them employees at the slaughter plant said they had seen the Pucketts' vehicle at the slaughterhouse late in the night. The thought that they had rendered their victims was gruesome and evil beyond words. How many years had this been going on? It was Maggie's thought that the slash marks and years found in the safe might represent other people they had killed over the years. She was gathering missing people's numbers now from those years to see how many numbers might add up. The thought made her sick.

It was a long silent drive back to the Bentley home. Maggie decided not to try to engage Hayward in idle chit chat. She knew he had to be terribly disturbed at what she and Geno had surmised. When they got to her car, Hayward turned to her and thanked her for meeting with Geno and him. "This has been a difficult night," he said. "I, in my worst thoughts after the Pucketts were arrested and I learned of their employment, came to the same conclusion that you and Geno have reached. I wanted so much to be able to give Victoria a Christian burial, lay her to rest in my family mausoleum. I will never get over this, Maggie. To think that these evil men were ultimately brought down by an innocent five year old girl, quite a remarkable story. I hope your friend realizes what a special little girl she has."

Maggie drove to her apartment and finally fell in to a fitful sleep. She had nightmares of dying horse, and Victoria screaming all night. The next morning, she went to the Cook County jail and asked the guards to being the Pucketts to an interrogation room. She specified they be cuffed behind the back and have leg irons. Two other officers would be with her. This would be the first time since the Pucketts were arrested and appeared in court that they would see each other.

Aaron and Elvis were brought into the room. Maggie thought they looked horrible. They were sunken-eyed and looked as if they'd lost weight. She asked if they wanted an attorney present and they only shrugged indifference. She had already notified their court appointed attorney she intended to question them, and he was there. He told the two they did not have say anything to Maggie if they chose not to.

Maggie told Aaron and Elvis all the mounting evidence they now had against them. Authorities had found the missing tire and wheel from Victoria's Porsche in their van. She told them about the earring belonging to Mandy Gillespie found in their van, the fingerprints of both Mandy and Victoria in the van, the hairs that matched Victoria, Mandy and Precious both in the van and at their home. She told them they also had multiple fingerprints of Mandy and Victoria in their home, the bloodstained sheet matching the DNA of Victoria, the charred dog tag found in the ashes of the fireplace. She told them of the diamonds they had found in the safe, along with the card with Geno's phone number and the money and list with Mr. Yoshika's name and number. She told them her father who was the sheriff of Brannon had interviewed their cousins and Mr. .Yoshika. All confirmed the two of them had been over the years selling horsemeat to Mr. Yoshika. She related that the cousins said that the twins had brought horsemeat down for them to eat as well.

Maggie explained, "Mr. Yoshika was deeply humiliated that he had been duped by you two. He believed your story to him that as an employee you received horsemeat for your own use and that you were honoring him by selling it to him." At this the two men smirked and said something under their breath that Maggie thought was "stupid Jap".

"How many others have you killed and rendered?" At this the men jerked their heads up in surprise. "Yes," she said, "We know you rendered your victims. You had the perfect murders, didn't you? How many years and how many people have suffered and died by your hand? To think you were brought down by a fire year old child and a couple of women old enough to be grandmothers. Some tough guys you are! When I walked out of the Custard Stand you thought you'd seen a ghost because you thought I was Victoria."

Elvis sneered and finally spoke. "Victoria was perfect, and you are nobody. You could never compare with Victoria. She was the ultimate." Salvadore Diaz, their court appointed attorney, advised the men to keep quiet.

"Never killed a kid," Aaron said, but I'd like to kill the little witch that was kicking and hitting us. How'd she know who we were? We'd never seen her before in our lives."

"She's a very special child," Maggie said. "Her father was a soldier killed in Iraq almost two years ago. Ever since he died, little Savannah has been able to sense things about people. She had been dreaming about the two of you for a while. She saw in her nightmares what you did to Victoria and Precious. She saw your faces, knew about your eyes, Aaron, and your thumbs, Elvis. She knew you killed horses. She was a very brave little girl to confront you, much braver than the two of you. You aren't brave. You kill and destroy, and you will die for it. Illinois has the death penalty you know, and with the evidence we have, even without a body, I think any competent lawyer can convince a jury of guilt beyond doubt."

"We ain't going to die by some needle," Aaron said.

Maggie turned, "Maybe not, maybe you want to think about cooperating and making a plea. Maybe something could be worked out that you two plead guilty and tell us whom else you have killed, and in return you serve life without parole. The decision is up to you. Talk it over with your attorney." Maggie then had the men taken back to their separate cells.

Some prisoners make a big deal of announcing a hunger strike. Aaron and Elvis, by some mutual consent, had both not eaten nor drunk more than a couple sips of water since they had been jailed. In addition, both their gunshot wounds were infected and not healing. They had been transferred to the hospital for IV fluids and antibiotics. Both were refusing treatment. It seemed rather than face a life sentence or death by lethal injection, the Pucketts wanted to decide their own fate. In the end they got their way. Even though they were forcibly given fluids and antibiotics, they both had contracted a virulent strain of staph infection. Both died within hours of each other.

Maggie was glad it happened that way. Justice was still served, just not by a court of law.

CHAPTER 19

▼

The town of Brannon has an Annual Christmas Parade on the second Saturday of December. Local businesses decorate floats and vie for best float award. The local high school bands march and play. Rival high schools each have floats, too, with homecoming queens waving to the crowds along the crowded parade route. Of course, the main float is always Santa's. This year in addition to Santa, there were some special VIPs on the float, throwing candy and waving to the crowd.

There with Santa was a smiling Savannah, along with Maci Joseph, Hailey McGuire, and Boo. Boo had on a big red bow tie and was "smiling" at the crowd alongside Savannah. Savannah was wearing a beautiful Christmas dress covered by a red coat, and much to the dismay of Jett, the ever-present pink, scuffed cowboy boots. Hailey was decked out in Christmas cowgirl style, wearing a black and red embroidered circle skirt with matching blouse with pearl snap buttons and lavish embroidery on the cuffs and yoke. She had on a red-fringed suede jacket to ward off the chill and, of course, she was also wearing black boots with an inlaid red floral pattern to match. Maci, being Maci, opted to keep the fun going and was wearing her special edition Christmas pajamas, red silk with white snowman embroidered all over them with matching housecoat and fuzzy slippers. Her hands were kept warm by a white rabbit's fur muff. The mood was fun and festive. Maggie and Jett were both in the crowd waving and yelling to "the girls" and Boo.

At the end of the parade a special presentation was made by the mayor of Brannon at the courthouse square, bestowing Bravery and Good Citizenship awards upon Savannah, Maci, Hailey, and Boo. It was a good time, enjoyed by all. Jett was happier than she had been in a long time, and Savannah seemed so, too. Standing also in the crowd with Jett and Maggie was Hayward Bentley. He had made a special trip down to meet little Savannah and Boo, Maci and Hailey. With him he had brought three checks, reward money for the apprehension of the Pucketts. Hailey, Maci, and Savannah each got a check for half a million dollars. All were overwhelmed and tried to decline the money. He wouldn't take it back. He said if not for their heroic action he might have never known what happened to Victoria, and the Pucketts may have never been caught.

Maggie asked Jett how Savannah was doing and was happy to learn she had not had any more nightmares since the "bad men" had been caught. She had suffered no ill effects from the whole ordeal of her near abduction and had reported that Star had told her afterwards that's why he has sent her to the Custard Stand in the first place. He didn't tell her before she went because he didn't want her to be afraid. Savannah talked about it all in a very matter-of-fact way, so Jett and Maggie both agreed it was best to let it be.

The next day, Jett decided to take Savannah to check out a horse riding school she had read about. The center had classes for all ages from beginning riders to advanced. You could learn English riding, western riding, or dressage. The school was having a Christmas open house that Sunday afternoon with special sign-up prices. Jett had decided they would both learn to ride and she would buy them each a horse in the spring.

The Equestrian Center had an indoor riding area so they could take lessons all winter. By spring, they should know enough to handle their own horses. When she told Savannah this, Savannah said she'd go with her, but the only horse she wanted was Star. Jett let that slide by without comment. She really didn't know what to do about Star. She had hoped after the drama with the bad men that Star would disappear. He had not.

The Equestrian Center was in a little town on the other side of Lexington. It was a longer drive than Jett anticipated, unless she was lost, which might be the case, she thought. As she and Savannah were driving down the little road where she thought the Center was, the car in front of her suddenly swerved. Instinctively, Jett put her arm across to brace against Savannah, even though Savannah was firmly buckled in. They both saw at the same time the car had hit a little dog. The driver had tried to avoid hitting the dog but its bumper had grazed the dog. The car sped on. The dog took a couple steps and collapsed.

"Mommy, stop," Savannah screamed." We have to help that little dog." "Is it dead Mommy? Please don't be dead little dog." By this time, Savannah was sobbing.

Jett was shaken too. "Don't cry, Baby, we'll stop and help the little dog. You stay in the car." She opened the trunk, got out the blanket she always kept there in her emergency box, and ran over to where the little dog lay limply on the ground. She could feel its heart beating so she knew it wasn't dead, at least not yet. Jett ran back to the car and put the dog in her lap and pulled out in the road.

Still crying, Savannah whispered, "Is the dog dead Mommy?"

" No Savannah, I can feel its heart beating. We'll take it to the Equestrian Center. It should be just down the road. We can find out from them where the nearest emergency clinic is."

Jett kept driving, looking at the numbers on the mailboxes. She was afraid she'd made a wrong turn because the numbers were not matching the address of the Equestrian Center, and she knew it should be close. About the time she started to turn around and back track, she saw a mailbox. On the mailbox was written Daniel Parker, DVM. Jett told Savannah, " Look Savannah, a vet lives here. Let's pull in and see if he's home. Maybe he can look at the little dog or tell us where to take him."

Jett got out of the car and ran to the front door of the house, quickly ringing the doorbell. She assumed Savannah was right behind her. When the door opened, Jett saw a very handsome smiling man. "Gosh he's cute," she thought, blushing under his gaze. For a moment she was dumbstruck. What was happening to her? She was stammering like a schoolgirl and blushing. Her stomach was doing a tiny flip just looking at this man. She stammered about seeing the dog get hit and she had it there in her arms and saw his mailbox. She was rattling on like an idiot, she thought.

Daniel was going through the same range of emotions as Jett. He had opened his door to find a beautiful woman face flushed with cold, eyes sky blue, and he, too, suddenly felt a catch in his throat. He was trying to concentrate on what she was saying, but his head was buzzing, and he was blushing. "She must think I'm nuts," he thought." I'm sorry," Daniel said. "You said something about a hurt dog?" Again, he stood staring at her, and she was staring right back.

"Uh yes, the dog," Jett said, lifting it up to him. "He got hit by a car."

"Come on in," Daniel said, "Let's take a look."

Jett was looking around the room and realized she was looking for a woman in the house. Had he been wearing a ring? "Stop it," she thought. "You are being foolish. What has come over you...?"

While he unwrapped the dog, Daniel was thinking the same thing. "I didn't see a ring on her finger. Surely she's married. She's gorgeous."

Suddenly Jett came to her senses enough to realize Savannah had not followed her to the house. She looked around and said, "Where's Savannah?" Daniel replied, "Savannah?" "My daughter," she said, "she was right behind me." "She wasn't at the door when you came up," he said. They looked out the window and saw Savannah getting ready to climb over the fence next to the barn beside Daniel's house. "Oh no, "Daniel gasped," Oh, God, no, he'll kill her."

"Who? What?" Jett said. Daniel replied, "The horse. He's wild. He'll kill her!"

The color drained out from Jett's face, and her legs felt like rubber as she saw a huge black horse rearing up, and whinnying in the barn paddock. Savannah was straddling the fence ready to jump down.

Jett and Daniel, forgetting about the poor dog, ran outside. Jett was screaming at Savannah to stop, and so was Daniel. Savannah looked their way and smiled and jumped on down.

It looked to Jett like Savannah said, "Star," but Jett couldn't hear her above her own screams. They weren't going to make it. The big horse was in a full run, charging right to the spot where Savannah stood smiling. Jett felt her world coming to an end. Her daughter was going to be stomped to death right before her eyes. Suddenly, the big horse skidded to a stop in front of Savannah.

Daniel, his voice barely a whisper, said, "I don't believe what I'm seeing."

Savannah was saying, "Mommy, it's Star. It's Star. Mommy, I finally found him." The horse very slowly lowered himself to the ground. Savannah threw her arms around his big neck, hugging him. She climbed upon his back and holding onto his mane, gave him a full hug. The horse got up! Savannah was on the big black horse riding! Daniel was standing in shock, his mouth open. After the horse took Savannah around the paddock, he once again kneeled to the ground allowing her to slide off. He then took off whinnying, kicking sideways and running all over the paddock.

"He looks like he's happy," Jett murmured. Daniel could only shake his head in amazement. After running around the paddock, the horse came back around and stopped in front of Savannah.

"Oh Mommy," she said, "Isn't he the most 'beautifulest' horse you ever saw? I told you Star was real. Star, this is my Mommy. Mommy, this is Star. Can we take him home, Mommy, can we?"

"Savannah, honey," Jett said, "This is Dr. Parker's horse."

Daniel said, "Actually it's my wife's horse, or was. She died. . ."

Savannah was petting Star and hugging him around his legs. "I told you Star was a real horse. I told you, Mommy."

The horse seemed as smitten with the little girl as she was with him. He nickered and nibbled kisses on her face, making her giggle. Daniel suddenly remembered the dog in the house. "Let's all go back inside. We forgot all about the dog."

Savannah turned to Star and said," Star, I'll be right back. I have to go check on the little dog."

Daniel and Jett both could have sworn they saw the big horse nod his head.

They all went back to the house where they found the blanket but no dog. When they found him, he was chewing on a pair of Daniel's shoes! Daniel examined the dog and said he probably had just been grazed and maybe knocked out from the hit. He now seemed fine. "He's one lucky dog to survive getting hit," Daniel said.

"Can we keep him, mommy?" Savannah asked.

"I don't know Savannah. He may belong to someone." Jett said.

"No he doesn't," Savannah said, "We'll name him Lucky, like Dr. Parker said."

"Well," Jett agreed, "He sure is cute. The little dog looked like some kind of beagle mix. "Tell you what. We'll put signs up and put an ad in the paper and if no one claims him, we'll keep him."

"Oh, goody," Savannah said," I'm going to tell Star." With that she went running back outside to the paddock where the horse stood waiting for her.

"I'm sorry," Jett said to Daniel, "I guess I need to explain about Savannah and Star. I don't know what I'll do now." She went on to tell Daniel the whole story, how Blake had been killed, and the dreams she and Savannah both had the night he died about him sending someone to take care of them. She went on to tell him that "Star" had arrived the next day and had been what Jett had thought was Savannah's imaginary playmate ever since. Laughing, she told him she has hay, water and sweet feed in her kitchen waiting for him! Savannah had also become somewhat clairvoyant during this whole period, with Star often telling her things before they happened or she dreamed things that happened. She further explained about her father's heart attack and the Puckett story.

Daniel interrupted, "Wait a minute, my minister gave a sermon about your Savannah and her grandfather not long ago. He didn't use names, but the story is the same. He based the sermon on having the faith of a child."

"Really," Jett said. She remembered the minister who had talked to them in the hospital. "Is your minister's name Reverend Jenkins?"

"Yes," Daniel said. "I heard about the shootout at the Custard Stand in Brannon, too. Gee, Savannah is famous," he laughed.

"Yes," Jett laughed back, "and she has been adamant through all this there really is a Star, and now she thinks she's found him."

Daniel then told her the abbreviated version of his story. He told her about Julianna and the horse, Sahara, and how she had saved him from being killed by her persistence in trying to tame him. He then told her of Julianna's cancer and how she'd died. He told Jett on the night Julianna died she asked to be taken to the barn and talked to the big horse. He described how the horse would kneel for her, just as he had for Savannah. He told her Julianna told him she would send someone for Star, and she had died with her arms around both of them. Jett was crying, and so was Daniel. "By the way," he said, "Sahara's real name is Prince of Sahara Midnight Star. Julianna always called him Sahara. I guess Star was easier for a child."

Jett smiled," She called him Star because she said he had a white star on his forehead, and he does."

"There is no doubt that Sahara, now Star, belongs to your Savannah," Daniel said.

Talking further, they realized both Julianna and Blake died on the same night, virtually at the same time.

"Let's go outside and help Savannah get Star in the barn. By the way, where were you headed when you came upon Lucky?" Daniel asked.

"The Equestrian Riding Center," Jett said. "I was going to sign Savannah and me up for riding lessons."

Laughing, Daniel said, "Did you ever take the wrong turn? You're nowhere near the Equestrian Center. Besides, you won't need to take lessons because I'll be happy to teach you and Savannah how to ride." As they walked outside it seemed so natural for him to take her hand in his.

Maybe theirs truly was a match made in heaven.

Made in the USA
Lexington, KY
30 September 2010